QUEEN of LEGENDS

FROST KAY

Copyright

Queen of Legends

First Edition

Cover by Sanja Balan
Editing by Ocean's Edits
Proofreading by Red Ninja Edits
Formatting by Jaye Pratt

DEDICATION

For my readers:
Thank you for giving me the courage to write.

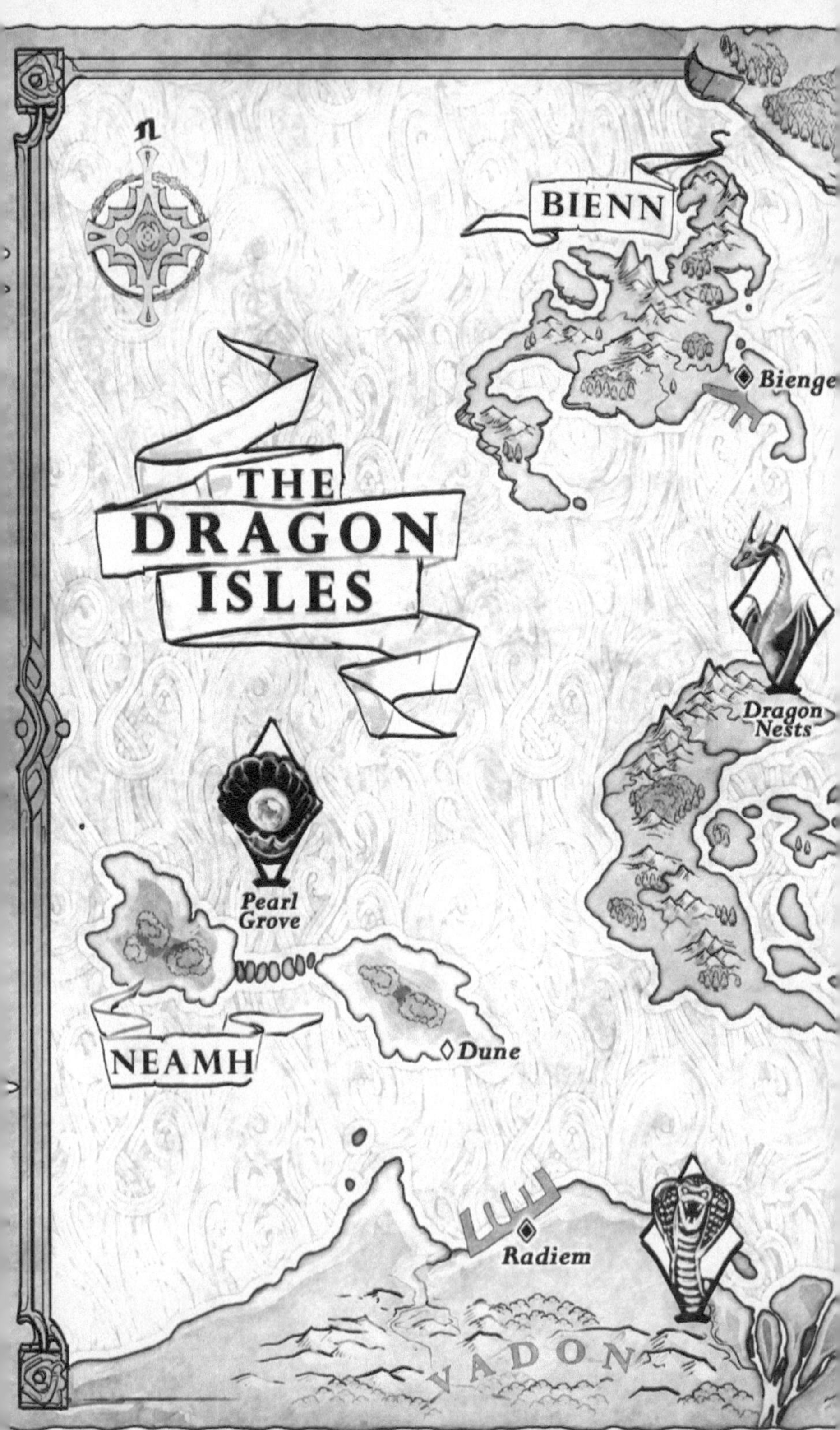
BIENN
THE
DRAGON
ISLES
Bienge
Dragon
Nests
Pearl
Grove
NEAMH
Dune
Radiem
VADON

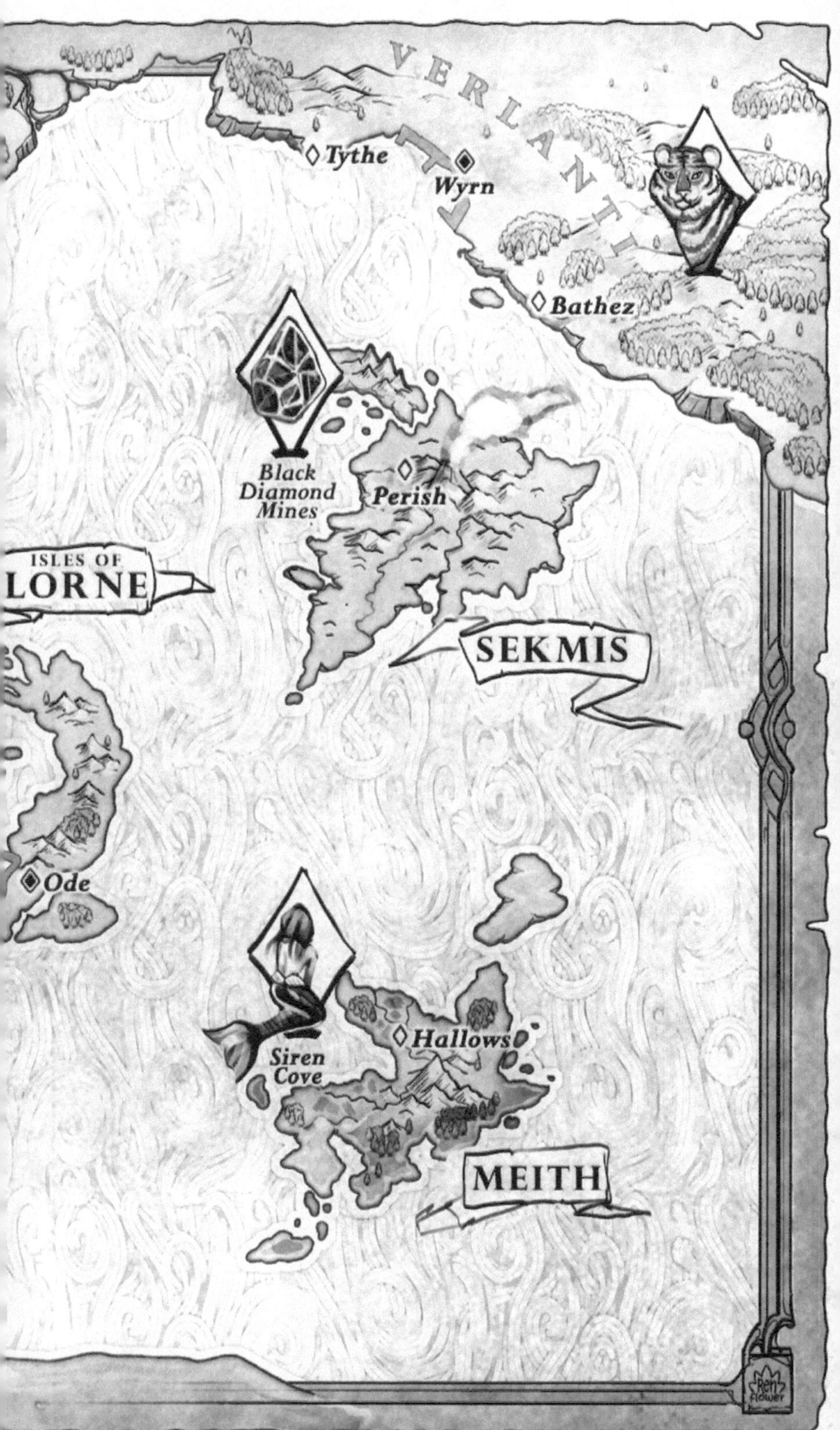
VERLANTI
Tythe
Wyrn
Bathez
Black Diamond Mines
Perish
ISLES OF
LORNE
SEKMIS
Ode
Hallows
Siren Cove
MEITH
Ren Flower

TABLE OF CONTENTS

PROLOGUE

The illusion of freedom is a trap I was once told.
It's like trying to catch the wind.
Or taste the sun.
An impossible feat.
The elves thought they could cage me.
To use me for their own evils.
But I am the wind.
My kiss holds the warmth of the sun.
The legend was born with me.
Their greed ends with me.

CHAPTER ONE

Wren

Wren ran a hand over her face. "That's the fourth "wanted" poster I've seen so far." Her husband was relentless. Soon she'd not be able to travel without being recognized.

Leif flicked a glance her way. "There's been seven, actually."

"Where?" Bram muttered, his dark brown eyebrows slashed together. "Down by the harbor, the two taverns, the brothel…?"

"And outside the duke's residence, the orphanage, and the fish market," Leif said, pleased with himself. Bram looked like he wanted to curse at Leif for noticing something he hadn't.

Bram's scowl deepened. "We haven't been anywhere near the duke's residence, or the orphanage, or the fish market."

"Ah, I may have scouted them privately in the early hours of the morning."

Wren sighed as Bram's face turned bright red. Leif knew just what to say to needle the man.

"You know you're not supposed to go out alone right

now!" Bram bit out through clenched teeth. The fact they were trying to stay unnoticed was the only thing preventing him from losing his temper entirely. "If you're caught—"

"But I wasn't. I know better than to get caught. Don't I, Wren?" Leif grinned at her. She had watched their entire exchange with a now-familiar feeling of resignation. Over the last two months she'd gotten to know the rebellion as best she could, particularly her watery dungeon companion and her aunt's point man for operations, Bram.

It was clear from day one that Bram did not like Wren at all.

Perhaps "trust" is more accurate than "dislike." He doesn't trust you.

Ever since Wren and Leif broke free from the Verlanti palace with the help of the miraculous blue dragon, she'd hardly had a single moment to herself. Her aunt, Vienne—the leader of the rebellion—had set Bram and Leif to be her constant companions. Leif she did not mind; she had grown to like and trust the boy. But Bram...?

If he had his way, Wren would have spent the last two months locked in a cell, away from trouble and any risk that she might contact her husband.

Her stomach twisted sickeningly, as it always did when she remembered the look on Arrik's face when he realized she was fleeing.

Don't think about Arrik.

"Perhaps you should listen to Bram," Wren said, deciding it was wise to side with the seasoned spy over his younger companion. "All it takes is one mistake and that's it, you're done for."

Leif stuck out his tongue. "As if I'd ever make a mistake."

"Pride before the fall," she retorted, arching a brow.

"As if you have any room to talk," Leif muttered, crossing his arms.

"Back on the topic at hand," Bram scowled, flashing a glare Wren's way as if it were her fault the conversation had been waylaid, "this is the sixth port town we've scouted in two months, and it's already full of people on the lookout for us. Especially for YOU."

Wren winced at Bram's tone, and pulled the hood of her ash-colored cloak tighter around her head. Wren had braided her crimson hair back and smeared it with the brown clay that built up near the rivers running through the forest in order to dull the color. It was already flaking off—it never lasted long, but her hair was one of the biggest giveaways of who she was after all, so she persisted in coating it in the disgusting stuff as often as she could. Wren knew she should cut all her hair off, but a rebellious part of her refused to even entertain the notion.

I am the Dragon Princess. My hair is part of who I am. I refuse to remove part of me for the Verlanti royal family.

"The wanted fliers," Wren murmured, wishing she had one to look at closely, "were they issued directly from the palace or—?"

"A few were from Soren, but the ones by the orphanage, brothel, and fish market were issued by your dear husband," Leif said. "With a substantial reward offered for your capture, unharmed. Clearly he knows who to target for help and how to bribe them."

Husband. The word didn't seem to capture what Arrik was.

"Unharmed, and even offering money," Bram said, chewing over the words. He cast a critical glance over Wren, who forced herself not to turn away. "One wonders why he'd go to such great lengths to get you back when it would be easier to have someone cut off your legs and drag you back."

Wren didn't reply. Bram wasn't the only member of the rebellion who suspected that Wren was in cahoots with Arrik, and believed she should be blamed for his actions.

As if I had any sway over him at all. As if Arrik would ever have listened to me.

A very small part of Wren knew this didn't quite ring true, but she ignored it. The prince was as good as dead to her.

"Regardless of the fliers," she said, "we still need to infiltrate the gentleman's club." A furtive look to her left, then her right; Leif and Bram followed suit, then crept down several back alleys until they reached the staff entrance to the club.

Despite his distrust of her, Bram nonetheless had worked well with Wren on other such missions, and respected her abilities. Wren could fight, and her time spent memorizing the passages beneath her father's castle on the Dragon Isles made her adept at sneaking around unnoticed. There was no animosity between the two of them, so long as they were *working.*

"You remember what to do?" Bram whispered, pulling out a wig from a bag along with pins. Wren hastily tugged her hood back and put on the black, long-haired wig just as Leif covered his own hair with a softly wavy, hazel-colored wig. The long hair was all he needed to pass as a young woman instead of a teenage boy—along with the dress he had on, hidden by his cloak. Leif helped her secure the wig with what seemed like way too many pins.

She eyed Leif's wig and frowned at Bram. "Why the devil do we get a wig now but I have had to put sludge in my hair for the last several months?"

Bram gave her a nasty smile. That was all she needed to know. He wanted her to be miserable. The miscreant. She then answered his earlier question. "Target the duke and his companion, Bellnai," Wren recited. "Leif targets the duke himself, since his tastes run…young."

Leif grinned viciously. "And if he thinks to touch me—"

"You'll avoid bloodshed at all costs or I swear I'll abandon you in there," Bram grunted, his dark eyes full of warning. "Now, off with you. I'll enter from the front as a guest. We have an hour to gather information before we abandon the mission, got it?"

Wren and Leif nodded. The information they needed was simple: find out where Prince Arrik currently was, and what he was doing.

It was easy for Wren and Leif to slip into the gentlemen's club as working girls. The place was loud and busy, even though the sun had barely set, with some patrons demanding three or four serving girls for them alone. Wren and Leif smiled easily at anyone who caught their eyes, snaking through the crowd before anyone could catch sight of them for longer than a second and recognize them from the posters.

The point was to fit in, not draw attention.

With these disguises, I doubt anyone would work it out.

Wren picked at the pink silk of her outrageously Verlantian dress. She had grown used to their flowy somewhat scandalous fashions over the last couple of months—she'd had to—but that didn't mean she liked them. Having the curve of her waist exposed, and the column of her back, and the line of her thighs, made Wren more uncomfortable than she could possibly say.

But she didn't show it on her face. Leif had taught her well how to walk and talk like a Verlanti serving girl, so Wren focused on that as the two of them homed in on the duke and his companion, proffering claret-colored wine from a golden pitcher. Both the duke and Bellnai eagerly accepted a cup, the two of them eyeing their new serving girls with approval. To their immense luck, the two were already discussing Prince Arrik when Wren and Leif came upon them.

"They say his barbarian wife tried to kill him on their wedding night," Bellnai said, reclining on his seat to sweep his gaze up and down Wren's frame. She resisted the urge to flinch. "Though I don't mind a bit of spice in the bedroom." His eyes twinkled and he winked at Wren. "What say you, lass?"

"I'm known to enjoy a tussle or two," Wren replied, exchanging a deliberately filthy look with Leif for the sake of their act, even as her stomach knotted. She hated this part. Bellnai and the duke traded glances, looking positively delighted.

"I heard it was the other way around," said another serving girl, who was fanning the highborn gentlemen with a gigantic palm leaf. "That Prince Arrik tried to kill the Dragon Princess. Like how he murdered his other wives!"

"Hush now," the duke scolded, though it was clear he was enjoying the gossip as much as the others around him. "We must not badmouth our dear prince, nor suggest he's done something that has not been proven. In any case, the Dragon Princess must be close by—Prince Arrik is due to arrive in town tomorrow after stopping by Kray's Village in the forest tonight."

So close.

A slight squeezing of Leif's hand on Wren's arm was all that stopped her from running off. Arrik was too close.

Kray's Village was right on the doorstop of a rebellion hideout. How the devil did he keep finding them?

"Oh my, it seems we're out of wine," Leif crooned, a sorrowful expression on his face. "We mustn't have that. Sparrow, can you help me?"

The name was a play on Wren's real name of course, a joke between the two of them. Wordlessly Wren nodded, bowing slightly for the duke and Bellnai, then retreated for the kitchen as swiftly as she dared, the back of her neck tingling from Bellnai's stare.

They caught sight of Bram on the way, trapped in an intense conversation with a drunk highborn lad who didn't look old enough to be inside a gentleman's club. With a mere look from Leif he disengaged from the youth, stalking out the main entrance while Wren and Leif made their exit through the servants' door.

Only once they were outside and wrapped in their cloaks once more—though the Verlanti early autumn air was just as hot and balmy as high summer—did Leif and Wren make their way around to the front of the building to reconvene with Bram. Between them and the other spy, however, was a guard shaking a small girl by her collar. Wren glanced toward the market street wrapping up for the night, then to where the well-kept cobblestone streets of the port town began to disintegrate into the dirt roads of the poorer district, and came to the conclusion the child had probably stolen something.

Despite the wealth of the kingdom, the highborn had taxed the lowborn into poverty. Anyone without a title was suffering or starving.

"Come on, Sparrow," Leif said, sticking to her code name as he tugged insistently on her hand. They both still had their disguises on; it would be easy for Wren to intervene on the child's behalf.

The guard shook the girl again and lifted his hand as if to strike the wee one.

Not on my watch.

One warning glare from Bram standing behind the guard was all Wren needed to know that helping the child was not in any way, shape, or form, something she should do.

Wren stepped forward to help the child anyway.

No one hurt the lowly in her presence.

CHAPTER TWO

Wren

If Wren couldn't help a starving child in need, then she had no right to call herself a Dragon Princess. She strode forward, bristling with anger.

"What's going on here?" she demanded, surprising the guard. He lowered his hand and then shook the little girl. Wren's eyes narrowed as the elven brute yanked the food out of the wee one's jacket and tossed it on the ground—half a loaf of day-end bread, well on its way toward becoming inevitable food for the pigeons come daybreak.

"This is none of your concern," the guard snapped. "She's a thief."

"Don't cause a scene," Leif whispered in her ear, grabbing at Wren's sleeve to steer her around the guard and over to a seething Bram. But Wren merely pulled out of Leif's grasp to address the guard who'd lifted the little girl off her feet as if to give her one more good shake.

"I can pay for that on the child's behalf," Wren said evenly, making to remove her coin bag from her cloak. The guard merely scoffed at her.

"Does no good to help these street rats," he growled, shaking the child as he spoke. "They deserve a good walloping."

The young girl hung in the guard's grip, covered in soot and dirt but with big blue eyes that pleaded with Wren for help. *Barely younger than Britta.* Wren's chest constricted painfully at the mere thought of her sister.

"I insist," Wren said, her voice flinty. "I'll pay double what the bread is worth. Let the girl go."

The elf's lip curled as he stared her down, but he tossed the child to the cobblestones. Wren flinched at the noise, and glanced over at the girl to make sure she didn't have any major injuries before turning her attention once again to the guard. She held out the coins as he closed the distance between them. Wren stiffened when he deftly knocked away the gold to the ground and closed his meaty hand around her throat.

Stay calm. Don't cause a fight unless you need to.

"Who are you to tell me what to do?" he spat, grip tightening with every syllable.

Her fight-or-flight response kicked in, dulling her surprise.

No choice but to move.

With practiced ease, she clapped both of her hands over the guard's ears. He yelped and let Wren go, clutching at his head. Her eyes watered and she wheezed out one cough before kicking the guard down to the ground before he could recover.

Dully, Wren scanned the lane and realized both Leif and

Bram had fled, though she knew they wouldn't have gone far. The little girl remained, sitting on the cobblestones and watching Wren fight as if she were an angel.

Or a dragon, Wren mused, grinning at the girl before sliding out a blade from her cloak. She punched the guard in the gut with the pommel of her dagger, cut off his coin pouch, collected her own, and then grabbed the girl by the hand.

"We need to leave," she urged the child, praying the little one would follow.

The girl nodded and started running alongside Wren.

"Get back here!" the guard wheezed as they rounded the first corner.

A second later, a whistle informed Wren that he'd called for backup. Her jaw clenched. The order of the Kingdom of Myths had told her a million times of the whistles that the guards kept on themselves, and yet she always forgot they carried them. Because of her oversight, they had only moments to get away.

"Where do you live, little one?" she asked the girl between heavy breaths, stumbling on slick cobblestones when they gave way to dirt as she took an educated guess and headed into the poorer district of town.

The child stared up at her with huge blue eyes, mouth slightly open as she tried to keep up with Wren's strides. "Your hair is coming off!"

"Don't worry about that," Wren reassured her. "It's a disguise." Hopefully, it would stay put. There were enough pins in it to lock-pick a hundred doors.

"Are you a hero?"

"I saved *you*, didn't I?" Wren said, slowing to glance around the corner of an old stone building. She peered back down at the child.

The girl nodded sagely.

"Then tell me where you live so I can take you there. I can't be a hero if I don't return you home!"

With a trembling hand, the wee one pointed to Wren's right. "Down there for a bit, th-then to the left. Mama isn't doing well. She can't work right now, which is why..." Her eyes filled with tears. "I'm not a thief, I swear!"

"I understand," she murmured, pulling the girl behind the corner of a thatched, whitewashed building. She bent low to avoid a guard she spied coming from the left, taking the moment to hug the girl against her chest. She was so skinny. *Too* skinny.

"Stealing because you're starving doesn't make you a thief," Wren reassured the girl, speaking the words into her filthy, straw-colored hair. "Or, at least, it wouldn't if the world were fair. Unfortunately, our world is not fair and there are consequences to our actions."

Wren snatched a glance to her left and right, then bolted down the next alleyway, then the next, and only just avoided running down a merchant crossing the next street with a donkey. The man fired a string of curses, but Wren merely ignored him to wind through the crowd on the busier street to find the next alleyway.

A flash of mahogany caught Wren's attention. Abruptly she stopped running, scanning the people in front of her to better focus on who she had seen. Lean and tall, built for swimming. Close-cropped, curly hair. An easy smile prone to laughter spread across his face.

Rowen.

Her breath seized and she blinked.

But then the man Wren thought she saw—for surely she had only *thought* she saw him, because Britta and everyone else she'd lost were currently weighing heavily on her mind—disappeared as quickly as he had appeared, leaving only a poor imitation of her best friend haggling in the street.

It's not him. Just another elf. Rowen is dead.

Wren shook herself when the little girl squeezed her hand. She peered down at the child.

"This is where I live," the girl announced quietly, tugging on Wren's wig when she didn't respond. In reality, Wren had no idea when and how she'd left the busy street to find the cramped, filthy back alley she now stood in. Numbly, she released the girl, who lifted a sheet of dirt-creased canvas to reveal the dark entrance of a hovel.

"Mama!" the girl cried, when a woman crashed into her and held her tight.

"Lillia!" the woman exclaimed, stroking her daughter's hair like her life depended on it. "Lillia, oh, Lillia, where did you run off to? I was so scared! You didn't go to the market, did you? I told you not to!"

"It's all right," Wren said, bending to her knees so that she was level with Lillia and her mother. The woman let go of her child to stare wide-eyed at her. She had big blue eyes, like her daughter, but with dark circles beneath them. Wren held out the bag of her coins and kept the guard's. No one would believe the family if they spent the gold, but Wren's mixed coins would be hard to trace back to any origin.

"Take this," she insisted. "Please use that money to feed the both of you until you're well enough to work again."

The woman gulped as she flitted her gaze from the heavy bag to Wren's face and back again. Eventually, the telling growl of hunger from Lillia's stomach made her decision for her, and she took the money.

"Thank you," she whispered. "How can I ever repay you?" Just then, a lock of Wren's real hair—washed clean of the brown clay used to dye it by virtue of the sweat on her scalp—tumbled free from beneath her wig. The woman's gaze rounded. She gave Wren a thoughtful look that told Wren the woman definitely recognized her.

Time to go. The bounty on her head was enough to tempt anyone.

"Look after Lillia," Wren said, smiling sadly at the girl. "Look after her the way I wish I could still look after my family."

The woman's eyes grew even wider. "You can count—"

Wren held a finger to her lips. "Can I trust you?"

The woman took one look at her daughter, safe from harm, and the coins in her hand that would feed them for months and nodded. "Of course. You are truly good and brave, Pr—"

"Call me Sparrow," Wren cut in, winking as she got back to her feet.

The woman wrinkled her nose at the joke. "Sparrow. My name is Francesca. I hope you do not forget us, as we will not forget you."

At this Wren laughed. "You are the kindest Verlantians I have met by far. Trust me, I will not forget you."

"Leave now. The watch should be sweeping through this part of town in the next half hour," the woman cautioned.

"Thank you." Wren gave the pair a small smile.

And with that, Wren left the mother and daughter, careful to take a completely different, winding path away from their hovel to truly ensure she was not being followed. She glanced up at the sky and scowled. More time had passed than she would have liked. Wren had to make her way back to camp as quickly as possible, and was in no way looking forward to the lecture Bram would inevitably give her on why her actions were dangerous, selfish, and wrong.

But she couldn't feel bad about helping Lillia and her mother. If faced with the situation again, she'd make the same decision twice.

Arrik was renowned for spreading death and destruction in the name of his father, King Soren, no matter how he'd tried to appeal to Wren to work with him. She was determined to atone for each of her husband's crimes against humanity, one good deed at a time. If her existence could negate Arrik's, then Wren knew she was doing something right with her life, even if she was half a world away from the life she longed to live.

She could handle a stupid lecture from Bram.

CHAPTER THREE

Arrik

Of all the tasks in the world that Arrik did not wish to do, retrieving his younger brother from an opium den was all the way at the bottom of the list.

Kalles had spent much of his time in drug houses ever since Princess Wren escaped and the Verlantian palace fell into disarray. Kalles was avoiding him, Arrik was convinced, but this time Kalles had taken things too far. His brother seemed to purposely visit the most obscure, out-of-the-way drug den he could possibly find. It was bloody inconvenient.

It also just so happened to be one of the most depraved and opulent opium dens in the entire kingdom.

Kray's Village was not a place Arrik ever enjoyed finding himself in. Why did his brother have to be such a pain? Kalles knew Soren would send Arrik after him, and it was never a pretty affair. So why did he continue on with the same song and dance at every turn?

Addiction is not reasonable. You should know that.

Arrik shoved the thought away as he wound his way

through the village—which had been set up within the forest specifically with the purpose of propping up the illicit activities of highborn degenerates with too much money and too few morals—Arrik made sure to maintain his haughty mask. It would not do for anyone who frequented the village to see how much of an effect the place had on him. Arrik felt like his skin was crawling, as if being in this place, standing here, looking at it, breathing its air, was enough to corrupt and sully his soul.

Or rip it apart with old memories.

Given the despicable things Arrik had done in his life, that was saying something.

All you need to do is retrieve Kalles and get the blazes out of here.

He exhaled through his nose and forced himself forward, mask in place, footsteps heavy with purpose as he marched toward the opium den.

And then stay by his side until he's sobered up. After that...

After that, Arrik would question his younger brother about the fact he'd given Wren a knife during their wedding celebrations and told her he'd killed his brides before they could spend a single night together. Like all of Arrik's brothers, Kalles liked to play games, but this was out of character for the youngest prince. While he didn't have the best of relationships with any of his half-brothers, he and Kalles had maintained an uneasy truce the longest. And despite Arrik's best efforts to never let anything affect him anymore, it bothered him that his brother had acted in such a way.

If Wren hadn't been so weak that night, Arrik was not certain he would have come out of her attack unscathed. As it was, after weeks of imprisonment in the bowels of his warship, there had been hardly any strength left in her muscles with which to attack him. But if the warrior princess had been at full health—the way Arrik had first spied her, a fiery blaze upon the back of a glittering dragon, taut and furious in battle—with a knife in her hand and him unsuspecting of this fact, Wren would have killed him, or at least wounded him grievously.

She had no idea how good it was for the both of them that she had failed. Soren was becoming more unhinged by the day. For some reason he was hyperfocused on Wren.

She made him look weak. The king will never let that go.

A pang of irritation spasmed in Arrik's temple. Had Wren only stayed put, things would be different now. If only he had told her what was going on sooner.

You couldn't. You can't jeopardize the plan for one woman.

He clenched his jaw and glared at a noble who dared look his way. The highborn man dropped his eyes back to his mug of ale.

Arrik knew the fault of their situation lay with him and him alone. His wife had been a prisoner, and him her captor. Of course she had wanted to escape. All Arrik had to do was tell her what he was doing, but he hadn't been able to trust that she would follow along with his plans. She was too unwieldy, too coarse...and irresistible.

And that was the problem.

He'd cared for each of his wives, wanting only their safety, but none of them had stirred him like the Dragon Princess. Arrik wanted to savor her wildness—to capture some of her spark and keep it inside himself.

She's making you soft.

There in lie the issue. Arrik couldn't afford to show any weakness or form any attachments. Everything rested on his ability to execute the plan, even if it meant losing the one woman he desired more than any other.

He had made a choice and now he had to lie in his proverbial bed. His wife obviously believed the worst in him and he'd used that to his advantage. Wren expected him to genuinely be on the hunt for her, hell-bent on revenge or imprisonment or whatever her darkest fears were about what her monstrous Verlantian husband would do to her, and he'd allow that. For now.

One day perhaps, when his plans were all over, he'd have the opportunity to reveal his intentions to Wren in full. And with a small bit of luck, perhaps she'd forgive him.

Stop being so naïve. She'll never forgive you.

Arrik shook himself and squared his shoulders. It would be best if he just wiped his lovely little bride from his mind completely. He had much more important tasks today.

Today was a day for other truths. Just not his own.

He rounded the corner and inwardly smiled as he came upon the opium den. The guards flanking the door, who were "discreetly" dressed like common men, straightened immediately at his approach. They did not hesitate in letting him or his men in. Who would dare refuse entry to one of King Soren's sons? Especially considering the fact that one of his sons was already inside.

Arrik's lip curled as he stepped inside. The madam of the place froze for but a minute before approaching and then bowing deeply. She rose and opened her mouth to speak when he held out his hand to stop her. She pressed her painted lips together and nodded regally, but Arrik noted a flash of fear in her eyes despite her calm countenance. He raised a finger to his lips, and she dipped her head. His message was conveyed. He didn't want his brother to know he was coming.

Arrik indicated to the left and the right, signaling for his warriors to move throughout the place in search of Kalles. He lifted a black scarf over his nose and mouth, then moved farther into the building.

The air was full of swirling, choking, purple smoke; he was careful to breathe in through a scarf tied around the bottom half of his face. Everywhere he looked there were silken curtains draped from the ceiling all the way down to the floor. Below his feet, innumerable carpets embroidered in lush, foreign patterns swallowed his footsteps. Every now and then Arrik came upon a recessed pit full of cushions.

In every pit, behind every curtain, and hidden in every corner, were the strung-out bodies of Verlanti's most depraved nobles, and the poor souls who had no choice but to serve them.

Slave women, and men, and ones far too young to really be either yet—children by any other name. Arrik bit his tongue to stop himself from yelling out at the immorality of it all. This was what he hated the most. Death, he could handle. But the use of innocents, or the blank, shiny eyes of those completely out of their minds...?

He hated it all. He wished to burn it to the ground.

"Prince Arrik, over here!" one of his warriors, on his left, called through the den, though his voice was muffled by the smoke and the curtains.

Arrik cut through the dim light and bodies, shaking off hands that gripped at his ankles and begged him to lie with them, until eventually he came upon a roped-off area with a bed large enough for ten people.

Kalles lay upon the bed with his feet hanging off the bottom, two women kissing his toes.

He was completely lost and utterly unaware—or uncaring—of who might see him like this.

Kalles was the youngest of Soren's sons, and the one who looked most like Arrik himself. His long, dark blond hair was splayed around his face, disheveled, tangled, and dirty. His heavy-lidded, cerulean eyes tried to focus, but Arrik could tell that Kalles saw nothing. He'd always loved outrageous fashions and colors, like his father, but where Soren's clothes were always immaculate, Kalles had a deep purple stain upon the jewel-blue silk of his shirt, and the buttons had been ripped off.

He was a complete and utter state, all of his own making.

"Disgraceful," Arrik muttered.

Arrik was ashamed to call him his brother. He was half-tempted to leave him here, to languish in his own filth and perverseness until he died. That's what Kalles seemed to want most days. Why did Arrik keep saving his brother?

Because you care for him.

He shoved the thought down deep. Affection killed. He needed Kalles to survive because he had information Arrik needed. And at the end of the day he was the only brother Arrik could somewhat tolerate.

"Pick him up and get him outside," Arrik ordered his warriors.

Kalles whined and then began to cackle as he finally managed to focus on Arrik. "The dutiful black knight coming to save the disgraceful youngest son? What did Father promise you this time? Another wife?"

Arrik kept his expression bland and turned on the spot, striding back out of the opium den with increasing fury as he stepped over the blissed-out bodies of lost souls. He yanked the scarf off his face once he was back outside, and nodded to his lieutenant. "Get the slaves out of here. Every last one of them. You have three minutes."

His lieutenant knew better than to question this and began barking orders. The rest of the warriors bolted inside, filling the den with the cacophony of panic-ridden slaves. The patrons of the den would be too drugged-out to notice what was going on, Arrik knew, and so would be slow to react.

He tipped his head back and closed his eyes and began counting. It always seemed to calm his mind and heart. Cries and shrieks filled the air as his men dragged everyone from the building and then placed them on the porch of a nearby alehouse.

...178, 179, 180...

"Everyone is out, my lord," his lieutenant said.

Arrik opened his eyes and dropped his head. "And the prince?"

"Tied to his horse so he won't fall off."

Good. God forbid Kalles fall off and break his royal neck on his way home.

He nodded curtly to his lieutenant and then moved back to the entrance of the opium den. Arrik lifted one of the torches that bracketed the entrance and lit it before tossing it inside. Immediately the place caught on fire. He turned his back on the place.

Good riddance.

He did not care for the screams rising from those who'd been taken from the building in tandem with the smoke as he left Kray's Village on his horse. Arrik did not intend to return.

Kalles swayed dangerously upon the back of his own horse, a beautiful white mare and the sister to Arrik's own stallion. In all honesty, he did not understand how he could sit upright at all. Kalles shielded his eyes from the late afternoon sun, his expression one of scandalized indignation at the fact he had to perceive daylight.

A small part of Arrik wanted to ask what had happened to his brother to make him like this. It was true that Soren pitted them against each other, and the dark elf court was a dangerous place to grow up, but once upon a time the two of them had gotten along well. Arrik would even have considered his younger brother his friend. Somewhere along the line, Kalles had turned into a spoiled, foppish, drug addict. Arrik considered how much time his younger brother likely had left before he overdosed and died. Years? Months? If Kalles kept traveling down the same path, it was days or weeks at most.

Part of him mourned. A larger part seethed with anger.

But an even bigger part told Arrik not to care. Kalles clearly didn't.

"I have been looking for you for weeks now," Arrik growled at his brother. "And yet every time you're in a new drug den, with a new wench or a new pipe in your hand. What is wrong with you?"

"Haven't you heard brother? *Everything.*"

"That we can agree on," Arrik muttered. "It's not like you to avoid me."

"I am not...avoiding you," Kalles said, slurring his words.

He chuckled. "Come now, I know you better than that."

He knew why. He wanted his brother to say it.

Kalles threw his arms out, wobbling in the saddle. "This is just...who I am, brother. If you're disappointed, then—"

"Enough with the games. Tell me why you gave the Dragon Princess a knife to murder me with on my wedding night." Arrik had promised himself he would wait for Kalles to sober up to ask his questions. But he couldn't wait, and part of him reasoned that Kalles might be more likely to give him an honest answer when he was too inebriated to screen his responses. His younger brother had a way with twisting words to his benefit.

It took Kalles a few moments to understand what Arrik had asked. Then he shrugged, tilted his face to the sky, and let out a horrible laugh. A garbled, choking sound. It was altogether more sad than mirthful.

"Why not?" he asked, glancing at Arrik out of the corner of his bloodshot eyes. "It's all fun and games in our family, isn't it? Maybe I wanted you to lose for once."

Arrik did not believe it for a second. Even drugged out of his mind, Kalles was capable of lying. He was a master at keeping secrets; he had been even back when the two of them had been close. Perhaps it was one of the reasons they *had* been close, for Arrik knew he could trust Kalles with anything he told him.

That was, until their father broke them apart. Arrik knew why. Two sons banded together against the king was bad news for Soren. Especially his smarter sons. It would not take much for them to overthrow him.

And so now here Arrik and Kalles were, divided.

"Do you really believe I would kill my own brides?" Arrik asked his brother. "That's what you told Wren. Do you believe it?"

"Didn't you? Simply by marrying you the poor women signed their own death warrants. What is that if not your fault?"

A thread of old guilt wrapped around his heart. Kalles always knew how to strike a person to the bone.

Arrik would get nowhere with his brother this way. Time to change tactics. "Where did the blade come from? I do not recognize it from your armory. "

Kalles merely smiled. "A friend," he said, eyes hazy and even more unfocused than before. He held up the loose rope and smiled. "I have lots of friends and yet none at all."

Arrik cursed. Even high, his brother had managed to untie himself. The wily little fox.

Kalles gurgled, and then his eyes fluttered closed, and he fell from his horse with an ungraceful thump.

Arrik dismounted his horse and touched his fingers to the base of his brother's neck.

A steady pulse, but Kalles was out cold.

Perfect. He was none the wiser about what his youngest brother was planning.

It was going to be a long afternoon.

CHAPTER FOUR

Wren

By the time Wren made it back to camp, word had been sent of Prince Arrik's movements and everyone was busy packing up to head to a new location. It reminded her of a bunch of ants scurrying to and fro. She wasted no time in searching out her Aunt Vienne's tent, knowing full well that Bram was likely already inside. He was probably tattling on her. If Wren was going to get chewed out for saving Lillia the little child, best to get it done with quickly.

She reached the flap that covered the opening of the simple brown canvas tent and paused. There were a cacophony of voices coming from inside, not just Bram's. Listening carefully, Wren managed to pick out Leif, Vienne, Bram, and Ever—her aunt's best friend and stalwart companion. But there was another voice Wren recognized, though she hadn't heard it since the day she escaped from the palace.

Josenu.

She entered the tent and, sure enough, there he was, the spy the rebellion had planted within Prince Arrik's very own retinue of guards. His dark, shoulder-length blond hair and gray eyes, along with his height and imposing figure, cast the ghost of Arrik himself before Wren, and her stomach flipped. What news of her vile husband did he bring?

You want to know more than you should.

Her jaw clenched. The fact she wanted to know more about Arrik not just for the sake of the rebellion but for herself was a disgrace.

Wren pasted on a smile as the group quieted. Leif cast a fervent glance over at her before dropping his gaze to the floor. Even Bram was avoiding looking at her, though Wren had fully expected a loud scolding from him full of every expletive the man knew—of which there were many. Were they speaking about her before or something else?

Wren's aunt tossed a map over several documents on the large, circular table that stood between everyone. Suspicion curled through her chest. What were they trying to hide? She was well aware that she was a newcomer and that several members of the rebellion—especially Bram—did not trust her, but something still felt off.

Wren knew better than to demand an explanation. She would come across as childish and entitled. Instead, she hung back at the entrance of the tent and quietly listened to the group's whispered plans for relocating the camp.

"There are soldiers flocking into every port town in search of Wren," Josenu said, flashing a look of concern her way before pulling his attention back to the map. "We will not be able to recreate this entire camp in one place. If you split our forces here, here, and here"—Josenu stabbed the central forest drawn on the map with each word—"then we should be able to avoid detection. You will have to stick to foraging and hunting in the forest though. It's too risky going into town to buy food."

At this, Ever frowned. "Game is scarce in this area," she muttered, clearly unhappy. "It will be difficult to feed everyone."

"Perhaps if someone hadn't made such a scene earlier," Bram growled, obviously insinuating Wren, "then the port town guards wouldn't be on such high alert."

"I wasn't recognized," Wren protested, speaking in her defense before she could stop herself. She took a step toward the group, feeling altogether like an outsider. What did she have to do for them to trust her? Was she not the biggest victim in this situation? And yet still they did not trust her. They expected Wren to be in cahoots with her husband—a man who had plundered her home, slain her parents, and dragged her away to be forcibly married?

"But I will hunt for food," Wren said, eager to make herself useful. "Game is hard to come by on the Dragon Isles too. Hunting in such conditions is something I am particularly good at. So let me be useful." A pause. "Please."

Vienne shook her head, looking so much like Wren's own mother that it caused her breath to catch. "That is far too dangerous. You cannot go alone."

"So send someone out with me."

"We cannot spare the men. Anyone required to protect you is too valuable elsewhere."

This rankled Wren to no end. She didn't need protecting.

Vienne was right about one thing though: anyone required to keep Wren safe from Arrik and his men would have to be a skillful person indeed, and definitely needed for more important missions than hunting. But Wren fit that bill all on her own. Several weeks of eating well and exercise had returned strength and function to her. She was fighting fit. She was born a warrior. If she were to face Arrik now, she would put up more than a good fight.

If she planned it properly, she might even beat him.

"A wealthy merchant will be visiting the next port city over that I'm familiar with," Leif chimed in. "I overheard it this morning down by the docks."

"Do you mean Delansh?" Bram asked, the perpetual scowl on his face deepening. "That place is full of pirates!"

"Exactly the kind of place a wealthy merchant would decide to dock his ship if he planned to deal with the rebellion, not the crown." Leif grinned. "And as it turns out, this particular merchant has sympathies for those enslaved in Verlanti. I think, with the right words, we can turn him to our cause. That will give us a safe, reliable source of foodstuffs and grain while we're being hunted. I think that's worth risking our necks against a few pirates, don't you?"

Everyone pondered this in silence for a while. It was a wildly reckless, risky plan. Wren's father had set up an entire naval branch just to deal with pirates; that's how dangerous they were. She'd only dealt with them herself a handful of times, and it had always led to casualties. Leif's plan was stupid and foolhardy.

It was also the only plan they had to work with.

Vienne sighed, running a hand over her face, then said, "It isn't a good plan, but it's the best we have. Leif, take point on this."

"I need the Dragon Princess."

"Absolutely not!" Bram exclaimed, outraged. "That's just asking to be caught. You saw how she acted today, Leif. Use your bloody brain here—I know you have one somewhere. We have to keep her out of sight."

That was out of line.

Wren took a step forward, but Leif held his hand up, gave her a sidelong glance, and smiled mischievously. A gleam she hadn't seen in his eyes since the night of their escape, deep in the Verlanti palace dungeons, filled her with a surge of adrenaline.

"This entire plan hinges on Princess Wren," Leif countered. "She's visible proof that the crown doesn't hold complete control over the Dragon Isles. What better indication is there than that to bring the merchant to our side? If we hold the Dragon Princess—"

"Then we hold the Dragon Isles," Josenu finished for him. He looked down at the map, tapping his fingers repeatedly as he mulled over something. "It will be difficult, but I think we should be able to keep Arrik away from the city for a day. Perhaps two. But I cannot make any promises. You will have to be quick."

"Then we do not have the time to lose," Ever said, snapping to attention and readjusting the positions Josenu had pointed out on the map. The tall, scarred woman was in charge of the rebellion's effort to free slaves in Verlanti.

Many of them joined the rebellion afterwards as a direct, pointed attack against their former captors, and so became Ever's most trusted compatriots.

If they were going to organize the rebellion camp into three separate bases and split their forces appropriately, Ever was the one to do it alongside Vienne.

Vienne nodded at Leif. "I leave the merchant to you, then. And take—"

"Bram," Leif finished, rolling his eyes even as the man scowled once more. "I know."

It became painfully clear that Wren was expected to leave the tent before anyone else, as they planned to continue their conversation.

The one they were having before you interrupted them. Just what are you planning, Auntie?

Her gaze lingered on the table, and the contents beneath the map, one final time before taking the hint and leaving.

It was therefore to Wren's surprise that Josenu followed her out.

"We need to talk," he murmured, lightly touching Wren's elbow to direct her away from the camp and into the forest.

Wren was torn between viciously refusing his request and satisfying her burning curiosity to find out what was going on. She never wanted to hear Arrik's name again if she could help it. But on the other hand...being ignorant was a weakness. Knowledge was power, even when that knowledge was unpleasant.

And she wanted to know. More than she should.

She nodded. "Then let us talk."

CHAPTER FIVE

WREN

"So how are things going at the palace?" Wren asked the question casually, though her heart was thrashing wildly in her chest. Suddenly, allowing herself to be alone with Josenu in the middle of the forest felt like a terrible idea. He was one of Arrik's personal palace guards.

What if helping you escape was all a ploy?

Her stomach knotted and she forced herself to keep her calm façade in place.

What if this was some twisted game of Arrik's just so he could capture you again?

She exhaled slowly, memories surfacing that brought both fear—and to her shame—a little thrill. The expression on the prince's face when he realized Wren was fleeing his side lingered in her mind far too often—when he knew once and for all that she was rejecting him—his politics, his plan, everything—in order to go off on her own and protect the Dragon Isles any way she could.

"I'll hunt you."

Wren shivered.

Three little words that haunted her at night.

"Princess Wren?" Josenu murmured, concern coloring his fine features. It was only in forcing her attention back on the guard that Wren noted just *how* fine those features were. A proud brow, sharp cheekbones, a perfectly straight nose. He was more beautiful than half of the Verlanti court—on par with Arrik and his brothers. Wren had never noticed before; Josenu had always been dressed in his on-duty guard uniform.

Now in casual clothes made to blend in with the lower classes, his handsome features stood out even more.

Josenu frowned, casting a shadow over his gray eyes. "What's wrong?"

"You look different in plain clothes," Wren said, which at the very least wasn't a lie. "It took me aback."

"Are you sure you weren't thinking, 'What if he's double-crossing the rebellion for the sake of Prince Arrik,' by any chance?"

Wren winced. Josenu was clearly a clever man; no wonder Vienne had trusted him to help Wren and Leif flee the Verlantian palace. "It may have crossed my mind," she admitted, slowly. "I'd be stupid not to but..."

"I'll hunt you."

"But...?" he prompted.

"You've helped me in the past. Until you give me a reason not to trust you, we're allies."

Josenu snorted. "How very diplomatic of you. It'll get you killed. Never trust anyone."

"Even you?" she questioned, eyeing the forest around

them, pushing past the roiling, twisting feelings inside her.

"Even me."

"How very comforting," she replied dryly. "What news is there from the palace?" Wren asked, changing the subject.

Josenu leaned against a tree, crossing his arms over his chest as he regarded Wren. An evening breeze gently blew his hair around his face, softening his features. For one traitorous moment, Wren wondered what Arrik himself would look like in such a situation: lowborn clothes, hair undone, at ease beneath a forest.

She wanted to see it, almost as much as she didn't.

Get yourself together. What is wrong with you?

"Queen Astrid plans to visit some of her favorite friends soon—you would do well to avoid straying into her path."

This gave Wren pause. She liked the queen. She had been perhaps the only member of the royal family who had treated Wren like an actual person. More than that: on the day of her wedding, Astrid had treated Wren like a daughter.

She's not your mother. They killed your mother.

Bile burned at the back of her throat.

Don't think about your mother.

"How can I know to avoid her path if I do not know who her friends are or where they plan to meet?" Wren rasped, trying to get control of her emotions. Something told her to keep her curiosity over why she should avoid Astrid to herself for now.

"I trust Bram to keep you out of trouble. Leif, on the other hand..."

"What about Leif?" Wren demanded, affronted. Was she

supposed to be wary of her only friend? He'd been nothing but a gem for weeks.

Josenu laughed, then held his hands up in surrender. "I only meant to say he seems the type to lead you into trouble simply because it might be fun for the both of you, or if it will satisfy your curiosity over certain matters. He's taken more of a liking to you than to anyone else in the rebellion. Just what did you say to him in the dungeons to appeal to him so much?"

Wren considered this. In truth, she hardly knew a thing about Leif, only that he was very capable of playing the part of a mad prisoner, and he had trusted Wren to save his life aboard the back of a fearsome dragon.

It bonded them.

He trusted her, so she trusted him. It was as simple as that.

Wren allowed a small smile to curl her lips.

Leif *did* seem the type to lead Wren into a bit of trouble. That gleam in his eyes when he insisted on Wren coming with him to meet the merchant flashed through her mind. He was definitely prone to a bit of mischief. And he wasn't nearly as serious as the rest of the rebellion.

Wren didn't dislike it. Given her circumstances, she was tired of safe and serious. She needed someone to be reckless with. His outlook on life was refreshing, and a break from the turmoil that roiled in her head.

Clearly, some of Wren's thoughts were obvious on her face, for Josenu took a step toward her, brows furrowing. "Don't be foolish, Princess Wren. You know you must be careful. Don't put everyone's lives at risk just to prove that you are useful."

That stung—because it was true.

Today she'd been reckless even if it had been an honorable decision. She didn't have the luxury to stray from the path that had been set before her. Too many lives depended on the success of her missions.

With a sigh, Wren's shoulders slumped. "I know. But this is all so stifling. Two months I've been with the rebellion, and if Bram had his way I'd be locked away, out of trouble. I basically *am* locked away, for all the freedom I actually have." Her family had never hidden her away in such a manner.

You also weren't believed to be the heir to the throne.

"Don't lose sight of what you're doing," Josenu said, trying to reassure her. "While the queen is away, King Soren is planning a party with his closest friends. He has brought women from the Dragon Isles as gifts for them."

"What?" she whispered. Though the evening air was balmy, Wren's skin suddenly became cold and clammy.

My people...slaves? For the Verlanti king?

She had to stop it. She had to—

"Wren." Josenu spoke her name without her title, placing a hand on her shoulder and gently squeezing it as if it might stop her thoughts from spiraling.

When the devil had he moved from his spot?

She blinked repeatedly and tried to ground herself in the moment.

The elven spy squeezed her shoulder once again. "You

need to be the woman who bided her time in the palace, collecting information and planning her escape, not a woman who is a hair-trigger away from doing something stupid. Keep your wits about you. Take a deep breath and *focus.*"

He was right. She was panicking. It was a struggle to get air into her lungs, and when she tried to breathe it stung like a thousand needles. She became aware, then, that the mention of Soren and what he was doing to her people reminded Wren of her own enslavement, and the torture that had been inflicted upon her. She had thrown her memories of her experience into a box that she never planned to reopen, but even Wren knew she could only hold back the trauma for so long.

Maybe that is why you're imagining Rowen?

"Deep breaths," Josenu said again, voice calm and soothing. "You can do it. You need to be at the top of your game to meet this merchant tomorrow. Otherwise, I can't do much to protect you."

"I'll hunt you," Arrik's voice echoed in her mind.

"Arrik…he…how is he doing?" Wren bit out. She had to know. Josenu blinked slowly and she went over her words and blanched. "I don't want to know about his wellbeing but about his movements—his plans," she growled.

His hunt of her and the rebellion had been relentless. Today—having to split the camp into three, thus weakening their forces—was further proof of his determination to find her.

Josenu hesitated. He let go of Wren's shoulder as if

suddenly remembering that she was a princess and he a guard, and stood a little straighter. She could glean no sense of what he was thinking from his face. What horrors was her husband subjecting the world to?

"He's doing what he does best," Josenu finally said—too carefully. "Taking care of what's important." A pointed stare at Wren. "He's sent men into the Dragon Isles to prepare the palace for his arrival. His and yours."

Wren snorted at his arrogance. "As if he will get me back and be able to do such a thing. They will fight him until the bitter end."

"Not if you're at his side."

She started. "I will *never* rule at his side."

Josenu studied her, his eyes roving over her face. "He has a way of getting what he wants, Princess. I've met no one who can outwit or outrun him."

"I've done both, haven't I?" she murmured.

"For now." His ominous reply made a shiver run down her spine.

"You are right about one thing," she admitted. "I need to keep my wits about me. Being emotional will get me nowhere." A pause. "How can you stand to work for him, even if you *are* spying on behalf of the rebellion? You seem too...good."

Too kind. Too concerned for Wren's wellbeing to be a heartless Verlantian.

Not all dark elves are evil.

It was a disturbing thought. Their kingdom had always been the monsters looming on the horizon.

"I'll take the compliment with thanks," Josenu replied, a wry smile on his lips. "And as for *how*...that is something you will work out, given time. Hopefully."

"And what is *that* supposed to mean?" She crossed her arms and arched a brow. The spy seemed to get more cryptic by the minute.

"It means be careful, don't underestimate Prince Arrik, and don't trust just anyone with your secrets and your concerns." He glanced back in the direction of Vienne's tent, then murmured, "Blood doesn't make someone honest. What you saw of King Soren with Arrik should be proof enough of that."

As the two of them made their way back to camp before Wren's absence could be noted, Wren pondered what Josenu had meant. Certainly, it was true that her aunt was clearly keeping something from her. But wasn't that reasonable, given the fact much of the rebellion did not yet trust Wren? Plus, no one owed anyone all of their secrets.

So why did he compare her to Soren, and the way he is with Arrik?

Just what was Vienne up to...and how was it going to affect Wren and the Dragon Isles at large?

She peeked at Josenu from beneath her lashes. And what game was the spy playing? Was he trying to sow doubts in her mind about her kin? Could she trust him? Or any of them?

Trust only yourself. For now.

Josenu was right about one thing. Wren had to keep her wits about her, keep calm, and think with her head.

"I'll hunt you."

And not only when she was dealing with her barbaric husband.

CHAPTER SIX

WREN

Wren didn't know what she had expected of the port city of Delansh, but it certainly wasn't this.

The city was a mess of confusingly-laid-out spindly streets, crisscrossing over each other with barely a single marketplace available for trading and shopping. The buildings, their roofs, and their doors were made of seemingly any material the residents could get their hands on—brick, steel, slate, wood, straw, rough cloth, mud, clay—which resulted in not a single street looking the same.

Smells of fish, spices, bread, smoke, and salt filled the air. It seemed to chase Wren everywhere she went, and only got stronger as she forced her way through thousands of faceless bodies toward the port proper.

The city was busy. It was hectic. It was stressful. It was overwhelming.

But she liked the chaos. She was just one face among hundreds trying to scrape out a living.

When Wren reached the port, Delansh finally opened up into perhaps the largest, busiest, sprawling market she had ever seen. All manner of ships were docked along vast timber jetties, sailors and merchants alike hollering for help or heaving immense barrels and boxes on and off the harbor.

She sighed, feeling all at once at home. The sea and ships had always called to her. It was where she belonged. Her lips twitched in humor. While she was comfortable in the port, it was nothing like home.

But many of these so-called sailors and merchants looked nothing like the kind Wren had seen before. Not on the Dragon Isles, even though people came from afar to trade there, nor in Verlanti or any of the other port towns Wren had since visited. They were all dressed as haphazardly as the city itself, often far finer than a sailor or a merchant had any right to dress.

Pirates, Wren guessed.

All in all, Delansh was perhaps the most bizarre, interesting place Wren had ever seen.

"Seems the Verlantian prince hasn't been able to reach Delansh yet," Bram muttered, as he, Leif, and Wren filtered through the early morning shoppers as if they, too, were merely here to purchase fish and exotic goods from pirate merchants. "That's good."

Leif nodded in approval. "Josenu *did* say we'd likely have a day's head start."

"Then let's not waste it. Where were we meeting this wealthy merchant of yours?" Wren asked, tightening her coin purse on her belt.

"In a tavern on the corner there," Leif said, pointing toward a building that looked as if it had seen better days.

Though the sun had scarcely been up three hours, the door to the tavern swung open and closed every few seconds, indicating that business was already booming for the day.

Wren wondered if the place had closed during the night at all, or if it merely remained open forever.

Bram's lip curled in distaste. "Dare I ask how you came to know about this establishment?"

"I've performed here more than once," Leif said, shrugging before leading the way to the front door of the tavern and waving them in. "My foreign appearance isn't so interesting to them here, so I can sing in peace." Wren regarded Leif curiously. Certainly, it was true Leif wasn't Verlantian or even Vadonese. But Wren had seen merchants with the same creamy skin and slanted eyes before, back on the Dragon Isles. They came from far, far to the east. She supposed that meant Verlantians were not used to the young bard's appearance. Given what Wren had learned of the nobility here, she reasoned that meant Leif had to deal with undue interest whenever he performed.

Most of it likely unpleasant.

That's how he learns so much.

Wren shared a smile with her friend. If people treated him as the object of interest—their entertainment for the night—he was likely to be privy to a whole host of things the rebellion might otherwise never know. It was a brilliant ploy.

That was, until Leif's face was plastered on wanted posters right beside Wren's.

As they made their way through smoke-filled air to a tiny,

circular table in an obscure corner of the tavern, a familiar unease began to creep up Wren's spine. She did not believe it to be a good sign that there had been such a light city patrol upon their entrance to Delansh. It was...suspicious.

Arrik would have sent a messenger along to increase the guard tenfold if he thought you might be here.

That was what had happened in the last few towns Wren and the rebellion had passed through, after all. Why would the pirate city be any different?

Does the Verlanti crown not hold much sway over the city?

Wren could only wonder. If the merchant they were meeting was sympathetic to the rebellion's cause, and had wanted to meet in Delansh, did that mean there were others within the city wall who might wish to rise against the Verlantian royal family, and the higher classes in general?

"Right," Bram huffed out once they'd sat down and he surveyed their surroundings. "Ale all around, then?" He waved a hand at the bar and held up three fingers.

Wren frowned at Bram in confusion, for though the man had clearly disliked the tavern when they were outside, and now he held himself as if he were right at home. He'd pushed his hood down and slid a hand through his hair to reveal the ugly scar by his right ear, and there was a glinting, clearly genuine gold chain resting across the hollow of his throat which hadn't be there before.

"How do you do that?" she mumbled out of the corner of her mouth, shifting the hood around her head to ensure her red hair did not show.

Bram kept a smarmy grin plastered on his face as he

replied, “Do what?”

“Fit in.” He was generally unpleasant to deal with but the man had skills when it came to subterfuge.

“He wouldn’t be very good at his job if he couldn’t fit in.” Leif chuckled. His gaze never stayed on one place for too long, constantly surveying their changing environment. When his shoulder tensed, she casually glanced behind her, lowering her lashes to observe the room.

A man sat there at a table, alone. Going by his odd but expensive attire, she assumed he must be one of the pirate merchants she’d seen out on the docks. He caught her look and nodded once.

Wren batted her lashes and lazily turned back to the table with a calmness she didn’t feel.

When their ale arrived, Wren had to fight not to snatch the tankard out of the barmaid’s hand out of sheer nervousness, though she was still careful to hide most of her face and her hair.

Leif, on the other hand, did not bother hiding his, clearly deciding that confidence would prevent suspicion—something which Wren, with her unique hair, could not emulate. When a tawdry bard stood up on the bar and began playing a tune on his guitar, Leif whistled along to the melody before pulling out a flute from his cloak and adding a harmony to the song, much to the delight of both the bard and the tavern’s rowdy customers.

“You know it?” Wren asked, when the boy’s harmony grew even more merry and complicated.

It was Bram who answered. “I’m surprised *you* don’t.”

Wren was about to demand he speak plainly, then scrunched her eyes as she decided instead to try and focus on the tune. It *did* sound familiar, truth be told, though she wasn't sure why.

Then the bard began singing, and it didn't take long for Wren to work out where she'd heard the song. Every town they'd traveled through she'd heard snippets sung on the lips of every lowborn—and highborn—reveler leaving a drug den or tavern or whorehouse.

"And though the prince indeed looked fair,
His good wives three he did so scare!
And now I say, without a lie,
Through fright or flee, they did so die!"

"Ahh," Wren sighed, fighting the urge to roll her eyes. After hearing the truth from Arrik's own mouth, the song held no amusement for her. At first, the lyrics had made her feel…sad, almost. They were a lie—if the prince was to be believed. Someone had murdered them. Had likely meant to murder *Wren,* too, though Arrik had ensured that did not happen.

No, you tried to kill him instead.

Now the lyrics merely annoyed Wren. She was fed up with hearing them—of feeling sadness, or guilt, or whatever else it was the words made her feel.

He has a hold on you.

Her fingers tightened around her cup. It was a dark truth that she never wanted to come to light. It shamed her. All she wanted was to be done with Arrik entirely.

"And what about the fourth wife?" the pirate-merchant who sat behind Wren bellowed, startling Wren so much she spilled half her ale across the table. She shook her hand off and wiped the excess ale onto her dark cloak.

Leif paused from his flute-playing to grin at the man. "I heard she tried to kill the fair prince!"

Wren couldn't believe her ears. Was Leif honestly admitting to what she *had* done? But the confession had the entire bar in fits of laughter.

"I'd like to see the woman who could do that," someone called out.

"She *is* a dragon!" someone else shouted. "If she really tried to off the barbarian prince, just imagine what netting her would get us in return."

"Hmm, I wonder," the pirate-merchant murmured, right into Wren's ear. Far too close.

She flipped around to face him, heart in her throat, and was met with a steely gray-eyed stare, slightly too-long brown hair tied carelessly back, and a roguish grin filled with perfect white teeth. He looked younger than Arrik and even Josenu. Closer to Rowen's age, if Wren looked closely enough.

She pushed thoughts of Rowen away.

"Take a step back," she muttered, pressing a blade against his thigh.

He smiled, mischief twinkling in his eyes as he leaned closer. "Or what, my lovely lady?"

"Gunn," Leif said, when it became clear the bar had returned their attention to the bard and his next song. "Nice of you to make yourself known."

Wren stiffened. This was their contact?

Bram huffed. "You took your time revealing yourself."

"I wanted to see what she'd do," Gunn said, still grinning at Wren and far too close. She wanted to move away but knew that meant losing to the clearly very dangerous man in front of her.

"And what did you want me to do?" she whispered, pressing the blade harder against his leg.

"Cry, maybe. Run out the tavern. Sing along as the bard slanders your dear husband." His lips tilted roguishly. "Or my personal favorite, fall madly in love with me, let me whisk you away as you lifted your skirts."

The distinct urge to slap Gunn filled Wren's veins. Instead, she matched his smile. "Sorry, crying and fleeing aren't things that dragons do. We do sing, but not about monsters who murder our family. As for the tossing of skirts..." She eyed him from head to toe before meeting his gaze once again. "I doubt anyone has lifted theirs in a long time for the likes of you."

Gunn's smile grew even wider, which Wren hadn't thought possible. "What a treasure you are. You're everything Leif said you were and more." He arched a black brow. "Now that we're acquainted, would you be so kind as to remove your dagger from my thigh?"

Wren slowly pulled away and stowed her weapon. The impertinent pirate swayed forward to lean on her shoulder, head sticking between Wren and Leif in order to address the both of them along with Bram. The blatant disregard for her personal space should have incensed her, but for some reason it actually made her like the pirate-merchant more.

He had no fear.

He'd fit right in on the Dragon Isles...if he weren't clearly a dirty thief.

"I heard from my favorite false bard that you're in need of a reliable source of supplies," Gunn said.

Leif clucked his tongue and sniffed dramatically. "A bard who is also a spy is still a bard."

"Yet a merchant who has a penchant for sometimes playing the part of pirate is always a pirate," Gunn pointed out. "That's a double standard if ever there was one."

"Yes, we need supplies," Bram cut in, before Leif and Gunn could further derail the conversation. "Food, primarily. Can you help us?"

"That depends. What can you do for me?"

"We can continue freeing slaves and fighting to take down the Verlanti royal family, which you seem to want to see happen."

"True," Gunn purred, stroking his chin. He glanced at Wren. "But if things were that easy, you wouldn't have brought along your pretty little princess to sweeten the deal. So what do you think I want, *personally*, from this deal?"

"Not that," she drawled, pulling away from his touch on her shoulder. She was disgusted for thinking she might actually like the pirate. He was a degenerate and a rake.

But then Gunn laughed at the look on her face, and Wren moved quickly from revulsion to confusion. "Oh, love, it's not what you think!" he protested, still laughing. "I have plenty of women who very much *want* to be in my bed. No, what I want is to trade—legally—with the Dragon Isles."

Wren scowled. "Do you enjoy making others feel uncomfortable?"

"When it helps me work out what folk *will* and *will not* do, yes. It seems we are similar in that manner."

"How do you mean?" she asked, leaning an elbow on the table.

Gunn mirrored her position. "You kept a blade on me and refused to let up until you understood my mettle."

"Your mettle sure, but your character not so much," she quipped.

"Such is life in espionage, my love."

"True. So what do you want?"

He smiled. "Straight to the point. I love it. Would you be willing to trade with me, Princess Wren, if you get out of this mess and return to your kingdom as its queen?"

"If you help us, then it would certainly be in the cards," she said, keeping her face as blank as possible. Any sign from her that someone else was, in fact, the heir to the throne, would not serve Wren any favors. "Once we *get out of this mess*, as you put it. It's a long road and I'm not sure you have the patience for it."

"Oh, I am the master of patience."

"Is that so?" she murmured.

"It is." He winked. "I've been waiting a lifetime for you to take me as your lover."

Wren smiled in spite of herself. "So we have a deal?"

"We do." Gunn was still smiling, but his grin had a new

edge to it—if not malicious, then devilish. “You must prove yourself to me. I need to see your mettle, my love.” Then, in one fluid movement, he knocked Wren’s hood off and swept to his feet to address the entire tavern, who caught sight of Wren’s red hair immediately.

He waved at the money-hungry crowd. “So get out of this mess. Escape the city, then we’ll talk.”

CHAPTER SEVEN

WREN

She was going to kill Gunn. She was going to gut him nice and slow, then feed his entrails to the carnivorous fish beneath the Verlantian palace.

If she, Leif, and Bram got out of the tavern alive.

The pirate had materialized out of existence, melting into the mob as they quickly organized their efforts to corner Wren into their custody.

"Leif," Bram muttered, as he positioned himself in front of Wren, "remind me to kill you after this."

Leif laughed like a madman. It reminded Wren of the way he'd acted down in the dungeons—when she thought he truly *was* mad. Given his current reaction Wren couldn't discount that he might actually be at least a little insane.

"If you can kill me after this, that means we're getting out alive," Leif replied, before sliding a dagger from his cloak and aiming it with pinpoint precision at their closest attacker.

It flew past the man's cheek, slicing it open before landing in the chipped wooden surface of the bar.

"You missed," Wren said, as she readied her own

weapons.

"I didn't," Leif replied, before grabbing Wren by the wrist and pulling her through the opening that had been made when their first attacker recoiled from the dagger. He flashed a grin back at Bram. "Cover us!"

"As if I have a choice!" he growled, ever the grump.

Wren ran by pure instinct, using her elbows and her knees and her knives to bash and slash her way toward the door along with Leif. The young man moved like water through the crowd, barely touching anyone. It was uncanny. He was as elegant as a dragon.

Aurora would have liked him.

The thought almost stopped Wren in her tracks.

Grief tore at her heart. Why was it that whenever she was in a dangerous situation she thought of the ghosts of her past? Her mother, her dragon, Rowen.

You need to get it together or you'll get your friends killed.

Wren exploded out of the tavern with Leif and she winced, eyes watering. The morning light reflecting off the waves just about blinded her, but there was no time to waste adjusting to the brighter surroundings. Leif pulled Wren through the curious crowd—whose eyes followed Wren's hair wherever they went. Her lungs burned as Leif forced Wren to move faster, their boots slapping against the slick cobbles of the road.

She tried to pull up her hood, but they were running so fast it wouldn't stay up. "We need to—" she gasped, when Leif scrambled onto the top of a ramshackle building and she followed suit, hauling herself up. "We need to hide my hair."

Her chest rose and lowered with her heavy breathing. She needed to train more to keep up with Leif.

"We just need to remain out of sight until the crowd forgets us," Leif called back, over his shoulder, clambering over another roof and scaling an adjacent, much taller, building. "There's a place on the docks I know."

Wren didn't ask what this place was, nor how Leif knew it. Given what Gunn had just done she wasn't inclined to put much faith in anything Leif knew, though Wren also had to acknowledge she had no other choice but to follow him.

One last time, she pulled her hood over her hair and followed him with a groan, her arms burning as she climbed after her friend. When she got her hands on Gunn, he'd wish he'd never been born.

The blackguard.

Below them, the noise of people shouting and clamoring through the streets after them all merged into one incomprehensible din in Wren's ears. The fact none of them had followed them onto the roof was a good sign—it meant they didn't know where Leif and Wren had gone. So long as she remained hidden behind chimneystacks and plumes of dirty smoke from fireplaces, it was possible they'd actually make it out of this alive.

"Will Bram be all right?" Wren asked Leif when they paused to catch their breath after climbing onto the top of a particularly tall roof. He didn't seem in need of the break at all—the miscreant. Climbing was clearly second nature to him; for Wren, however, it was a skill she had been forced to dramatically improve over the past two months. Her muscles still weren't used to it. She'd never been one for climbing and preferred swimming.

The bard nodded, then peeked down to survey the streets well below them. "Man's a monster in close combat range. I wouldn't worry about him—nor let him *know* you worried about him. He hates that. On second thought..." Leif chuckled. "Let him know, because he hates it. I want to see how he'd react to the Dragon Princess being concerned for his wellbeing."

Wren shook her head in frustration and pulled a face. "I don't get you, Leif. Do you actually care about anyone in the rebellion, or are you merely sticking around because it's fun?"

"Can't both be true?" he said in a singsong voice.

"I don't know. Can they?"

You like and loathe the prince. Can he not have it both ways, you hypocrite?

Wren blew out an annoyed breath at her own thoughts.

After checking that the streets finally seemed to have calmed down, Leif turned his attention properly to Wren. He squeezed her hand gently. "I haven't told you how I came to work with the rebellion, have I?"

"...no." She cocked her head and waved a hand at him to continue.

"I was kidnapped when I was eight and brought over to Verlanti as a slave. I escaped, and the rebellion found me half-dead by the side of a road. I don't remember it, if I'm honest—Ever told me I was delirious at the time—but, since I had nowhere to go after they saved me, I stuck around. I *am* loyal to the rebellion…it just isn't where I want to be my whole life. And perhaps my sense of humor doesn't exactly make it seem as if I care about the people who saved me." He shrugged halfheartedly. "But I do."

Wren squeezed Leif's hand, feeling wretched for questioning his intentions. Her friend hadn't had an easy life so far, not in the least. She could not possibly understand his way of coping with things. Could she expect him to understand *her* way of coping in return?

Are you even coping? You're haunted by the past and keep trying to push it away so you don't break down. And you keep seeing—

Wren froze, catching sight of a dark-skinned man on the street.

Rowen.

It's not real.

She rubbed at her eyes and looked again. He was still there.

"Get me down there. Now." Her voice rose an octave.

"Wren?"

She rushed to her feet, wobbling like she was drunk. "I need to go. That's Rowen. That's—"

"Your dead husband?" Leif murmured, following Wren's gaze to the man currently standing below them, talking with another man with even darker skin.

Wren didn't trust her voice. She merely nodded as the man began to waver before her very eyes. She glanced at Leif, who studied her, lips pressed firmly together.

He'll call me crazy. I'm seeing ghosts, that's all.

"Then let's ask your dead husband why he's not so dead," Leif said, not letting go of Wren's hand as he led her toward the easiest way to scale down the building. They descended as quietly as possible and, though Wren's muscles heavily protested against it, she followed Leif when he redirected their descent in order to land in a very narrow side street barely wide enough for them to squeeze through.

She dropped his hand and raced forward, only for Leif to catch her by the arm. She frowned. What was he doing? He held a finger to his lips, then interlaced his fingers with Wren's once more and carefully crept to the end of the side street. Wren pressed into his space and peered around the bard's head.

The man was gone.

Rowen had disappeared.

You're losing your mind.

"I'm *sure* I saw him," Wren whispered into Leif's ear, feeling crazy and overwhelmed. "He was there. He was—" Grief clogged her throat and she swallowed hard. Rowen was dead and yet she kept seeing him everywhere. Had she finally cracked? "I saw him," she choked out.

But can you really trust your mind?

"I believe you. I'm not saying you didn't. But he isn't there anymore, and we're still wanted. So let's make sure we're safe before trying to find him."

Wren stilled, eyes filling with tears as she stared at Leif. "You really...believe me?"

Leif turned his head in the narrow space, locking his dark eyes on hers. "People always see more than they admit to seeing. We call folk mad just because we don't want what they see to be true. Then we discount them and throw them away. But *you*...you looked out for me in the Verlantian dungeons and saved my life even though it meant you were almost captured once more. It did not matter to you if I was 'mad' or not."

"I don't understand how that relates to you believing what I saw," Wren said, wiping her tears away. "Do you think I'm insane?"

He laughed softly. "It means I trust you. And if you saw Rowen, then I know you must have, or your mind at least believes you did. Either way, we'll look for him."

Wren's chest constricted, though the pain was welcome. Leif really was on her side. He might be part of a rebellion that wasn't convinced of her trustworthiness, but that did not matter to him.

He was her friend. Perhaps the only one she had.

"Thank you," she murmured, feeling exposed and comforted at the same time.

"You don't need to thank me. We're family now, you and I."

She blinked repeatedly, trying to break into sobs. Since her capture, she'd felt so alone and adrift. "I always wanted a brother," she managed to reply.

Leif nodded. "And I a sister."

They shared a warm look before Wren glanced down the lane.

"You said you knew somewhere on the docks," Wren said, offering Leif a small smile. She tightened her hood as much as she could. "Take me there, please. I don't think we're getting out through the gates."

As swiftly and as silently as possible, the two of them made their way to the docks. With a furtive glance all around them, Leif pulled Wren off a jetty—she braced herself to hit water—and they landed on a very narrow stretch of sand even narrower than the street they'd just been hiding in.

Wren raised an eyebrow. That was unexpected. "*This* is the place you know on the docks?"

"I never said it was a *good* place."

She couldn't argue with that.

At least nobody can see us down here. They'd have to be swimming right by us to notice us.

With a heavy sigh, Wren leaned against the stone wall beneath the jetty and sagged down until she was sitting on the damp sand. Her legs dangled into the sea, and her cloak and trousers were quickly taking up water, but she didn't care. She was exhausted and the sound of the water made some of the tension in her muscles leak away. Even thousands of miles from her homeland, she felt at home. The ocean connected her to her roots.

"That was some test Gunn put you through," Leif said, plonking himself down beside her, cross-legged. He looked as bright and alert as ever. He scratched his ear. "He could have done me a favor and skipped this whole part just this once, though."

"Wait, *what*!?" Wren demanded, glaring at the bard. What in the blazes was he going on about? She waved a hand around her. "This was all a bloody test? A test of what?"

"Gunn won't work with someone who gets captured easily. They have to be as good at escaping an angry mob as he is."

Wren thought of how the pirate had slipped out of the tavern, using her as a diversion. A fire began burning in her stomach. "Does Bram know?"

"He does not."

She wrinkled her nose as she thought of Gunn, but then smiled. The pirate had made a mistake playing with her. "He's going to regret messing with me. I'll get him back."

"Of course you will." Leif's expression was feral. "He doesn't know what he's gotten into. So what's the plan, Dragon Princess? We going to cause some chaos?"

"Do you know which ship is Gunn's?" Wren asked, scanning what she could see of the docks from their tiny hiding place. The sea gently lapped at her knees, informing her that the tide was coming in. They had perhaps another fifteen minutes before the strip of sand they were sitting on would disappear beneath the water.

A little shiver ran down her spine. It reminded her of the Verlantian dungeons.

Leif nodded, then pointed over to their right. "It's the one farthest out on the dock. The most respectable-looking ship out of them all, if you can believe that."

"Gunn *did* make that comment about being a merchant who only sometimes acts like a pirate," Wren commented as she eyed the ship. "Does that mean he *is* a merchant?"

The bard shrugged. "Around these parts, the titles are almost always interchangeable. But I can get you to the ship."

"Good. Then let's go before the tide comes—comes..."

She blinked slowly as a ripple of water moved in their direction. The tide? Not likely. She pursed her lips.

"...Wren?"

She was no longer listening. The disturbance in the water had nothing to do with the tide. At first, she thought it was a shoal of small, glittering fish, but then several narrow-tipped spines protruded from the sea, and she felt something nudge her boot. Her breath caught.

It can't be.

Wren scrambled onto her knees until she was waist-deep in the water, chest heaving as she held out a shaking hand toward the face that hovered just beneath the surface.

An inky blue dragon snout nuzzled against her palm and her heart skipped a beat.

Behind her, Leif sucked in a breath and scrambled closer to the stone wall. "That...how does that bloody creature keep finding us?"

"What do you mean, 'keep finding us?' This is the first time I've seen him since we escaped." She ran her fingers over the dragon's slick scales and hummed a soft note of welcome, which the beast reciprocated, pressing farther into her palm.

When Leif did not respond, Wren asked, not taking her eyes from the creature: "What are you not telling me?"

"The dragon may have been following us from port town to port town," the bard admitted. "I didn't tell you—didn't tell anyone—because I was concerned the dragon would draw attention to us. And us, in turn, would draw attention to *it*."

"Him," Wren corrected, stroking the dragon's long nose. She could barely make out his unnatural eyes beneath the water, but they were watching her intently. "Trove is a male." The name had been in her head ever since the dragon had saved her life.

She glanced over her shoulder at Leif. "You should have told me."

Her friend rolled his eyes. "And have you expose us?"

"I thought you liked a little chaos."

Leif sighed. "I do, but that dragon will be the end of us. He's too conspicuous."

He had a fair point, not that she'd let him know that.

"Keep watch," Wren told Leif, turning her attention fully to Trove. A song escaped her lips, the hums and trills that only the dragon would understand. He growled into her hand, almost a purr, before closing his eyes. Wren ran both hands along his snout as far as she could go, struck with the insane desire to mount the beast once more and escape Verlanti forever.

Away from Arrik and the royal family and the rebellion and the ghost of her husband who would not let her be.

Leif's hand on Wren's shoulder brought her back to stark reality. There would be no escape today or in the coming weeks.

"We have to go," he murmured, clearly uncomfortable with interrupting her song. Trove flicked open an eye and trained it directly at the bard, though he made no move to intimidate or attack him.

Leif was right. Running away would solve nothing. With a

final stroke of Trove's nose, she got to her feet, and the dragon melted into the sea as if he had never been there.

The urge to cry caught Wren's breath in her throat. But she couldn't. She had a job to do, and people to protect.

And Trove would be back.

She flashed a toothy grin at Leif, who eagerly matched it as she stepped out of the water and wrung out her cloak. "Let's catch ourselves a pirate."

CHAPTER EIGHT

Wren

"How does that dragon—Trove—keep finding us?" Leif asked between heaving breaths, his thin arms straining against the waves.

Wren glanced over her shoulder and grinned at her friend. When it had become clear they would not be able to access Gunn's ship by sneaking on via the port, she'd made the suggestion that they simply swim to the ship instead. She was a strong swimmer, after all. Leif, it seemed, was not. Just like how Wren had struggled with scaling buildings when the rebellion first took her on.

Wren glanced out of the port toward the open sea and smiled. "I think Trove must like me," she mused, cutting through the water like a seal.

"How much farther?" Leif gasped, choking on seawater as another wave passed them.

"We're almost there."

"You said that ten minutes ago," he groused. "So wait...is the dragon bonded with you?"

Leif changed subjects at a dizzying pace. She kicked

harder and smiled as she spotted a shadow of Trove pass beneath her. "He's at least considering it." The thought warmed Wren's entire body. Which was saying something; the water they were treading was growing colder with every passing minute toward evening. She flicked a glance at Leif.

He offered her a tired smile and Wren's grin grew. Only Leif would follow her into the ocean with a haphazard plan and swim with her for several hours. She'd been blessed with a wonderful friend.

She reached the ship and clung to the side as Leif caught up.

The bard studied the side of the ship, a frown shadowing his face while he caught his breath. "Well, since we have no dragon to fly us up on deck…how do you suggest getting on board? It isn't exactly my area of expertise."

"We use our daggers," Wren explained, fishing beneath the water's surface for the two weapons attached to her belt. "Don't worry about stabbing through the hull. The wood is far too thick for our daggers to do much more than dent it."

"If you're sure…" Leif looked decidedly uncertain, but Wren had no doubt he'd follow her lead.

"Trust me," she whispered.

"I already do."

Bracing herself, she stabbed her first dagger above her head, then used it to lever herself up just enough to stab the next one above it. It was tough-going, slow work, but so long as she kept her breathing even and made sure not to dangle from the blades, she eventually made her way up to a porthole on the lower deck.

With some clever knife work, Wren pried the window open. Trusting that Leif was right behind her, she pulled herself through the small space, silently slipped to the floor, and popped to her feet, daggers in hand in case she had to fend off any surprised sailors—or pirates. No one was around.

She stuck her head back out of the porthole to wave a sodden, very sorry-looking Leif through the window when it became apparent the coast was clear.

Leif collapsed in a shuddering pile on the wooden floor. "I am never—*never*—doing that again."

"Never say never." Wren chuckled, helping her friend to his shaking legs before scanning their surroundings. By some stroke of luck they seemed to have found themselves in the cargo hold.

Jackpot.

Leif lifted a solid gold candelabra from one of the crates and whistled lowly. "Gunn's newest acquisitions are stunning."

Wren rolled her eyes. "It's just gold."

He snorted. "Excuse me, little miss black diamond princess."

It was her turn to snort. "Do I look like a princess to you?"

Leif arched a brow. "To be honest? You resemble a drowned rat."

"Lovely," she grumbled, searching through boxes and bags nearby. She sighed when she found a collection of fine linen shirts and trousers. Finding a pair that would fit Leif, she threw them at him, then wasted no time in struggling out of her sodden clothes.

Once Wren was dressed in dry, stolen clothes, she turned to discover Leif gawking at her, still holding his pants.

"What?" she demanded, suddenly feeling very self-conscious.

A pause. Then, "Nothing," Leif murmured, pulling his shirt off in the process. "You've just never gotten undressed in front of me before. You're usually such a prude."

Wren considered this. It was indeed true that she used to be far more protective over who saw her naked and vulnerable. But she trusted Leif not to take advantage of such a situation, though in truth Wren herself was surprised at how easily she had been able to get changed in front of her friend.

She flashed him a grin, then tossed him a thick-woven cape when she unearthed some from a mahogany box, before pulling one on herself. "I guess I must be becoming less a princess and more a feral dragon."

"Just so long as you aren't so exposed around other strange men," Leif countered, getting dressed behind a barrel. "As it stands, I prefer not having an audience when I'm getting dressed."

"It was your choice to look," she retorted, staring at the far wall to give him his moment to dress. No one liked to be ogled.

"I didn't really look. I gave you privacy as soon as you started undressing. I was just surprised that you didn't order me to turn around."

The situation was a far cry from when Arrik had charged

into the room Queen Astrid was helping Wren get dressed in before their wedding. A shiver went down her spine as she remembered the way the prince's eyes prowled across her skin, hungry for something she hadn't been prepared to give him. A hot flush crept up her neck and set her ears on fire as she thought about the way she'd hidden behind a plant to obscure her nakedness. He'd probably thought she was a spineless ninny at the time.

Why does it matter?

She pulled at a wet lock of her hair, willing unwelcome thoughts of Arrik away from her head. He didn't have any place here.

"...said he was more merchant than pirate, but I beg to differ. Wren. Wren?"

"Huh?" Wren blinked, then realized Leif was wandering around the cargo hold, investigating the contents of boxes, barrels, and sacks as he passed them wearing his newly filched clothing. She shook her head and was quick to catch up to him. "What do you mean?"

Leif waved toward the open box in front of him. "I mean that these goods have almost certainly been stolen. See the crest inside the box?"

Wren peered at the symbol. Her eyes narrowed. "That's...the Vadonese coat of arms."

"Exactly. And since when have Verlantian merchants ever successfully traded with Vadon?"

"That would be never." Wren considered this. "Does that change anything? If Gunn is more pirate than he is merchant? In all honesty, we're all criminals and traitors to the Verlanti."

"Good point. If anything, it might work in our favor if he largely works beneath the law." Leif shrugged, as if it didn't matter much to him at all, then headed for the door that led out onto the lower deck proper.

"You mean you don't know?" she asked, arching a brow.

The bard gave her a ghost of a smile. "I know Gunn, and he's as good as they come." Leif gave her a piercing look that made Wren want to fidget. "But not everyone shares all their secrets."

She shuddered her eyes. If only he knew.

He suspects though. You need to be careful.

If Wren didn't watch herself, it would be so easy to confide in Leif. But that would put Britta in danger. Her sister needed to be kept hidden until Wren had sorted everything out and recaptured the Dragon Isle throne.

With a glance in her direction, Leif tried the handle of the exit only to find the door locked. She reached forward to try her hand at picking the lock, but the bard held his hand up and then pulled out a tiny bag of tools from the waistband of his trousers. Where the devil had those come from?

"So you are a thief now? Or a bandit?" Wren teased, as Leif held his ear to the door whilst he worked away at the lock. "Did you steal your tools too?"

He stuck out his tongue. "I always come prepared. Plus, you learn a thing or two when you work with Bram. *Ah*, there we go," he said, satisfied, when the lock clicked and the door swung open. Going by the bustle and thumping of heavy footsteps overhead, it was clear that mostly everyone was on deck, preparing the ship to leave port.

"We don't have much time before they leave the city," Wren concluded, noting the failing light through the porthole in the cargo hold before closing the door behind them and lifting the hood of her stolen cape to conceal her hair. "We need to find Gunn as soon as we can. Getting stuck on this ship isn't part of the plan, and there's no way you can swim back."

Leif said nothing, though he nodded in agreement, and together the two of them prowled through the dark lower deck as silently as they were able.

"Who's there?" a man slurred.

Wren froze, spotting a sailor. He blinked at her through bleary eyes and then promptly passed out, slumping against the wall, his bottle of spirits clanking to the floor.

Leif whistled out a breath. "That was a close one." A pause. "Wonder what kind of rum that is. Smells delicious."

"Get your mind in the game," she muttered, stepping past the sailor.

"My mind is *always* on games."

Wren's eyes widened as another older sailor swung out from behind the stairway to the upper deck, his back to them. Leif darted forward and knocked the man unconscious and caught him before he hit the floor. Her friend tucked the sailor back behind the stairs and brushed his hands off.

He gave her a wry smile. "You were saying?"

"That you're amazing," she chirped before sneaking up the stairs.

All around them was organized chaos. Cargo was being

brought on board, while the final loads of cargo to be brought *off* the ship were being hurriedly taken down the gangplank. It was clear the ship would be leaving imminently.

"There," Leif muttered, surreptitiously pointing toward the telltale figure of Gunn by the prow of the ship. The man was laughing at a sailor whilst wildly waving his arms. Wren gritted her teeth and imagined he was regaling his companion with his antics from the tavern. She still didn't know how she was going to get back at him, but it wouldn't be pleasant, that much she knew.

Together, Leif and Wren stalked toward the merchant-turned pirate, thankful for the anonymity their cloaks granted them as they wove between cargo, thick coils of rope, port workers, and sailors. It was only when Gunn's companion left to continue with their duties that Wren decided to approach him, waiting until the pirate was by the mast of the ship before leaving Leif's side, dagger in hand.

"So I got out of your mess," she breathed into the man's ear, before slicing her dagger through the side of the man's cloak to stick it to the mast. All at once Gunn turned round, though Wren had the element of surprise and used it to her full advantage. She bowled into the man and bodily pinned him to the mast, pulling out her other dagger to point it directly at his jugular. "Now get out of mine," she purred.

For a moment a flash of admiration filled Gunn's gray eyes. Then he let out a raucous laugh. "I must say, I'm impressed. Not many people can sneak up on me." His gaze trailed down Wren's figure and back up again, then flicked to Leif. "In my own stock, no less. But I told you to get out of the city, did I not? You're still in the port."

With a growl, Wren nicked Gunn's throat with her blade. "I'd rather say that successfully boarding your ship despite all of its security is more than a fair test of my abilities," she said, waving out toward the intimidatingly large, muscular bodyguards the pirate had posted all across the deck of the ship. They were heading toward them now, intent on pulling her off their captain. "Now call them off, and work with me as you said you would, or we'll report all of your illegal cargo to the crown. I doubt Soren would smile upon you for it. I hear he's very temperamental these days."

Gunn's lips stretched over his perfect teeth into a feral grin. "So you would just walk up to King Soren and tell on me? You, who's wanted by the crown and hunted wherever you go? I highly doubt that, Princess. No matter how bold you are, I doubt you're that stupid."

"I'm fairly certain my husband would do something about it. Something tells me he doesn't take too kindly to pirates."

This, at least, caused Gunn to pause in his mirth, though the smile did not slip from his face. "I see you more than live up to your reputation as a princess of dragons." A nod at Leif over Wren's shoulder. "You did not exaggerate when you told me I'd meet my match in her. I like her fire."

"You cannot even begin to match Princess Wren," Leif said, his confidence in her warming Wren up from the inside.

The pirate took a moment to consider this, then waved at his men to stand down. "Get the dagger away from my throat and we can trade, as you wanted. I think I'll enjoy seeing how your little drama with your *husband* will play out, Princess Wren. My sources say his hunt for you has been quite ferocious."

She smirked, pulling the blade out of Gunn's cloak before removing the one she held at his throat. She didn't care for the pirate's petty reason for helping them out—she knew he had far more reasons than drama alone to help the rebellion, if Leif was to be believed that the pirate was against the slavery the Verlantian Court benefitted from. All she cared about was securing food for the rebellion and proving that she could be trusted with dangerous work on their behalf. Even though the marriage had been forced upon Wren, her connection with the crown had tainted her reputation. It was unfair, but so was life.

"Bring them as much grain as they can carry," Gunn ordered his men. He bowed graciously to Wren, though the filthy look on his face made it look anything but gentlemanly. "A gesture of good faith, if you will. I will contact you in time with the rest of the promised shipment. But be warned, Dragon Princess: playing with fire will lead to you getting burned."

"Good thing I like a little heat," she countered, collecting the grain with Leif before leaving the ship without another word. Her boots thumped against the boardwalk and she felt like whooping in victory, but even now she could feel Gunn's gaze pinned to her back. She wasn't quite sure what to make of the pirate.

"You did it," Leif breathed, hugging the sack of grain closer to his chest.

"*We* did it," Wren corrected, even though Gunn had made their task as impossible as he possibly could.

She eyed the ships bobbing in their slips and savored the brine scent of the sea. A haunting melody filled the air as they passed the nearest ship, and for a moment, if she closed her eyes, Wren could pretend she was home. But it wasn't to be. All her worries and stress rushed back in.

Bram was going to be so angry they'd lost him earlier.

"It's going to be a long walk," Leif lamented as they moved around the edge of the city.

Wren sighed. That was an understatement.

Her skin prickled and she swept the area, searching for the source of the feeling. Her breath seized and she froze.

The prince.

He almost blended in with the shadows, but his silver-white braids were a shining beacon. Wren dropped the sack of goods and pulled a dagger from her hip, taking one step toward the man who'd ruined her life.

"Wren?"

She glanced over her shoulder at Leif and then back at the prince.

Except that he was gone.

Wren searched the darkness for any sign of him. There was nothing. Was she hallucinating Arrik now too?

"What's wrong?" Leif asked, stepping to her side.

"I thought I saw something," she murmured. "It's nothing."

She sheathed her weapon and took a step back to get the grain.

"Are you okay?" Leif questioned.

"Yeah. Let's just get home."

Wren wasn't okay. Not by a long shot.

It was full dark by the time they made it back to camp. As if he could sense them, Bram thundered toward the camp entrance the moment Wren and Leif set foot over it, murder written all over his face. Vienne was quick to follow him, her own face unreadable.

Here we go again.

Wren held her head high as she met Bram head on.

"You irresponsible *wretch,*" Bram spat, pointing at Wren. "That's the last time you're *ever* being trusted with a mission." Then at Leif: "Just what in the blazes were you thinking? You let her pointlessly put her life on the line for a fool's errand!"

With a satisfying thump Wren and Leif chucked the bags of grain they'd hauled back from Gunn's ship at Bram's feet. Satisfaction swirled in her chest as Bram's eyes narrowed on the foodstuffs.

"I never said we failed," she argued, making sure to intonate every word with care and precision. She turned her attention to her aunt. "If this isn't the proof you need to know that I can work as a spy for the rebellion—playing by the ridiculous rules set by our allies whilst also avoiding our foes—then I don't know what is." She crossed her arms and stared down her aunt.

Vienne had to side with her. She *had* to. The older woman was Wren's family, after all, and she had succeeded in her mission.

But the head of the rebellion shook her head. "Do not leave the camp—that's an order," she added on when it became clear that Wren would argue. "I don't want another word from you on the matter. Do as you're told."

Wren tossed her shaking hands in the air and choked down all the horrible words that wanted to escape. Hateful speech wouldn't change her aunt's mind. It would only prove Wren to be immature.

Vienne turned on her heel and left without another word. Bram gave Wren one last glare before he followed in Vienne's footsteps.

Wren had been dismissed.

Ignored.

She'd done everything that had been asked of her and yet still it hadn't been enough.

Though Leif accepted her, and Gunn had accepted her, she was never going to be accepted as part of the rebellion, and now she knew it.

"They'll never trust me," she whispered.

Leif winced. "That's not true."

Wren dropped her hands and met her friend's gaze evenly. "Don't lie to me. I'm just a tool."

She picked up her sack of grain and began stalking into the camp.

When would she ever be free?

CHAPTER NINE

ARRIK

That Arrik had to act as part of Queen Astrid's retinue as she visited friends was pure torment. He'd managed to sneak away for a day to meet his spy within the rebellion. It had afforded him a chance to see Wren.

She'd stared at him like he was the wolf and she the hare.

It would have been easy to stay out of sight but he'd wanted his wife to see him. But what was more, he'd wanted a proper glimpse of her to make sure she was okay.

It's more than that and you know it.

Even now, Arrik wanted to chase after her. To corner her and see how she'd react to him. Though Arrik knew fine well why she'd escaped the palace instead of trusting him—in her place he'd have done the same—there was a feral urge in him to act exactly like the villain Wren clearly thought he was. Thoughts of chains and his bed flashed through his mind.

She'd be shocked by your thoughts, you beast.

When he captured her once again, would she scream at him? Would she attack him? Would she come at him, eyes blazing and daggers out, full of the life and fight Arrik had witnessed when he'd destroyed her life on the Dragon Isles?

He ached for that version of Wren so badly it physically pained him.

Get a hold of yourself. Your wife isn't truly yours. Focus on the mission.

He was acting as a guard for his stepmother, so Arrik had no choice but to bear the brunt of that pain with no hope of tackling it head-on.

They were traveling through Novenport, a one-day ride from the pirate city Wren had been chased through, a pack of Astrid's personal guards as well as her simpering, loyal subjects in tow. Arrik didn't trust a single one of them to follow his orders unless the queen herself willed them to. The ladies in her company were of course holding everyone up, insisting on visiting every shop on the central street to peer through windows and flirt with the upper class.

At this rate they wouldn't make it to Astrid's new residence before nightfall. Soren had gifted the keep—built at the highest point of the upper-class living quadrant of Novenport—to his queen as a means of apologizing for his last illicit dalliance, though he had never openly admitted to the affair. But Queen Astrid never seemed to mind when the king was unfaithful...so long as she received some kind of outlandish gift in return for infidelity. Their relationship was mercenary. His stepmother was just as unfaithful...only much more skilled in hiding her affairs.

The whole thing put a bad taste in Arrik's mouth. Marriage was meant to be between two people, not the whole bloody world.

"What a beautiful afternoon it is," Arrik heard Astrid comment from her carriage. It was open to the sunshine, though the moment a single cloud appeared in the sky he knew they'd have to stop so the removable, gilded roof of the blasted thing could get put into place over the carriage. He was dreading having to slow the procession even more, so he silently hoped the sunshine would stay. He hated how high-maintenance his stepmother was. A little rain never hurt anyone.

"A single drop of rain wouldn't dare fall upon your head, my queen!" one of her guards called back. The foolish man blushed when Astrid smiled at him, her dark eyes twinkling at his praise.

If only he knew what she was really like. He wouldn't be smiling so much then. She was poison wrapped in a pretty package.

Eventually, their agonizingly slow walk through the main street of Novenport resulted in them taking a turn to the left to head for the gates that allowed access to the upper-class quadrant. It was full of low-lying, smooth stone walls, opulent golden rooftops, and immaculately designed gardens large enough to hold fifty regularly sized households within them.

Arrik despised them all. It was everything that was wrong with the kingdom.

He glanced to the sky in the west: they had perhaps an hour left of light before the city descended into darkness. Though the days were warm, it was autumn after all. Once night hit—and it would hit quickly—the city would grow cold and unwelcoming, and even in the nicer parts of Novenport the most unsavory types of people were likely to come out. He wanted to avoid them at all costs. Though he was itching for a fight, the last thing he wanted was to spend more time on this ridiculous job than he had to. His father had sent him along as punishment. Soren knew how much Arrik despised playing guard to the queen who couldn't keep her hands to herself.

He closed his eyes for a moment.

Flaming red curly hair and a fair face flashed through his mind. Arrik snapped open his eyes and glared ahead. The bloody woman haunted his thoughts at the most inopportune moments.

A prickling along the back of his neck had his eyes narrowing and scanning his surroundings. Someone was watching them.

You spoke too soon and cursed yourself.

They stepped through the gates and movement down a side street informed him that they were being followed. Arrik loosened his sword from its scabbard, exchanging a glance with the captain of Astrid's personal guard. The man, at the very least, had noticed the movement too, and with a series of signals readied the rest of his guards into action. Within a few cacophonous moments the company of guards had Queen Astrid and her friends corralled together in a group—the better to protect, with his stepmother in the middle—and had prepared for a fight. Only now was Arrik thinking that they really should have insisted on the queen's carriage having its top installed from the beginning of their journey. It would have been so much harder to attack her within the confined, protected space.

She was a sitting duck for arrows.

Is that such a bad thing?

That wicked thought had his lips twitching, but he tamped it down. Soren would tear apart the world if his queen were murdered. He'd pin it on one of his enemies and wage another costly war.

This was why Arrik hating being allocated to doing such jobs when he didn't have full control over the situation. One false move and he'd lose everything he'd been working toward.

They proceeded through the upper-class quadrant for almost fifteen minutes in careful, wary silence. Whoever was following them clearly hadn't wanted to be spotted, and Arrik entertained the notion that they had withdrawn now that their presence was known. His hands clenched the reins, and he scanned the area once more.

No, someone was still following them.

A man launched himself from a golden roof above—using the setting sun behind him to conceal his presence—and landed squarely on Arrik's back. He grunted, reaching for one of his several daggers.

"Son of a—" the captain of the guard spit out, but Arrik himself stayed silent as he calmly and efficiently rolled the attacker off his back and skewered him to the cobblestones with his spear. The man cursed and pulled on the spear in his shoulder, his face creased in pain.

Arrik jumped from his saddle, yanked the spear from the man, and began scanning for the next attack.

"You move, you die," he growled at the man he'd wounded.

The man nodded, clutching at his bleeding shoulder.

To his left, several men rushed out from the shadows to keep Astrid's guards busy. Arrik saw it for what it was: a distraction. He turned on the spot and barely managed to parry the heavy great sword that a man as tall as he was had struck him with.

"What are you doing if not protecting the right?" Arrik spat at the captain of the guard after he disposed of his would-be assassin in a few quick moves. But the captain was currently outnumbered by four men, and all of his guards were dealing with the attack on the right. He huffed out a breath and leaped to the captain's aid, ensuring at all times that all blades were facing away from Queen Astrid and her now screaming and crying company of idiotic friends.

Ridiculous ninnies.

He should have seen the blade coming that slashed down his left arm. He should have, but like the first assailant this new attacker had used the setting sun to his advantage to sprint toward Arrik unseen. The dagger slashed across Arrik's bicep, making him deeply regret only wearing a breastplate and no other metal armor, only leather. It had been a long, hot journey to Novenport, and it was supposed to have been a simple—boring—tour.

You were just complaining about being mind-numbingly bored. At least this got your blood pumping.

Arrik's attacker was no match for his sword. Only after Arrik had dispatched him did Arrik finish helping out the captain with his opponents, then finished off every other attacker.

Even then, men who tried to flee he shot down, one by one, with his bow and arrow.

Wren would have dispatched them all from above before they could have dealt a single blow against me, Arrik thought despite himself, as he heaved in a breath and counted the queen's retinue to confirm that they had not lost a single member of her party. *Wren and her dragon would have obliterated them all.*

Except Arrik had ordered her dragon shot from the sky, and Wren was on the run from him. He was the monster of the story, not her.

"Continue on," Arrik ordered, his bad mood turned thunderous in the wake of the blood and flesh strewn across the street and the cut on his arm. He didn't give a single person an opportunity to rebuke him, though it was clear Queen Astrid's guards wanted to stop and tend to the injuries some of them had sustained. But he had no patience for the fools. If it hadn't been for himself and the captain—the only decent fighter in the queen's retinue—likely everyone would have died. This attack could have cost Arrik everything because of their incompetence.

It unnerved Arrik to no end how easy it was for things to fall apart when he didn't have his own men beside them. But more than that: the attack on them had clearly been coordinated. *Planned.*

He eyed the attackers strewn about the ground and studied their clothes. Stooping low, he dug through the pockets of the nearest slain man, discovering a pouch full of mixed gold that could have come from anywhere.

He clenched his jaw and stood, dropping the coin purse on the ground.

This hadn't been a band of scraggly, hungry drug addicts or desperate peasants. They would never possess that much gold, let alone gold from the isles and the south. Someone was trying very hard to hide the origin of these men.

He huffed out a breath and pushed his silver braids from his face. Plus, Arrik wasn't even sure Queen Astrid had been the target. Rather, it felt like...

It felt like Arrik himself had been the target.

Not the first time, nor the last.

If that were the case, he'd have to do some investigating as to who knew that he was expected to be in Novenport, and when. Yet that was a subject to research on another day. He glanced in the direction of the assailant he'd wounded, only to spy a bloody spot on the stones. Arrik growled underneath his breath.

"What is it?" the captain asked.

"The man that attacked first. He's gone. Send someone to find him. He's our only lead to figuring out who ordered this attack."

"Done."

He watched in silence as the captain of the guard began to bark orders at his men. For now, Arrik had to see the queen safely into the keep and tend to his arm and pray that nothing else got botched.

Thankfully, the keep was already full of servants, who took over from Arrik in organizing everyone into rooms and to general comfort and safety. A woman tried to usher Arrik into a room so that she could clean his arm, but he fought her off.

"I am more than capable of doing it myself," he bit out, in no mood to deal with the hopeful look on her face that implied she wanted something more than simply thanks in return for helping him. The pain in his arm was bothering him more than he expected, considering it wasn't that deep. He imagined his overwhelmingly irritated mood had something to do with it.

By the time he reached the quarters that had been assigned to him—much smaller than Arrik supposed was befitting a prince, no doubt a deliberate move on Soren's part—he collapsed onto the bed and let out a heavy sigh. He was fed up. Of life, of war, of court games, assassins. He had things he wanted to do. Needed to do. And Soren was keeping him busy with, well, busywork. It was deliberate, and they both knew it.

The devilish snake.

Had the king himself ordered the attack to get rid of him?

No, that didn't make any sense at the moment. Soren wanted Arrik out of the way, yes, but still on his side, ruling the Dragon Isles with the unruly red-haired princess. Soren could not have that if Arrik were dead. Sure, the king was angry that Wren had escaped their clutches, but not enough to send assassins after him.

So who?

He somehow doubted it was Kalles, even though he'd encouraged Wren to murder him. His brother was still throwing himself into every drug den he could find.

Some time must have passed, for the next moment Arrik blinked, the window into his room had grown dark and he had bled all over the white sheets of his bed. The servants would hate him.

"Great," he muttered, ripping his torn shirt away with his armor to attend to the wound. But just then the creak of the door opening caused him to pause. "I will come for food when I need it," Arrik called out, assuming it was a servant. "So you can—"

"Last time I checked, you waited on me, Arrik, not the other way around," Queen Astrid said in her dangerously silky voice, entering the room and quietly closing the door behind her. She swanned over to him and knelt at his feet, dark eyes twinkling. "Though perhaps I can be convinced to serve you just this once."

She had come dressed as scandalously as if she were going to one of her husband's revels. As if Astrid expected Arrik to be a wanton and willing partner for whatever illicit activities her clothes implied she wanted. The sheer, silvery material across the woman's ocher skin left very little to the imagination. Any other red-blooded man would have found it nearly impossible to turn her down. But Arrik was having none of it; he knew Astrid was a viper not to be trifled with. When she began tending to his bleeding arm, he let her do so, though he remained silent. Flatly turning down his stepmother always led to dangerous consequences. He needed to tread carefully.

"That was a close call out there," Astrid said, keeping her tone conversational, though when she glanced up at Arrik from beneath her eyelashes there was nothing casual about the bedroom eyes she gave him. "I was lucky the king put you in my retinue for this trip. I am sorry you got hurt."

Arrik gritted his teeth, feeling a migraine coming on as a result. She was baiting him to say something—anything—and he was determined not to give her anything to work with.

Eventually, Astrid finished cleaning and wrapping his arm and gave his bicep a pat. "That wasn't too deep. It didn't cut into your muscles. Which is good, considering what I would like to get up to with you tonight..."

"We have been through this before, Queen Astrid," Arrik said, keeping his tone even. He pulled his arm away from her touch and her face hardened. "I am not interested. How could I commit such a great badness against my lord king and father?"

The queen stood up to her full height; with Arrik sitting on the bed she reigned over him. There was no warmth of seduction left to her presence, only bitter anger and a willful vengeance Arrik knew the queen was happy to inflict upon all who displeased her. "You have no right to dismiss me," she seethed. "I am your queen—"

"Married to my father, as I recall."

"Do you wish to die, bastard prince?" she demanded, bristling. "Keep denying me like this and you will see how easy it is for me to have you killed." A pause. "And my men *never* fail."

The fact she had no qualms about openly threatening Arrik showed just how ugly Astrid was. And safe in her power. As if she deemed herself invincible.

Not forever, you witch.

Arrik kept his gaze and voice steady as he said, "Give it your best shot. I am not afraid of you, stepmother."

He wasn't, though part of Arrik wondered if he should be. She was vicious. None of her rivals ever survived.

The queen laughed then, an ugly sound that sent Arrik's spine crawling. "We shall see how unafraid you are in due course," she said, sauntering back to the door and slamming it with a resounding echo.

Once Arrik was left alone, he made a mental note to put another soldier on Astrid's trail. Something told him the previous one was either dead or now completely under her sway.

Do not eat or drink anything whilst in her company or her home.

He glanced at the darkened window and sighed, knowing it was going to be a very long and hungry night.

Astrid was known for her poisonings. Arrik had good reason to suspect she had killed at least one of his wives as punishment for him denying her advances. Whether she was responsible for all of them, Arrik did not know.

It was another thing he longed to investigate. Instead, he resigned himself to a long and thankless night of trying not to think about food, about the men who had attacked him, and about the Dragon Princess.

The one woman he'd let escape on purpose and lived to regret.

CHAPTER TEN

Arrik

"You're not going to stand there all night like a grumpy old man, are you?" His stepmother pouted, full bottom lip sticking out like a plump slug.

Two days stuck in Astrid's company felt like a lifetime.

Arrik kept his expression schooled as she ran her pointed nails over his chest plate and hid his shudder. "I'm here for your protection, my lady. I can't indulge tonight." Or any night. Indulgence led to weakness and weakness led to a knife in one's back. "The king tasked me with your safety. What would he say if I abandoned my duty?"

She rolled her eyes. "That man cares nothing for me. If I died tomorrow, he'd feast and appoint one of his many wives to take my place."

That was true. Soren only cared for pleasure and wealth.

Arrik nodded to his warrior stationed at the door to take his place. It was time for him to move to outside patrol. There was only so much of Astrid that he could take in one sitting. Plus, his stepmother was about to get emotional, handsy, and then mean.

"Soren cares for you," he murmured, removing her hand from his chest. "I need to secure the perimeter. Enjoy your evening, Mother."

He hated calling her Mother because she'd wasn't his mum, but it always established a wall between them.

An angry glint entered her gaze and she huffed, turning in a sea of silk, and flounced back to her group of miscreant friends.

Good riddance.

He strode from the room, down the stairs, and out into the back courtyard. The chill of the night surrounded him along with the scent of the sea and pine.

Arrik inhaled deeply and savored the quiet of the night. Astrid always tried his patience. Her persistence disgusted him but he couldn't outright rebuff his stepmother in public. She was queen after all.

It was a delicate game he had to play—be firm enough that she would go away but not harsh enough that she'd turn the full force of her wrath upon him. His stepmother was a force to be reckoned with. Soren had chosen Astrid for her family's land and her beauty, but what the king hadn't known was how vile and ruthless she was. It was no mistake she became his first wife and consort.

Arrik had seen her destroy families, topple criminal organizations in the name of justice only to take up the mantle of leader in secret, and sanction more assassinations than his royal half-brothers combined.

Astrid was a devil parading around as an angel.

A high whistle followed by two low notes cut through the

air.

That was Shane's call. He was supposed to be at the castle. What was he doing here?

Arrik's eyes narrowed and he scanned the surrounding area. A hooded man stood between the hedges of the elaborate garden to the prince's left. Shane slowly melted into foliage.

Things must be dire if Shane had come from the palace.

Arrik moved through the darkness, tailing his second-in-command. The prince made sure no one noticed his departure, and entered the labyrinth of exotic brush, trees, and flowers.

Shane pushed his hood back slightly so Arrik could see his gray eyes glittering in the moonlight.

"What's wrong?" he demanded.

"Cathal caught wind of the rebel camp and has sent men in."

The prince cursed underneath his breath. Did Cathal have a spy amongst the rebels too? "How close are they?"

"Close enough that your wife and our plan is in danger. Cathal can't get his hands on her. It would be better if she were dead than for your brother to capture her."

It wasn't great news, but he could get in touch with his spy within the rebellion and get the camp moved in a matter of hours.

He eyed Shane. There was another reason his friend was here. "What else? You wouldn't have made the journey just for that."

Shane sighed and pushed his long black hair from his face.

"I received news that some Vadonese agents have slipped into Verlanti and are seeking to unite with the rebellion."

Devil take it. Just what he needed.

"We need to move our timeline up."

"My thoughts exactly. Do you think your wife will go for it?" Shane crossed his arms. "You've made a show of hunting for her everywhere. She's no friend of yours."

"She'll have no choice. This is bigger than her vengeance. She'll make the right decision."

He hoped.

"That's surprisingly optimistic of you. You really think she won't kill you on the spot? You trust her that much?"

Arrik chuckled.

He trusted no one but he was an expert at reading people. His dear wife had a heart of gold and was merciful despite her temper. Did he trust her? No. Did he think bringing her in was worth the gamble? Yes.

If she didn't kill him.

Shane gave him a thoughtful look. "The dragon lass got to you, didn't she?"

More than Arrik wanted to admit. There was something about the fierce princess that he couldn't help but admire and covet. He wanted to *possess* her.

Dangerous thoughts.

"She's a tool, nothing more." It tasted like a lie.

"Don't lie to me. Lies among allies will get everyone killed."

Arrik grunted. "I desire her."

"Nothing wrong with wanting your wife. Downright

natural if you ask me."

It was more than that. He wanted to keep Wren. But he couldn't. And she didn't want him anyway. In her eyes, he was a monster, and for good reason.

Arrik didn't deserve the princess. All he would do was sully her with all the darkness he kept inside. He had too much blood on his hands to possess someone so precious.

"She'd stab me before she'd let me close." He shook his head, the silver beads in his hair clinking softly. "It would just muddle things to take her to bed."

"Then the decision is made. Use her for our purpose, and don't let your attraction distract you from what's important."

Arrik nodded.

It was wise.

It was the plan.

Then why did he want to hesitate?

CHAPTER ELEVEN

Wren

Three days had passed since Vienne banned Wren from leaving camp, and she was about to lose her mind.

Following Josenu's advice, their section of camp had moved farther into the forest. That had been two days ago; they hadn't heard from, nor seen him since. This only served to further infuriate Wren, for she hadn't been able to talk to Josenu privately when he'd come to warn them to move camp again. She was desperate for news.

But it was more than that.

Leif had been sent out on a mission almost immediately after they'd returned from Gunn's ship, and he had been gone ever since. Wren more than half suspected that her aunt had sent Leif away so he couldn't enable her impulses more than he already had. Vienne wanted to isolate her. It meant she had nobody to talk to. No friends. Josenu was her next-closest shadow of a friend, so Wren had hoped she'd have an opportunity to speak with him simply to talk to *someone.*

Yet even that was not a privilege afforded to her.

Helping Bram out—however displeased he'd been by the notion—had kept Wren's thoughts on the present. On what needed to be done *now*, then tomorrow, then the next day. With no spying missions to busy her body and soul, all Wren could do was languish in her memories of her family.

It was torture.

The fact that Britta must be so scared, alone without her or her parents. Her sister wouldn't even know she was alive. No one back home would know.

She huffed out a breath, setting down the knitting needles in her lap.

Then there was the fact the ghost of Rowen seemed to be following her wherever she went, taunting her. Leif had believed she had truly seen him, but now she had some distance from the incident she wasn't so sure. It was easy for the mind to play tricks, especially if you were grieving. Wren's own mother had told her that, once upon a time.

And yet still, drowning in memories of her departed loved ones was far more appealing than the alternative:

Thinking about her beastly husband.

Much to her shame and chagrin, her thoughts kept circling back to the enemy prince.

It had been difficult not to think of him, not least because he was hunting for her even as she sat there doing nothing and feeling useless. But it had been ripping through the pirate city with Leif, then verbally sparring with Gunn, that had truly caused a torrent of thoughts of Arrik to flood Wren's mind.

It was almost as if...she missed the thrill of being in his

company. Of the conversations they exchanged, even when they had been angry and full of venom. In the days leading up to Wren's escape, however, none of the conversations she'd had with Arrik had been angry. They had almost been soft. Almost been trusting. Like the prince had been opening up to her, and all she had to do was open up to him in return and things between them would transform.

She thought of all the guilty glances she'd stolen of his huge, domineering size, so at odds with his soft hair and elegantly-carved face—especially on the rare occasions he'd dared smile.

She thought of his lips on hers after they were married.

Her fingers clenched around the knitting needles and she squeezed her eyes closed, hating that she couldn't shake him from her thoughts.

Don't think like that. Stop it, Wren! He's the reason your parents are dead. You're barely chattel to him, a means to an end. He needs you to legally rule the Dragon Isles and that is all. Any compassion or kindness you saw in Arrik was all a ploy to make you drop your guard. Including the smiles. Including the kiss.

She exhaled heavily and opened her eyes to stare blurrily at her lap. Her father would be ashamed of her for her lack of control. Wren angrily began knitting once again.

"Watch those stitches!"

She grimaced at the sharpness of the old woman's voice. Wren had been corralled into a knitting group to help prepare clothing and blankets for the ever-growing rebellion. She was no fan of the boring work even on the best of days, but it was something to do.

Today was not the best of days.

Mum would have had this done in half the time.

Wren rolled her neck and stared glumly at the shoddy fabric in her hands that was supposed to be a blanket.

Half the time and ten times as good.

Her heart constricted in her chest, making her feel altogether unable to breathe. She needed to leave now before she broke down and cried in front of everyone.

Clutching her knitting in her arms, Wren nodded at the old crone. "I will continue this back in my tent." She barely got it out, not waiting for a response before she fled. Of course, the moment she got back to her tent she unceremoniously dumped the knitting in a pile on top of her blankets, then collapsed to the floor to try to pull herself together.

Tears stung her eyes at the mere thought of her mother; she dug her fingers into the plain fur rug to ground herself. Her good, strong mother who could knit anyone under the table with her eyes closed. She was always knitting. When Wren had once asked why, she'd responded by saying it helped take her mind off troubling things. Wren had never known what these "troubling things" were, though she imagined they were to do with the scars that wrapped around her mum's neck, and her difficult, mysterious past prior to landing on the Dragon Isles.

She blinked up at the pile of blankets and her abandoned project. Knitting wasn't helping her keep her mind off things. It was making it worse. She had to do something else.

She had to hunt.

Nobody had brought game in from the woods since before Wren and Leif secured the trade with Gunn. The grain he'd given them wouldn't last forever, and people couldn't live on bread alone. They needed meat to keep their energy up.

This is a bad idea.

Wren lurched off the floor and rushed to her bow and quiver which rested on a plain wooden trunk at the end of the bed. She snatched them up and snuck out the back of her tent. Her shoulders hunched up by her ears when someone yelled, but it wasn't for her. She released the breath she was holding when she managed to make it to the tree line. Wren cast one last glance on the camp and then crept deeper into the trees.

Freedom. At last.

Nobody was around to stop her. Bram was in a meeting with Vienne, and Ever was busy attending to things in the kitchen. Josenu was in the Verlantian palace, and Leif was wherever Wren's aunt had ordered him to be.

Not that he would stop me, Wren mused as she padded through the glum light permeating the forest. *Or would he? Perhaps he would ask me not to go for my own good. If Vienna and Bram realize I've flouted their orders, then there's no chance they'll ever let me out of the camp grounds again.*

A branch crunched beneath her right foot.

She didn't care.

Wren couldn't find it in herself *to* care. A dragon was never meant to be imprisoned, regardless of whether that prison was a rebellion campsite, the icy-cold depths of the

Verlantian dungeons, or the sun-strewn paradise of Arrik's bedroom.

Stop thinking about his bedroom.

She scowled at herself.

There were more important things to think about, like what the people of the rebellion needed to eat. If Wren returned from her hunt with prey in hand, then she reasoned more than a few hungry mouths would sing her praises. Perhaps if public opinion changed about her presence, she'd be allowed outside the camp again. And Wren needed all the support she could get, surrounded as she was by the folks who were still half-convinced she was in cahoots with her Verlantian brute of a husband.

For a while Wren wandered, a silent presence gliding through the forest without a single target in mind. But the moment she began spying the telltale signs of a deer moving through the undergrowth, all of her finely tuned senses came back to her as easily as breathing. She'd never enjoyed hunting like some did. Taking a life didn't bring her joy, but she understood the necessity of meat.

It was over an hour later when Wren finally caught sight of the creature. A stag.

Her breath stuck in her throat.

He was beautiful. A tall, well-muscled stag in the prime of its life. Wren had been told game was sparse in the forest, so the beast was clearly a clever one to stay out of sight of its would-be hunters. It was a travesty that he wouldn't see another day.

A pang of sadness hit Wren as she came to terms with the

fact that *she* was its hunter today. But it was the stag or the people of the rebellion. The creature would feed many mouths.

Creeping as closely as she dared, Wren pulled out her bow and nocked an arrow. The wind, coming from the west, rustled the leaves above her. Wren readjusted her aim to account for the wind. The stag moved from a patch of grass to nibble on a cluster of daisies a few paces away.

Wren took a single step forward, the deer in her sights. She inhaled and pulled back on the drawstring.

I'm sorry, my friend.

Snap.

Her brows furrowed and she slipped into stillness just as the stag did the same. She swallowed hard as something under her foot had given way beneath her weight, and that was when she realized what she'd just done.

Blast it all.

Wren had stepped into a trap.

CHAPTER TWELVE

Wren

Wren took a moment to breathe and absorb her surroundings.

So she'd stepped into a trap…

It hadn't killed her instantly, which meant it was likely not meant to be fatal. Scanning the underbrush, then the tree above her, Wren noted the barest hint of a rope entangled through leaves.

A net, then. The moment you lift your weight off the trigger, it'll ensnare you.

She briefly entertained the notion that she'd be able to out-speed the mechanism of the trap and get away unscathed. But Wren knew she'd be fooling herself; she wasn't nearly fast enough to get away from the automatic trap. There was nothing else she could do but shift her weight, accept her fate, then pray she had enough time to cut herself free before the person who set the trap returned to check if it had been sprung.

Here goes nothing.

Bracing herself, Wren forced her eyes to stay open as she

lifted her foot and was hauled up, up, up by a rope around her ankle. As she ascended, Wren watched the beautiful stag jolt and then flee.

It was ironic that her prey had watched Wren become someone *else's* prey.

A thick-woven net enclosed around her once she was dangling high above the forest floor. It knocked the wind out of her, but Wren knew she had to jump into action sooner rather than later, so she fought through it.

Struggling against her bonds, Wren peered below her to inspect the fall she'd have to absorb. No more than three times her height, she deduced, relieved. With the soft blanket of autumn leaves on the ground she'd likely come out of the fall bruised but otherwise unscathed, so long as she fell *properly*.

Her stomach rolled and her heart picked up speed.

"Don't panic, don't panic, don't panic," Wren murmured as she struggled for one of her knives. Her heart rate had accelerated, adrenaline coursing through her veins informing her that she was, conversely, very close to panicking. She'd let her confidence put her too much at ease within the unfamiliar woods. Her aunt had been right, and so had Bram.

She should have stayed put in camp.

If there had been no rope tied around her ankle, it would have been easier to get her daggers, but her movement within the net was limited. Her bow and quiver were tangled in the net, too, and her sheathe was caught at an angle that prevented her from moving much on her left side. Scowling,

Wren wriggled and shifted until finally her right hand grasped the well-worn handle of the dagger she kept on her belt.

When the blade was free, she brought it up to inspect. It was sharp—she'd fixed the edge of the blade a few days ago—but the net ensnaring her and the rope around her ankle were thick and well-woven. Expensive.

Just whose trap did you stumble into?

It didn't matter. She needed to get out now.

Wren tore at the net with her blade. Panic continued to bubble in her chest all the while. At the rate she was going, she would be lucky to escape the trap in its entirety within the hour. The blood rushing to her head made it difficult to think.

She peered back the way she came through the forest, then kicked and struggled within the trap until the rope spun her around to face the opposite direction. It was important for her to know where the hunter who had set the trap would come from. Given she'd come from the rebel camp, and that the rope was far too high quality for it to have belonged to them, it was a reasonable guess that the trap's owner had come from the opposite direction.

Wren kept her eyes trained on the ghost of a path sneaking through the trees, barely more than a squashed footprint of grass here and there, and continued hacking at the net.

Whether because of sheer adrenaline or luck, after about fifteen minutes Wren had managed to cut away enough of the net that, once she tackled the rope around her ankle, she'd be free. If she could grab on to the net on her way down, she should be able to get a decent amount of momentum behind her by swinging.

With some effort, Wren lurched herself into a sit-up, grabbing at her ankle. The net was in her way, but Wren tried to see through it so she could concentrate on getting her leg free.

A crunch through the trees froze Wren to the spot, much like the triggering of the trap had done. The crunch was followed by the snapping of branches beneath feet, and the confident strides of not one but multiple people. Going by the weight of their footsteps, Wren concluded they were men, and likely armored.

Soldiers? Trappers? Someone looking for a reward?

Move now.

Whether the original hunters or armored soldiers, Wren couldn't risk being found by *anyone*.

Between a lone hunter and multiple armored soldiers, she knew which she'd have preferred to find her. But today was not Wren's lucky day—or week, or month, or entire godforsaken year—so with what felt like bile rising up her throat she hacked at the rope around her leg.

She could hear voices now, thick with the Verlantian accent she'd heard from Josenu and the other palace guards. Of all people, Wren *definitely* couldn't run into palace soldiers.

What if they're Arrik's men?

Wren panicked, blood running simultaneously cold and hot. She thought she might be sick.

What if Arrik *is here, just behind those trees?*

She had to get free. She had to. Otherwise a fate worse than death was waiting mere moments away for her. Neither Arrik nor Soren would forgive her.

With one last hack of her dagger, the blade blunted by thousands of tiny rope fibers, Wren forgot all about her plan to swing from the net and fell in an inelegant lump. She landed painfully on her shoulder—not at all how she'd been taught to fall—and agony shot all the way down to her fingers. But she had no time to waste by wallowing in pain. Her shoulder wasn't broken or dislocated, and she'd at least managed to avoid damaging her bow and arrows when she fell. All things considered, it could have gone much worse.

Knowing that heading straight for the rebel camp would mean certain death for the lot of them, Wren made a split-second decision and careened to her right, following the path the stag had made through the trees. Out of the corner of her eye, she spotted the flash of armor shining silver in the sun.

That was too bloody close.

Every breath Wren drew in was ragged and bruised.

It felt like her heart was going to burst from her chest like some kind of vicious monster.

What if they saw me? What if they saw me? What if they saw me...?

The ruined trap would be a sure-fire giveaway that a human, not an animal, had escaped from the clearing—and recently. Even if the soldiers hadn't specifically spotted Wren fleeing for her life, it wouldn't be difficult for them to work out which direction she'd gone and follow out of curiosity.

So she kept running and jumping, over fallen logs and tripping on vines, knowing that to stop meant death. She didn't even listen for whether the soldiers were in pursuit; she couldn't afford to. But at least she knew this part of the forest from when the rebels had moved their camp. Wren was beginning to recognize specific clearings and giant trees, giving her an indication of how to redirect herself toward the new camp once she was sure she wasn't being followed.

If she just got a little farther she'd be free. Around this tree, then down to the burn snaking through the valley, then—

A hand clamped over Wren's mouth and she was yanked against a hard, warm body.

CHAPTER THIRTEEN

Wren

Despite all her training she screamed against the large, callused hand that pressed tighter against her mouth.

Calm down and fight.

Wren stomped her foot into her captor's instep, earning a grunt from him, but his hold never loosened. If anything, he tightened his grip. She clawed at the hand covering her mouth, noting how her captor's shadow swallowed her own. He was clearly large and—going by the force with which he pressed against her mouth—much stronger than she was. She needed to release the panic and focus on his weaknesses.

Think, Wren, think.

She didn't have the element of surprise. She'd lost a dagger to the trap. And her bow and quiver were uselessly locked between her back and her captor's chest. There was no way she could unsheathe her sword either.

Wren acted on instinct. She latched her teeth on the skin of his palm and bit until she tasted blood. The man hissed yet didn't release her. She needed something else.

Elbow him in the gut and then the groin. Then run.

She released his hand and jammed her elbow into his muscled stomach. Immediately, he let go and roughly spun her around to face him.

Her stomach dropped and she blinked repeatedly as if to dispel the nightmare before her.

Her husband glared down at her and roughly wrapped his arm around her waist and yanked her against him, trapping her arms. Arrik put a finger to his lips, warning her to stay quiet.

Him. The monster.

Horror mixed with something else entirely froze Wren to the spot, dissolving the scream in her throat. Arrik's face was painted with an intensity so fierce that she couldn't catch her breath.

Move. Do something. Scream!

He must have seen her thoughts flit across her face because his brows slashed down and he shook his head slowly. Wren opened her mouth, and he slapped his other hand over her lips and bared his teeth, releasing a low, soft growl.

A warning that sent a shiver down her spine.

Slowly, very slowly, Arrik bodily moved Wren until she was pressed between him and a tree, out of sight of the now fast-approaching assailants. The bark bit into her back and her heart thundered as she labored to breathe. Arrik's attention snapped to the left and she followed his gaze. She stiffened as several soldiers came into view.

Was he hiding from his own men?

Wren frowned and turned her attention to the prince. She

studied his ferocious profile as he tracked the soldiers' movements. Even now, he was attractive. High cheekbones, full lips, a jaw that could cut glass.

He destroyed your family.

Evil shouldn't be so beautiful. It was disgusting.

The soldiers moved closer and she squeezed her eyes shut for a second.

This was it. Arrik had her. She was surrounded.

So then why is he hiding you and willing you to keep silent?

She snapped her eyes open and watched, heart in her throat as the soldiers paraded past where the two of them were hiding. Her pulse thundered in her ears when he turned and his pale silver braids tumbled into her face. His scent, fresh sweat intermingled with sage and citrus, assaulted her. It should have been repulsive.

It wasn't.

The sound of his breath was calm, heavy, and collected, where Wren's was rapid and fleeting. She could feel his heartbeat against her chest. He turned his attention on her.

The prince loomed over Wren, his ice-blue eyes piercing daggers into hers. There were bruise-colored shadows beneath those eyes, as if he hadn't slept in months. That observation satisfied her. After all the crimes he'd committed, the beast didn't deserve to have a decent night's sleep.

Lastly, Wren focused on how Arrik felt pressed against her. He wasn't wearing plated armor—only supple, deeply tanned leather—so she could feel every inch of his tightly-muscled body against her. She wanted to wriggle away but knew, instinctively, that would only make things worse.

He held her gaze and warmth bloomed in her stomach as he studied her face. His lips turned down as if he wasn't pleased by what he saw there. She prickled and glared up at him. He didn't get to judge her. Not now, not ever.

Her husband readjusted his grip on her mouth and winced slightly.

Wren kept her expression fixed in place.

Was he hurt? If so, she could use that to her advantage. At his full strength and at such close quarters, there was no chance of Wren overpowering her foe. But if Arrik were hurt...

She might stand a chance.

The soldiers faded from sight and the forest descended into silence.

Wren thought he might finally give her some breathing space, but he didn't budge. She stared at the hollow of his throat for a few seconds, trying to work out how she was going to escape. He had the advantage, but it was clear he didn't want to attract the soldiers' attention any more than she did.

Maybe there was an easier way out of this. The prince seemed to have been warming toward her in the palace before she'd betrayed him. It was clear he liked her body. Perhaps she could seduce him. Her stomach knotted at the idea.

Do what you must to escape.

Wren exhaled heavily through her nose and lifted her chin to look at her dark elf husband through her lashes.

She blinked slowly when Arrik's proud face was contorted into the most lascivious expression Wren had ever seen. His eyes were clouded with something that might have been desire, or possessiveness, or victory, or all three. Just a hint of color crossed his cheeks, his full lips quirked into the barest of smiles. Wren could see the sharp points of his canines. When he noticed where her attention was, he licked his lips.

Wren couldn't look away. What had caused that kind of reaction? She'd not even started her seduction. She took stock of their positions and blushed. Her entire body had curved into his without her knowing, and she hated it.

The man's a monster.

A few strands of Arrik's pale hair—normally pulled back into perfect braids—blew in the wind, softening the sharp angles of his face. *A monster.*

It was sinful how good he looked. How eagerly Wren was reacting to him after months on the run from him.

Why can't he look like a monster?

"Silence suits you," Arrik drawled, smirking with those devilish lips of his that Wren hated admitting to having thought about on one too many occasions when sleep escaped her. "I like you meek and quiet."

Lies.

Those were the last two things Wren were. The mere *notion* of being meek and quiet unleashed her rage—of which she had many untapped stores—all directed at one gargantuan target.

Wren wiggled her fingers against his chest and smiled

beneath his hand before she thrust her hands out, pushing the brute of a man far enough away so that she could knee him in the groin. He stumbled back cupping himself.

She wasted no time unsheathing her sword, and then launched herself at Arrik.

Today, he would die for his crimes against her family.

CHAPTER FOURTEEN

ARRIK

His wayward wife had taken the bait.

Arrik tossed Wren a feral grin before swiftly moving out of reach of her blade.

He knew she'd react to the *silent* comment. It was ironic that she thought he'd prefer such a thing. He'd always adored strong women, and his fiery princess was one of the fiercest he'd ever crossed paths with.

He *loved* it.

"Don't you remember the last time you tried to attack me, my beautiful wife?" he teased, spinning to avoid the next thrust of Wren's blade. Time to rile her further. The sooner they could get this part over with, the sooner he could deliver his deal. "Emphasis on *tried*."

With a growl, his Dragon Princess aimed another attack at him—easily avoided, again—but then surprised him by pulling out a dagger with her left hand and bowling into him to slash at his injured arm. The edge of the knife sliced into Arrik's leather armor.

Your wife is out for your blood. Tread carefully or neither of you will get what you want.

Wren's chest heaved with anger, and he forced his eyes not to linger. Distraction would be the death of him.

"Good thing there will be no *trying* today, only *doing*," she hissed.

"I can think of something far more appealing to do with you," Arrik goaded before he could stop himself.

A delicious blush spread across Wren's face, equal parts rage and embarrassment.

Perfect. He had her, hook, line, and sinker.

She growled and swung her sword at him once more, her movements a little more wild than before.

Arrik yanked his sword from the sheath at his hip and parried her blow. He assessed her form as she circled him looking for any weakness. Wren was clearly no stranger to dual-wielding a sword and a knife; the smaller blade in her left hand was just as deftly handled as the long blade in her right. Given that he'd largely only witnessed Wren handle a bow and arrow before—to alarming effect—the fact she was so capable with blades as well sent heat streaking thought his stomach.

There was something titillating about a woman who could match swords with him.

She was potentially just as good with a blade as he was...when she wasn't flustered.

"The only thing you'll be doing with me is begging for your life," Wren seethed through gritted teeth, their swords clanging when she aimed for Arrik's kidney. It brought her closer to him once more, so Arrik grabbed for Wren's left hand to attempt to pry the dagger from it.

Wren slid from his grasp as easily as water, her crimson hair trailing behind her like a flag of fire.

He sank into the familiar steps of swordplay—the next minute full of the clamor of steel on steel as the two of them attacked, defended, and jumped away, only to repeat the intricate dance again and again. For that was what it was: a dance. He hid his smile as his bloodthirsty little wife lost her wild edge and settled in for a battle. Her movements flowed from one into another. If he wasn't half in love with her already, just fighting with Wren was enough for him to want to keep her forever. She was his match.

"You're not meant for love, but for war."

He gritted his teeth and tried to ignore Soren's words. Since he was a child, the king had always told him he wasn't good enough, that he was less than everyone around him, and yet he always expected more from Arrik than anyone else in Soren's company. As a child and young man just coming into the bloom of youth, he'd pushed himself to be better than everyone else to win the king's approval. His actions hadn't gained his father's approval. It had, however, turned him into Soren's personal tool.

You are not his to command. You control your own fate.

He looked down at the woman who haunted his dreams—who he'd longed to meet again.

The princess who had screamed from the back of a dragon as she took out his men.

The dragon who'd fearlessly attacked him in the ruins of her father's castle after she'd already lost everything.

The one pawn that had turned Arrik's life upside down by refusing to bend to his will.

He wasn't a devout man by any means, but he thanked every star that Wren had not been so easily broken. Her resolve—her determination, her passion—lit a fire in him that burned as brightly as her hair. He'd always lived his world in the gray. And he'd liked it that way. Nothing could hurt him if he didn't care, but this woman, this Dragon Princess, had ruined everything.

The world was starting to gain color and he was catching feelings.

It was problematic.

You don't want it to stop.

It was a shameful secret that he'd never reveal. Arrik knew that it would be the end of him if he ever did.

"How's life on the run treating you, darling?" he growled the next time their blades slid against each other sinuously and they were brought within touching distance once more. He spotted tiny flecks of green in Wren's deep blue eyes.

"I'd say it's better than being shackled to you and your family," she replied, trying once more to surprise Arrik with her dagger. But he never fell for the same distraction twice, and he parried the blade away with the pommel of his sword.

"Something tells me the rebels don't give you as much freedom as you desire. Are you not, in any other sense of the word, their prisoner?"

It wasn't far from the truth.

Josenu had reported how the rebels were treating his wife in the camp. He'd let her escape his prison only to enter another. One far from his family's grasp.

A shadow of doubt crossed her face, and something in his chest clenched. Perhaps things were worse than Josenu had led him to believe?

She must have seen something on his face, because her expression blanked a second before she lunged at him, her sword aimed at his stomach.

Not today, my vicious darling.

He laughed heartily, though in truth the woman's attacks were getting ever more precise—and dangerous. "I've clearly hit upon a sore spot. If you're going to be a prisoner either way, why not rule a kingdom? Come back to me and—"

"*It isn't your kingdom to rule!*" Wren shouted, sparks flying from her sword when it screeched against Arrik's. "The Dragon Isles will *never* be yours."

"Have you forgotten everything we spoke about before you betrayed me?" Arrik countered, knocking Wren's sword from her hand with a strike of pure brute force.

She gasped and her gaze followed the arc of her blade's fall—well out of her grasp—and back to Arrik. His wife pulled another dagger from her waist and sank into a defensive position, contempt and determination reflecting in her eyes.

This had gone on long enough. It was time to reel her in.

"Do you remember what passed between us?" he asked softly, the wind rustling through the trees above them.

She flinched like he'd struck her. "Why bring that up now? You'd have said anything to stop me killing you in your sleep!

You're a liar and a murderer."

"I have lied. And I have killed. But I did not lie to you, Wren, and your life is safe with me." He meant it. "Three days prior I could have captured you. I let you go. I have been protecting you for *months.*"

Saying her name aloud gave the Dragon Princess pause, and in that one opportune moment Arrik closed the distance between them until they were standing toe-to-toe. With a hooked finger he tilted Wren's chin up to face him. Her eyes were swimming with fury, her lips contorted into the most delicious snarl Arrik had ever seen. Any moment she could stab him—and yet she paused. Maybe she felt the same pull he did?

"Why would I believe anything you told me?" she uttered, voice barely audible over the throbbing of his heart. "You've never given me reason to trust a word you said."

"Have I not, wife?"

"Don't call me that," she snapped.

For some reason, that irked him. "We are bound together whether you like it or not, *wife*. Did I not save you from the worst of my father's wrath? Did I not keep you out of the dungeons, and allow you your freedom within the palace?"

"The freedom of a slave is not freedom at all."

"But even so—"

"You murdered my family!"

Now they were getting to the heart of the issue.

She dug the tips of her daggers into the flesh at the base of his spine. A dangerous embrace. He exhaled, taking a chance that could change everything.

"Nothing I can say will bring them back. They died at the hands of my kingdom, but their blood is not on my hands personally," Arrik replied carefully. The daggers dug in farther, breaking the skin, trickles of blood dripping down into his trousers. He held her gaze as her blue eyes filled with tears.

"You led the attack," she snapped. "I lost everyone!"

"I did. I've led many attacks, and no doubt you would and have done the same thing during times of war. I won't ask for your forgiveness because I can never remove the pain of loss that you suffer. I am sorry for your agony. The loss of kin…" He exhaled heavily, reliving the loss of his mother all over again. "…can break you or forge you into something strong, better."

She sucked in a sharp breath, one traitorous tear dripping down her cheek.

Time to push.

He slid his sword-wielding hand around Wren's waist to pull her closer to him, feeling the blades keenly. "Wield your grief into something powerful."

She lifted her chin slightly, his callused fingers brushing against the soft skin of her chin. "You killed my *husband*."

"*I* am your husband."

"You—" Wren bit out, then paused.

Arrik watched her search his face for…something. He wasn't sure what. It would be easy to knock her out. To drag her back to his secret lair. Part of him *wanted* to, after all. But that would go against his well-laid-out plan. He needed her compliance, her surrender.

The dark part of his mind purred at the idea. Of her pliant, beneath—

Wren blinked back her tears and her expression intensified, like she could read his scandalous thoughts. Perhaps she could. She'd enchanted him and it was a problem. Shane was correct that she was a distraction. One that would be the death of him.

"Do you really believe that I would ever help you? I'd rather see you dead."

"Nothing is stopping you." A challenge.

She gritted her teeth, and he felt her hands shaking. Arrik kept his breathing slow and even despite the burning pain in his lower back. The hair at the nape of his neck tingled as he inhaled the wild scent of her—salt and jasmine.

She pressed the blades deeper as she stared defiantly up at him. "Why aren't you fighting me?" she demanded. "Fight!"

"I'm done fighting you, wife. My life is yours if you seek it."

He stilled completely as Wren released a frustrated yell and pulled her blades from his back. She shook in his arms and glared up at him. Angry tears poured from her eyes.

"Why can't I kill you? Why am I so weak?"

"You're not weak, my darling."

"You deserve death."

"I do." It was the truth. His life wasn't pretty despite the palace he lived in or the title that adorned his name. His privilege was dripping in blood.

She shook her head and glanced away. "I hate you."

"No, you don't. Not any more than I hate you."

"I want to hate you," she whispered. "I want to, but—"

"I know the feeling," Arrik found himself saying, because it was true. He smoothed his fingers down Wren's chin to her neck, tracing the line of the throbbing artery there. If it was anything to go by, then her heart was beating just as fast as his was. "And yet…I find that I need you."

She released a bark of grim laughter. "You need me? You mean you need to use me?"

"We need each other."

Wren's attention snapped to his face. "What are we doing?"

"Nothing and everything."

A long moment of silence passed as she stared up at him. What was she looking for?

"Why can't I escape you?" she whispered.

"Because we're inevitable," he murmured back.

He blinked slowly as she lifted up on her toes and pressed closer. Wren gave Arrik a ghost of a smile, and he found himself captivated by the gleam that entered her eye. His attention moved to her lips that beckoned him as she pressed her chest against his. His body surged to life and Arrik stooped lower to meet her as unchecked desire filled him. What was it about this woman that temped him so?

To kiss her. To kiss his wife, the Dragon Princess.

He cocked his head to the side, finding a better angle. Just a little taste. He felt his own eyes closing as he lowered his lips to—

A violent knee to his manhood knocked Arrik to his knees. He grunted and glared up at his vile little dragon. She kicked him in the chest, toppling him onto his back. She then scrambled to snatch her fallen sword off the ground and took off running.

"Wait!" he growled, climbing to his feet as pain threatened to make him heave.

She never paused as she sprinted through the trees, disappearing like the nymph she was.

"You're a fool."

His father's taunt echoed in Arrik's mind. How could he be so stupid to believe she would kiss him willingly? The man she believed was responsible for her family's deaths.

Don't lose her.

He worked through the pain and recovered quickly, crashing through the trees after her. Arrik smiled as he caught sight of her cloak. He pushed himself faster and closed the distance between them in a manner of seconds.

Before Wren even made it to the forest proper, Arrik grabbed her hood and yanked hard. She cried as he threw her mercilessly to the ground, dropping down on her to hold her in place.

"Pretty little trick," he breathed, wrapping his hands around Wren's wrists, pinning them above her head to stop her from moving. He growled as she wiggled beneath him, making him want to act like the beast she accused him of. She was so petite compared to him. Wren was curvier than the elven women of his culture, and shorter, but he...loved it. Why was she so appealing?

His little dragon gnashed her teeth, squirming beneath him, and released a pitiful growl. Arrik found himself throwing his head back in laughter. "Was that supposed to be frightening, wife? It was tiny. Just like you."

"I'm not tiny. I'm..." she trailed off as a shadow crossed overhead, along with a whip of air that snapped through Arrik's hair.

Arrik yelled when a massive force slammed into his side, tossing him through the air. He rolled and landed on his back, breath knocked out of him. His eyes widened and he wheezed as a massive paw settled on his chest and held him in place.

A dragon.

A massive, glinting, midnight-colored dragon, its jewel eyes slits as they took in the sight of its prey. *Him*. He was the prey.

Was this how he died? All of his countless battles won, and kingdoms conquered, for what? For a creature of the isles to dig its claws into his flesh and rend him asunder.

Not today.

He bared his teeth, refusing to be cowed by the dragon. His mother had once told him that beasts always attacked when they sensed weakness. He'd give the dragon none.

"So is this the plan, wife? To have your beast do your dirty work?" he called to Wren. "I didn't take you for a coward."

"You use your men in that capacity. It is fitting, don't you think?" she crooned just out of sight.

"Perhaps, but you'll never escape if you let me die. You'll only seal your doom, and that of your people."

It was the truth. Soren would kill her and forget any sort of peaceful settlement of the Dragon Isles. It would be a bloodbath.

The dragon snarled, causing the hair along his arms to rise.

"Leave him be, Trove!" Wren barked.

The dragon pushed its nose against Arrik's chest, crushing him into the dirt and resolutely ignoring her.

He was going to die.

"*Please,* Trove." His wife began humming a sweet melody, and the spines along the dragon's back lowered. A low vibration rumbled through the creature. Ever so slowly, the dragon slithered off of Arrik.

He drew in his first full breath and sat up, wincing. He'd cracked at least one rib.

He registered the dragon at Wren's side, gently nosing at her with the same sharp-toothed mouth that had meant to tear Arrik apart.

Bloody beast.

He lunged to his feet when she jumped onto its back. With one final look at him, she nudged the beast and they leapt into the air, dragon and rider one seamless creature.

Arrik could do nothing but stare in awe, and struggle to comprehend the sight of his wife escaping upon the back of a dragon.

A *dragon*, in Verlanti. When had there ever been dragons in Verlanti? But more than that: a dragon that had meant to kill him but Wren had called it off.

"I'm coming for you," he whispered to the silent forest.

As if she heard, Wren glanced over her shoulder and met his gaze. He smiled and bowed to her.

This first round was hers—as he'd meant it to be.

Arrik would leave her alone for the moment, but not forever.

He was Wren's just as much as she was his.

The Dragon Princess simply didn't know it yet.

CHAPTER FIFTEEN

WREN

Stupid, stupid, stupid girl!

Angry tears fell from her eyes only to be snatched away by the winds.

You should have killed him.

An ugly sob broke free as Trove descended to a clearing in the forest, near the edge of a wide river she recognized as being barely an hour's walk from the rebel camp. As Trove landed with a whoosh of air, Wren slid off his back and stumbled, barely catching her balance. Wiping her stinging face with her shirt sleeve, she released another sob. This had been the first time she'd flown through the sky since Aurora died.

Since *Arrik* had torn Wren's entire world apart.

She wrapped her arms around her body, shuddering with grief that threatened to tear her apart. She should have killed him, taken vengeance for the lives he'd destroyed.

Your father would be ashamed.

Wren screamed and dropped to her knees, the wet earth seeping through her leggings. Trove settled around her, placing his heavy head over her lap and protecting her back with his gargantuan body. She stared at the beautiful creature that offered her protection and comfort. She didn't deserve it, and yet Wren couldn't find it in herself to move away.

His warm breath heated her thighs and belly as he stared up at her—the silent sentinel.

"How are you—why are you here?" Wren bit out, still not quite believing what she was seeing. What she was experiencing. Trove was here, far away from the sea, and he had saved her from Arrik.

He had saved her from imprisonment or worse.

Trove wouldn't have had to save you if you'd taken care of your husband.

Husband...more like personal devil.

The dragon responded by trilling out a few notes, then closing his eyes before humming in a much deeper, plaintive tone. The song was disjointed and keening, but it was enough to cause her tears to fall in earnest. She clutched at Trove's fin-covered head, openly mourning regardless of who might hear her.

After all: who would dare attack a dragon?

"Thank you for saving me," she cried against his scales, chest heaving with every breath. "I don't deserve it, but th-thank you."

Wren felt like she was breaking into a thousand pieces. So much loss, and for what? Greed. She'd made a promise to herself in the Verlantian palace to move forward and gain justice for her family—for her people.

You failed.

When the chance came, she'd shied away.

Would she be forever haunted by her past? The loss of her family seemed to make it impossible for her to struggle out of the quagmire that meant to drag her down into despair. Not only that, but her mind had begun to crack.

"I saw Rowen in the pirate city," she found herself telling Trove, who was still singing his sad song. "And before, too. I *know* I saw him." Even now, his face was seared into her memory. She hung her head. "Leif claimed that he believed me...but how could he? Rowen *died.*" Wren clutched her head and glanced at Trove. "I'm chasing ghosts and showing mercy to monsters. What is wrong with me?"

The dragon flicked his gaze to Wren, slit pupil expanding for a fraction of a second as if in answer.

"Everything?" Wren choked on a garbled laugh. "You're not wrong." She pressed her palms to her eyes. "If Rowen was here, he'd tell me to stop whining and move forward." *But he's not here.* Wren dropped her hands onto the ground on either side of her hips and dug her fingers into the wild grass. "He was my friend, my confidant, my love." She smiled despite the tears. "He could swim as well as any dragon. Well, almost," she added on, when Trove *harrumphed* in indignation.

Wren gazed out in front of her, focusing on nothing. "Why do I keep seeing him? Is it the guilt? Does he have a twin I don't know about? Am I simply going mad?"

The latter seemed the most likely.

Of course, Trove had no answer for her, but now that

Wren had opened up the floodgates of her mind, she found that she couldn't stop confiding in the beast. All her thoughts and feelings of the last few months burst free.

"I wouldn't be seeing ghosts if I'd saved my people in the first place. If I'd protected them. Now the Dragon Isles will be ravaged for jewels and slaves and God knows what else, all because I'm not there to help them."

"You take too much on, daughter."

She blinked hard as the memory of her mother's advice echoed through her mind. "Logically, I know everything is not on me, but..." Wren gritted her teeth and shook her head. "I'm all that's left. Britta is just a child. She has no one else, and neither do my people."

Trove stopped singing, lashing his tail painlessly against Wren's side. He was listening, and he could understand in his own way, and that was all that mattered to Wren. She'd kept everything bottled up for so long, it was a relief to finally speak it.

Her bottom lip wavered as she prepared to bare an ugly truth, one she didn't even want to acknowledge but had to. One that would lead to her downfall and potentially her death.

"I can't kill him," she said, whisper-quiet, into the scales that adorned the top of Trove's head. Wren traced soft circles against their luminous surface. Part of her heart broke at the confession. "The prince, I mean." She couldn't bear to say his name out loud. "Somewhere in that prison of a palace, part of me began to trust him. I don't have feelings for him...but we have a bond I can't explain." There was something there. Something intangible and unknowable between the two of them. Something dangerous enough that Wren really *had* almost kissed the prince, before coming to her senses and knocking him to the ground.

She wished that "something" would disappear forever.

Her stomach churned and bile burned the back of her throat. "He destroyed my world and yet…I couldn't kill him." She began to tremble. "I won't kill him."

It was ugly.

Unfortunately, it was true.

A song fell unbidden from her lips; her trembling slowly passed as the sun moved across the sky. Trove joined in.

For a while the two of them sat together, singing in a language no other creature in Verlanti could understand. The songs sounded odd away from the sea. Not wrong, but different. Wren became aware of how truly far away from home she was—and how dangerous it was for Trove to be so far from the water. Arrik had seen him, and no doubt his soldiers, too. They would be on the hunt for the dragon now.

They were rare and valuable.

"You have to go," Wren urged the creature, hugging Trove's head before standing up and brushing the soil from her aching legs. Slowly, the dragon uncurled to face her, but he made no move to fly away. "You cannot be here," she urged, a few seconds of immobility later. "Leave, Trove."

The dragon did not move.

"*Go*!" she cried at the beast. "Go and leave me here! You don't belong at my side. It means death. Everyone close to me dies, don't you understand?"

It was clear in Trove's endlessly dark eyes that he understood, at least to some degree, what Wren was doing. He butted her in the chest and crooned once before pulling away. The dragon launched into the air, and she whooped as he gained altitude, his majestic wings taking him higher and higher.

She swallowed down more tears as he cut through the sky, leaving her behind. Once again she was alone. Wren wished he could have stayed, but it was too dangerous for everyone. If the dragon stayed around, protecting her, he would die. And what was a Dragon Princess if she was unable to save her dragon? Wren had already lost one, once.

She would not be so foolish as to make the same mistake again.

CHAPTER SIXTEEN

Wren

The camp was in an absolute frenzy by the time Wren forced herself to return, hazy-headed and numb from both her encounter with the prince and her hideous truths she'd bared to the light.

"What's going on?" she asked Ever, who was trundling past with an armful of leather armor toward the weapons tent.

The older woman arched her eyebrows at Wren in disapproval. "I see you've returned. I trust you know your aunt isn't happy with your disappearance." When Wren didn't reply, Ever dumped the armor into the arms of a passing woman and said, "Soldiers have been spotted in the forest, much too close. We have to ready for an attack and move the camp. Come, I'll take you to Vienne."

Guilt twisted Wren's stomach.

Had they tracked her here?

Were they Arrik's men coming for his revenge?

She exhaled slowly and tried not to let her fear cloud her thoughts.

He hid you from the soldiers. He didn't want them to know you were here.

So what did it all mean? Was he just toying with them? Or was there something else going on?

Wren rubbed her temples and then dropped her hands when she noticed Ever studying her. It was not the time to dwell upon it. She'd no doubt hash it over during the sleepless night to come.

Nodding her head politely, she followed Ever to Vienne's tent, knowing that in all likelihood Bram would be inside too. Stars, she disliked the man. He was as prickly as a porcupine and twice as mean as a bear. Wren doubted he even knew how to smile. But it was better for her if they were both there so she wouldn't have to repeat her story twice. Better to tell them both about everything that had happened today, lest they lock her up for lying.

Well...not everything. She'd keep Trove's visit a secret.

Wren thought of Trove, and how he'd wanted to come with her. To protect her. Not for the first time Wren wished she had left with the dragon instead, and flown all the way home.

Don't be a ninny. Stand up straight and accept your lumps like a warrior.

She sucked in a breath through her teeth and entered the large canvas tent that housed her aunt and served as their war room.

The first thing Wren noted was that Leif had finally returned. He, at least, looked relieved to see her rather than furious, but when he made to walk toward her Bram thrust out an arm to stop him.

She schooled her expression and stared down at her aunt, who had yet to look up from the map on the table in the center of the room. Vienne slowly set down her quill and lifted her head, eyes snapping with anger.

"Did I, or did I not, tell you not to leave camp?"

Wren kept her mouth shut. It was not a rhetorical question.

Her aunt's face turned red and she slapped a hand against the table, straightening to her full height. "No, I *ordered* you. And what did you do?"

"I went hunting," Wren offered, because it was the truth. It felt like a thousand years had passed since she'd decided to run off into the forest in search of game. So much had happened.

Vienne waved at her. "Yet you have come back emptyhanded! What did we all say to you? Game is scarce in the forest! Are you really so arrogant that you believed you could somehow magic a rabbit or a pheasant or a deer out of nowhere?"

Wren kept her tone even. "I'm not so arrogant to believe that I alone could find meat for the people. I had nothing else to do and I wanted to be useful. There was a stag—"

"Then where is it?" her aunt cut in.

She swallowed down her ire and managed, "Something stopped me from being able to fell it."

Bram huffed and tossed his hands in the air. "I thought you were supposed to be a far superior hunter to anyone else in the rebellion. Yet when you have a *stag* in your sights, you lose it?"

"Like I said—"

Bram prowled forward into her space, his features contorted in fury. "So much of our bloody fight hinges on *you* being a piece we can play, yet you flagrantly ignored that *again* to run off as if nothing matters but what you want! You're just a foolish little girl who—"

Wren held her ground and kept her hands at her sides. Just barely. Boy, did she want to knock the look off his face. "If you would just listen—"

"Bram is right," Vienne said, face hardening. "I'd thought I was too harsh on you, banning you from leaving camp, but all of his suspicions and fears were right on point."

"What do you mean?" Wren asked, proud that her voice didn't waver.

Her aunt pushed away from the table and pointed a finger at Wren. "You're becoming a liability. I thought my sister had raised you better but..."

"Don't you dare," Wren said gutturally, stepping away from Bram. She glared at her aunt. "You don't get to speak of my mother. You may share blood with her but you are not my family. Family would never treat each other this way. It's shameful."

Vienne jerked as if she'd been slapped. "What is shameful is your actions and lack of responsibility. You're leaving us no choice but to restrain—"

"I met Prince Arrik," she snapped.

Finally, *finally* the lecture stopped. Everyone froze, all eyes on her: Vienne, Bram, Ever, and Leif. Leif recovered first, blinking away shock before observing, "You've already run into the soldiers in the forest, haven't you?"

Wren nodded, feeling sick to her stomach. "I walked into a bloody trap set for a deer. Stupid, I know, but I was watching the stag. I barely got out in time to run from them."

Vienne's eyes narrowed. "And the prince?"

"We..." Wren struggled through the memory, trying to find the right words. Now she had some distance from the situation it was easier to start putting things together. Prince Arrik hadn't wanted his soldiers to see her. He hadn't gone for a maiming blow or even a knockout blow when they'd fought. Once again, he'd tried to entice her.

She pursed her lips, ignoring Bram scowling in her direction.

In the Verlantian palace, what seemed like a million years ago, the prince had wanted a truce with Wren. He'd wanted her on his side—acting the obedient wife in public whilst being herself around him and only him.

Why? Just what was he planning?

Rebellion?

"I think he has plans for the throne," Wren concluded, speaking her suspicions aloud for the first time and in the process, realizing how true they sounded.

Ever snorted. "Everyone has designs on the throne. That is nothing new. Try again, Princess."

Wren ran through her encounter with her husband once again. Arrik hadn't wanted to bring Wren in because that meant she'd be under Soren's watch once more, likely imprisoned. Why didn't he want her to be underneath the king's thumb?

"He wants me." She looked around the room. "I don't think he wants to see me hurt."

Bram went bug-eyed, the tendons in his hands threatening to snap. "Oh, you *think* this? That's all right, then, we'll take your word for it! He is a master manipulator, *Princess*. He has killed hundreds without remorse. I knew he'd corrupted you in the palace."

"You have no idea what I went through to survive in the palace because of the prince," she spat. "If you'd shut your mouth for a bloody moment and listen to me, I'll tell you the whole story!"

Don't let your anger get the best of you.

She was tired of the rebellion dismissing her, especially when she *was* important to them. But she wasn't just important because she was the Dragon Princess.

She was useful in and of herself.

"Tell us, Wren," Leif said, gently squeezing her hand and nodding in understanding. His presence helped ground her, and she took a deep breath as she ordered her thoughts.

"Back in the Verlanti palace," Wren began, "in the weeks after our forced marriage… Arrik told me something interesting. Well, several things. First: he was not responsible for killing his wives. Each and every one of them was targeted by an assassin."

"And you believed him?" Bram spat out, disbelief plain as day on his face.

Wren turned on him. "Yes. Because he explained this to me after killing one of these very assassins sent to kill *me* the night of our marriage."

Silence.

Wren lifted her chin and stared down her nose at her aunt. "The second thing he told me is this: though he's bastard-born he is, in fact, Soren's oldest son. Since the king has acknowledged him as his child, then that means—if it became public knowledge that Arrik was the eldest—he'd have the support *and* the claim to the Verlantian throne, should Soren be ripped from it."

"Even if this were true," Vienne said, chewing over Wren's news, "that doesn't mean the prince would work with us. For all we know he's just as likely as his father to stamp us out. Given his track record, I'd be inclined to say this is true."

"I never suggested otherwise."

"So what's your point?"

"My point is..." Wren glanced at Leif, hoping to get some kind of confirmation that she wasn't mad to say what she was about to say.

Funny, checking I'm not going mad from the boy who's the maddest of us all.

Leif merely smiled at her, urging Wren to continue. "My point is I think we might be able to *use* Prince Arrik—if we play our cards right. He wanted me on his side, back in the palace. He needs Lorne to successfully fight against his father. It is the key to taking the throne."

A very nasty look of understanding passed between Vienne, Ever, and Bram then, and Wren knew they had concluded the wrong thing from what she'd said.

"So we should let you go back to him to rule the Dragon

Isles together, is that it?" Bram asked, an ugly grin on his face. "God, you really are just the prince's whore, aren't you?"

She flinched, the words piercing her to the very soul.

They're not wrong, are they? Your heart quickens when you think of him.

"*Bram*," Vienne warned, though it was clear she agreed with him. She turned to Wren. "You must see how this looks to us, Wren. You purported to be against the prince, and yet, at the first chance you get, you run off to have an illicit meeting with him."

"But it wasn't like that!" Wren gritted out. "I tried to end him. We fought and I wounded him—"

"Yet you didn't kill him. And now you're back with us, which means he wanted you to return to us. He is hoping to ensnare us, Wren, and you have foolishly been tainted by your time in the palace with him into believing that he speaks the truth."

"I am not foolish. You are for not looking at the bigger picture," she replied, rolling her shoulders back and standing tall. "Using the prince could change everything."

"Or it could get us all killed," Ever retorted. "Chances are that your husband let you go to get to us. Every moment we spend arguing is dangerous. We need to settle this now."

Vienne nodded. "If you leave the camp without authorization, I will be forced to tie you to my side."

"You'd do that to me?" Wren asked.

"I'd do it to my own mother if it meant getting rid of Soren."

Wren was thankful she'd sent Trove away and kept him a

secret. She couldn't even trust her last remaining blood relative to not fall prey to the siren call of power.

She bit back her reply and held her tongue.

When it was clear she had nothing further to say on the matter, Vienne sighed in satisfaction, taking her niece's silence as confirmation that she wouldn't try any other funny business. Any respect Bram might have had for Wren had clearly disappeared, replaced with the same dismissive look he'd had when she was first brought to the rebellion.

She could see it on his face. He viewed her as a foolish little girl who had fallen in love with the villain. It made her sick.

Only Leif looked like he believed her. A glint in his eye told Wren that he was likely going to investigate her version of things on his own, to check for himself the truth of things. It should have been a cause for relief—she still had Leif, and he believed her—but all she felt was tired.

Pure, unadulterated exhaustion. Any time she tried to do *anything* on her own she was stopped in her tracks. She couldn't effect any real kind of change no matter what she did.

Everywhere Wren turned, someone was trying to bind her to their cause.

"Now that we've got that out of the way," Vienne said, breaking the awkward tension in the room, "it is high time we met with our benefactor. If we have the prince to contend with as a separate force from his father, then we have even more cause to move faster."

To Wren's surprise, Ever did not look in the least bit

pleased. With a huff of disapproval, she left the tent. The woman had not once disagreed with Vienne in the entire time Wren had been with the rebellion. She took it as a sign that she was not going to like who their benefactor was in the slightest.

"Who *is* this benefactor?" Wren drawled. It was surprising they'd not banished her from the tent yet.

For a moment it seemed as if Bram was going to tell her that it wasn't for her to know, but then he said, "Lord Idril. He was married to King Soren's cousin."

"And a nasty piece of work," Leif added on, wincing. "He's a dark elf who delights in keeping slaves as much as our dear king. Ever was one of Idril's, back in the day."

Wren's lip curled in distaste. "So then why work with him at all?"

"Because needs must," Vienne said, "and sometimes you have to work with unpleasant people to meet your goals."

"He couldn't possibly be worse than Soren," Wren whispered, resisting the urge to shiver when she thought of the king's slimy fingers on her skin and his dreadful mouth on her lips.

Leif gave her the most minute shake of his head—too small for anyone else to see. It spoke volumes. "Prepare yourself," he muttered, promptly sending a shiver down her spine.

Perhaps Idril *was* worse than Soren. And if that were the case...

Wren believed more and more that she should have flown off with Trove, never to be seen again.

CHAPTER SEVENTEEN

WREN

The camp split once more—a message came from their other two camps, informing them that they'd done the same—and Wren was hauled off with Ever and Vienne. She shouldered her pack and once again wished Leif were with her, though she was supremely grateful that Bram was not. He hadn't stopped throwing glares her way until he left the camp.

The moody blighter.

But the bard and Vienne's right-hand man were under orders to follow the prince's soldiers and quietly redirect them so that they didn't follow the rebels making their way to Lord Idril's residence. Everyone would regroup there.

Wren eyed their procession. Just how big was the dark elf's abode? It had to be a veritable palace to be able to accommodate the entire rebellion. She rolled her neck and focused on putting one foot in front of the other. She'd find out more about their secretive benefactor in time. Although, from Ever's reaction, Wren didn't have high hopes that she'd like him.

"What are you thinking of?" Ever asked, glancing over her

shoulder. "I can practically feel you staring through my back."

"Nothing of consequence," Wren muttered as Vienne shot an annoyed look her way. Her aunt was still just as angry as she'd been several hours ago. Even now, Wren's skin crawled. If she hazarded a guess, Vienne had set at least four guards to watch over her. She snorted. As if she planned to take off running through the forest back to Arrik. If anything, it was a relief to be moving in the opposite direction as her husband.

"If you say so," Ever retorted with a gruff chuckle.

"Just remember we're not the enemy," Vienne added, arching her brows.

It didn't feel that way.

Though Wren hadn't been restrained, she was nevertheless not allowed to venture out of her aunt's sight. Considering the dense pine trees as they headed farther and farther into the forest, "out of sight" wasn't very far at all. The moment she put even a single step out of place, Vienne's gaze snapped to hers, warning Wren not to even attempt leaving her side.

No matter where she was, it seemed she was a prisoner.

Her thoughts turned to the prince and about what he had said—that she was just as much a prisoner with the rebellion as she was in the Verlantian palace. Wren swallowed hard. She was just a chess piece to be used by either side for their own games, with no will of her own. It would have been easier to discount what Arrik had said if she herself hadn't been coming to that same conclusion. So what was she going to do about it?

The closest she'd come to having her own will was when her husband had asked her to trust him, and rule with him.

But how could that be? How could that *be the situation wherein you have the most free will?*

It was unfathomable.

Her greatest enemy had offered her power and freedom.

It has strings and you know it. Don't forget what he's done.

Yet the way Vienne, Ever, and Bram had discounted her observations about the prince and his motives only served to incline Wren to trusting her own instincts more and more. They had never served her wrong before—not on the Dragon Isles, not in the Verlanti dungeon, not in trusting Leif, not when she escaped upon the back of a dragon.

And if that were the case...

Did that mean Wren should trust everything Arrik had told her too? Was siding with him actually the best thing she could do right now, despite everything he'd done?

She shook her head.

It was too difficult a situation for her to work through right now when a meeting with Lord Idril was imminent. She needed her wits about her for that, if Leif's comments were anything to go by.

Prepare yourself.

"Stop," Vienne said in a clipped, hushed tone, holding out a hand to make the rest of their group pause.

Wren peered through the darkness and the trees, wondering what had caught her aunt's attention. Then she saw it: a flash, there one moment and gone the next. It reappeared a few seconds later.

Torchlight reflecting off armor. Wren had experienced it plenty of times before to know exactly what it was.

Soldiers.

Josenu had warned them about the increased patrols happening throughout the forest. They had been lucky so far in that they hadn't come across any of these patrols—Arrik's own soldiers earlier that day notwithstanding—so it felt like an inevitability that they'd finally happened across one.

Nobody moved. A single motion, a single noise, a single word, would give them away. Wren hardly dared to breathe. Her attention wavered away from the soldiers and to the edge of the forest. It would be so easy to use the distraction of the patrol to slip away from the rebellion forever. Find Trove. Follow her own path.

Running away is never the right decision.

Before Wren could ponder the idea further, the patrol disappeared, and Vienne motioned for the group to continue.

Half an hour of silent trekking later, they came upon Lord Idril's residence. It appeared quite suddenly. One moment Wren was surrounded by trees and the next she was standing in front of the high stone walls of a castle.

It was larger than the Dragon Keep.

"It's stunning," she gasped, momentarily awed by the towering, dark, smooth-stoned surface of the castle. It reflected the forest back at them. Every few feet the stone was punctuated by lanterns and torches, hundreds of them in total, twinkling like stars in the inky night sky.

It should have been quiet. The forest had been silent after all, and it was the middle of the night. But music, singing, shouting, curses, and dancing spilled from open windows.

The group approached the castle, only to be halted by a huge elf dressed in armor from head to toe. He stood at the base of the stairs and sketched a bow to Vienne. "My lady, Lord Idril awaits your arrival." He scanned the group. "Accommodations have been made for your people and animals."

"Thank you, Satire."

"My pleasure, my lady."

He nodded to the guards at the entrance to the castle. They pulled open the double doors and Wren flinched at the cacophony of sound that rushed out to great them. It was the loudest thing she'd heard since the Verlantians stormed upon the Dragon Keep.

Her aunt drew near to Wren's side. "Keep your mouth shut and your head down. Cover your hair."

Wren nodded and yanked up her hood over her curls. Even if she wanted to say anything, no one would be able to hear her over all the racket. Her pulse leapt as they ascended the stairs and entered the castle, footsteps echoing absurdly loudly on the flagstones. For a few moments there was nothing to be seen but a wide, empty corridor, adorned on both sides with sumptuous curtains and tapestries. A male servant dressed in nothing but a gaudy robe and a translucent veil directed them up a grand flight of stairs to a large room filled to the brim with bodies.

Dancing bodies.

Writhing bodies.

Wren blinked slowly and coughed as embarrassment heated her face.

Barely-dressed men and women slid against one another, and the heady scent of sweat, drugs, and incense filled Wren's nostrils. She swiped at her nose and tried to breathe through her mouth. A woman to her right jostled Wren and gave her a sloppy smile. Wren pressed away, but there wasn't anywhere to go.

"Aren't you pretty!" the woman trilled.

Vienne pushed the woman away. "Begone with you."

The woman cackled and melted into the crowd.

"Let no one touch you," her aunt commanded.

"Not a problem," Wren muttered back, even as her head began to throb from the smoke.

Keep a clear head, keep a clear head, keep a clear head.

Another veiled servant appeared and cleared a path to the back of the room. The wall was gilded, and adorned with painted humans in compromising positions. Wren frowned. At least she didn't have to wonder what kind of person Lord Idril was any longer. It seemed he was just as depraved as his king.

Their group was taken to the dais at the back of the room. It was built into the stone along with two occupied chairs that looked like thrones.

Interesting. Lord Idril considered himself king.

Wren made sure to stay as out of sight as possible, at the back of the group. Vienne didn't tell her not to, which meant Wren could only assume that she had done what was expected of her.

It was easy to tell who Lord Idril was. He was sprawled over the larger, throne-like chair, his chest exposed and his feet bare. The only clothing he had on were a pair of leather trousers. His pointed ears were heavy with golden jewelry, setting off the deep auburn of his long hair, which was twisted into the loosest of braids. Even from where Wren stood she could tell he had piercing blue eyes. Sharp eyes. The kind of eyes that missed nothing, even when the elf who those eyes belonged to was laughing easily whilst a woman curled onto his lap, pawing at his chest, while another sat on the floor, playing with the hem of his trousers.

Wren's lip curled in disgust as she noted the dainty gold collar adorning the women's necks that connected to a long chain that Idril held in his hand.

"Later, later," he promised the woman sitting on his lap, sweeping her back onto her feet and sending her on her way. Looking more closely at the woman as she walked away, Wren could tell they were of a similar age, and her face wore the kind of bland expression only drugs could be responsible for.

Everything about this place seemed *wrong*. Tainted.

Lord Idril and his depraved *court* made Wren's skin crawl. She wanted out. *Needed* out.

"Vienne," Lord Idril purred, turning his attention to their group. Wren self-consciously tucked her hair behind her ears and made sure her hood was still secure.

Her aunt stepped forward to greet him.

"It has been too long since we've convened in person,"

Idril said.

"I agree," Vienne said, "though I am here now."

The elf lord scanned the entire group, his eyes pausing on Wren. Idril straightened in his throne, then, focusing his attention on Wren even though she desperately wished he would look elsewhere. The way his eyes saw through her felt *oily.* Invasive. She knew, instinctively, that Lord Idril was looking at her not as a person but as an opportunity. A possession.

She had to get out.

"We have everything prepared in the north to attack the dark elves," Vienne said, shocking Wren into listening once more.

What is this? Taking out the elves?

Slowly, Idril turned his gaze away from Wren and back to her aunt. A knowing grin spread across his face. "Excellent. My dear cousin-in-law has always hated surprises. I almost wish I could be there to see his face. We'll strike before he has a chance to reroute his forces to defend them."

"We're attacking the dark elves?" Wren muttered to herself, trying to make sense of this move. All around her, members of the rebellion shushed her. Vienne fired a warning glare in Wren's direction. For weeks now the rebellion had kept her out of their plans, but now, in the presence of a highborn elf lord of Verlanti, they were openly talking about dismantling the entire kingdom and her aunt was angry that she had asked one little question?

"And what have we here?" Lord Idril purred, unfolding out of his chair as elegantly as a jungle cat to stalk toward her. Forcing herself to stand her ground as the man closed the distance between them, she swallowed a mouthful of cloying air and wished she could hit herself for drawing more attention than she needed to.

She had no doubt she would not like whatever was going to happen next.

Her hand dropped to the dagger hidden beneath her cloak.

Well, he wouldn't like what would happen either if he stepped over any lines.

The rebellion members parted and Idril made his way to stand before her, forcing Wren to tilt her chin up to match his stare. He didn't look like Soren at all.

"Hello, little peach," Idril said, smiling sweetly as he scanned Wren from head to toe. When she said nothing, he reached out and slid her hood down, eyes widening when he spied her crimson hair.

"*Ah*, us redheads must stick together," he murmured, for only Wren to hear, flashing her a grin that was anything but pleasant. The blue of his eyes seemed familiar to Wren, but she didn't dare dwell on why.

"It is a pleasure to meet you, Lord Idril," Wren finally said, when it became clear he was waiting for her to speak. She nodded politely. "I can only apologize for interrupting just now. It was not my place to speak."

"Hmm," Idril murmured, gently stroking Wren's hair as his eyes noted every permutation of her face. Watching her every move like a hawk.

Like he held a secret about her that only he knew.

Then Idril waved a pointed, long-fingered hand around the room, an easy smile on his face. “Get comfortable, little peach, and enjoy what the night has to offer. We shall speak again over the next few days. You can be sure of it.”

Wren’s stomach dropped.

It sounded more like a threat than a promise.

CHAPTER EIGHTEEN

Arrik

His father was in a foul mood. Which was saying something, because whenever Soren wasn't in an exultant, hedonistic stupor he was always deep in the bowels of rage. But his mood now was different. Aimed at something very specific.

Arrik was taking the brunt of it.

"They stopped our ships *again*," Soren spat, guzzling down a goblet of wine. A petite serving girl wearing the barest slip of a dress promptly refilled it, before topping up the goblet of Arrik's brother, Cathal, the heir to the throne. He had taken to sitting in on all meetings between Soren and Arrik recently, claiming that it was his right as future king to keep abreast of all that was going on.

Which was a bloody joke.

His brother was frightened of what Arrik might be planning. In truth, Cathal was right to be afraid; after all, even their father knew he was a disappointment next to Arrik. But it was all part of Soren's games that he pitted his sons against each other—all the better to keep them attacking each other rather than uniting against the king.

But Arrik no longer cared about any of that.

He worked alone.

But you don't want to, do you? You want your pretty little wife by your side.

"But we hold the isles," Cathal drawled, lecherous gaze sliding over the serving girl as he spoke. A nasty smile curled his crooked-toothed mouth that Arrik wished to punch. "Why can't our ships go through? This wouldn't have something to do with you and your runaway savage bride, would it, brother?"

Arrik ignored him.

"If we can't make it through the isles to trade with Vadon, there will be trouble," Soren warned. "The people of Lorne are stubborn, far more stubborn than I ever thought possible. Though, given the antics of your *runaway savage bride*—" Cathal's grin grew wider at his father using his words to describe Wren "—I should have expected this."

"There was a reason the Dragon Isles always held the sea," Arrik said blandly. "Their navy and people alike are tough as nails."

"But you *destroyed* their navy."

"No, I destroyed what needed to be destroyed in order to conquer the place. Taking Lorne by surprise by attacking on Princess Wren's wedding day meant the Dragon Isles didn't have *time* to get their naval forces together properly. To have destroyed all their ships and killed all their people would only be a disadvantage for us going forward. After all, would you be willing to send thousands of Verlantians to run their navy to replace all the people we massacred?"

Soren hissed through his teeth at Arrik's observation, but

he knew he was correct. Verlantian forces were already spread far thinner than the king was willing to admit aloud, and he knew no elves that he trusted would be willing to move to the unforgiving Dragon Isles to toil and labor away for no reward. Keeping the people and ships of Lorne alive was the sensible thing to do.

"In any case," Soren muttered, which Arrik took as a victory, "this cannot keep going. Idril has been complaining for weeks now that his shipments of slaves are not going through either side of the isles. He's causing a ruckus in the upper circles." The king's eyes sharpened through their wine-induced haze on Arrik. "My fool of a cousin should never have married him."

"His gold was worth it," Cathal commented. "From what I hear."

Soren snorted into his cup. "She didn't live long enough to spend any of it." The king leveled a glare at Arrik. "Idril will offend me no further. Take care of him."

Now *this* was an unexpected turn of events. Lord Idril had always toed the line of acceptable conduct in the face of the king, but the two of them ultimately had more in common than they had disagreements. For Soren to have Arrik *take care of* Idril meant things were far more fraught and unsettled than he was letting on.

He suppressed a smirk. It only worked in his favor.

His bride needed another unexpected visit.

"Done," he said, inclining his head at his father. "I'll leave at once."

"And, Arrik..." Soren added, when he was halfway toward the door and basking in the livid expression on Cathal's face at him having been given such an important mission. "...find that wife of yours."

"It shouldn't be long."

"I hope that's the case. Deal with Idril, grab the wench by her pretty red hair, and drag her with you to the Dragon Isles. I need Lorne under control...by any means necessary."

Arrik knew what that meant. Torture Wren to break her, or torture her people in front of her—and don't leave her any option but to serve Verlanti in bringing Lorne to heel. He knew by now of course that *nothing* could break Wren. After all, Arrik had already taken everything from her and still she fought him.

Heat curled in his lower belly.

Which was why she was the perfect equal to him, and why Wren was so imperative in Arrik's plans.

Cathal laughed uproariously as Arrik left, his previous anger overwritten in the face of their father's threat. Arrik would have loved nothing better than to run a sword through his brother's contemptuous face, but he knew there would be a time and place for that.

Just not today.

Too bad.

He returned to his chambers and closed the door behind him, sensing a familiar presence. Arrik was not surprised to find Ronan, his third-in-command, waiting for him. The burly auburn-haired man stood to attention when he caught sight of Arrik, then relaxed into the corner chair when Arrik waved him off. Looking at his face, he could tell Ronan was exhausted. Beneath his beard and freckles, his skin was ashen.

Not surprising, since he'd entrusted Ronan with tailing Queen Astrid over the last few days.

"I take it you have news?" Arrik asked, collapsing onto his bed with a sigh. He pinched the bridge of his nose. He, too, was supremely tired. Ronan, along with Shane and Josenu, were the only people he trusted enough to ever show his fatigue.

And Wren.

Ronan huffed in confirmation. "She visited a few friends—nothing special, the usual revels. The normal indiscretions."

Arrik sneered, remembering her proposition. The woman made him sick. "But then…?"

"She traveled to Delansh. In disguise."

"*Delansh?*" Arrik swung upright, fatigue chased away by curiosity. "And what exactly is in Delansh?" The pirate city had been the last public place Wren had been seen. Where she'd been chased through the streets by a reward-hungry mob but had somehow still escaped.

Ronan smiled grimly. "She met with a pirate by the name of Gunn. I couldn't make out what they discussed though, without giving myself away."

Gunn. Was the pirate giving Wren up? Or the rebellion?

"I can work with that for now." He sighed and waved a hand toward the door. "Go get some rest, Ronan. You can start tailing her again in two days. And my thanks."

"Next time you want someone to spend four sleepless days tailing the queen, might I suggest sending someone far spryer than me?" his friend complained.

Arrik barked out a laugh. "You're twenty-four, Ronan. Same age as me. We are hardly in our graves." Although sometimes he felt twice his age. Growing up in Soren's court made one grow up quickly.

"Yet I can feel it in my back," Ronan teased good-naturedly, cracking his spine as he stood and made for the door. "The rebellion has some truly acrobatic spies in their midst. I think we had one of them locked up in the dungeon, actually—the one who escaped with the Dragon Princess. You should lure him over to your side."

"Ah, yes, I'm sure my natural charm will convince them to work with me. Go get some sleep, you wretch."

Arrik watched as his friend left. The door closed with a quiet click, and he stared out at the plants that secluded his bath, mulling over what Ronan had told him. He ran a hand over his eyes. He needed more people at his disposal whom he trusted. The problem was that Soren and Astrid and his brothers had everyone else in their pockets. Gold, power, and secrets were currency. While Arrik was a collector of secrets, his family always seemed to get the upper hand with the promise of higher social standing, riches, sexual favors, or the promise of complete and utter ruin.

But not for long. He held the key.

Wren.

He needed more leverage. He needed more people.

He needed his wife and her new compatriots.

A few hours later, Arrik was roused from slumber by a knock on his door, then the light of a torch approached when someone let themselves in. His eyes flashed open while he wrenched out the dagger he kept beneath his pillow, believing for a moment that another assassin had been sent to dispatch him. Then he spotted the scar-covered face of his second-in-command, Shane.

He pushed back the covers and swung his legs over the side of the bed, glaring at Shane.

"Don't come sneaking in like that," he growled. His empty stomach clawed at him, telling him it was well past time to eat. *How long was I asleep?* "I could have killed you."

Shane chuckled as he closed the door. "I wouldn't consider knocking repeatedly and then waving a torch in front of your eyes *sneaking in,* you fool. You were completely out of it. If I were one of your brother's assassins, you would be dead."

Arrik rubbed a hand over his face. "I haven't been sleeping well lately."

"You haven't been sleeping well for as long as I've known you."

"Thanks for that. Any news?"

Shane's scars were slick and shiny in the light of the fire. They were one of the reasons Arrik knew the man would always fight with him to take down the entire corrupt Verlantian monarchy. It was the reason he got the scars, after all. They twisted around his mouth, frightening and grotesque, when Shane grinned.

"The rebels have moved to Lord Idril's estate, as you expected."

"Is the Dragon Princess with them?"

Shane nodded. "They arrived last night."

"Does Idril know who she is?"

"I'm not sure. Some of our contacts seem convinced he does. Others believe him too drugged-out to have caught on to it yet."

"Good. That's good. Soren wants me to *take care* of Idril. I told him I'd leave today."

"Surely you need to rest, Arrik," his friend protested, concern coloring his face even through his scars. "It's the middle of the night already."

But he was already on his feet. "I have rested enough, and it will take close to a week to reach Idril's castle. If I leave now, I'll be able to catch him by surprise at the end of one of his ridiculous revels."

"If you're sure," Shane murmured, sounding unconvinced but ready to obey regardless. "I'll arrange the horses."

Arrik splashed cold water on his face and changed his clothes as he concocted a plan of what he'd do upon arrival at Lord Idril's estate. He knew he couldn't afford to mess things up when he got there, and that he'd only have one chance to both deal with the dark elf and get Wren out before Idril got his hands on her.

His wife was key to everything, and everyone knew it.

The key to a successful rebellion, the key to uniting the Dragon Isles...

The key to overthrowing Soren and Arrik successfully ascending the Verlantian throne.

She would change everything.

They would change everything.

CHAPTER NINETEEN

WREN

"I'm not wearing this."

Vienne stared Wren down. "You don't have a choice."

"I can't—"

"It cannot possibly be as bad as what you were expected to wear in the palace."

"It's definitely worse!"

Wren stared at the flimsy material lying on her bed. Even her Verlantian wedding dress hadn't been as shockingly insubstantial as this, something which Wren hadn't thought possible. At least that had been white. This ankle-length dress was made of wisps of sheer material the color of her skin, with tiny pinprick jewels sewn in to artfully protect her "modesty." Worse: it was attached by one simple clasp at the back of the neck, making it far too easy for someone to undo the dress and send it tumbling to the floor.

There was more substance to the jewelry that came with it than the dress itself: heavy bronze necklaces, rose gold bangles, and a pair of dangling earrings pitted with pearls and black diamonds Wren highly suspected came from the

Dragon Isles.

Five days had passed since the rebels arrived at Lord Idril's castle. Five days, and Wren hadn't seen hide nor hair of the elf lord—nor, as it transpired, much of anyone else. Which was a blessing and a curse.

She'd sat in her sumptuous room or wandered the dark corridors, trying and failing to talk to the staff in the kitchens or the women silently cleaning bathrooms and banquet halls. Wren had thought she was going to go insane with how little anyone wanted to speak a single word to her. What was everyone hiding? Had Vienne given a command for everyone to ignore her? Or had their master commanded them to never speak?

Even Leif had made himself scarce. Stars, she longed for some witty back-and-forth banter, a combative debate, or teasing and insults. It sounded liked she was pining over her beastly husband. Which was absurd and disturbing because he was her enemy.

Vienne sighed and rubbed at her temples. "Why must you be so difficult?"

Wren ignored her aunt and ran her finger along a necklace.

Leif and Bram had returned that morning, but all Leif had promised was that they'd catch up after the dinner party that evening. He had much to tell her. She had wondered what in the blazes he'd been referring to, but then Vienne had finally deigned to grace her niece with her presence.

And a *present.*

If one could call it that.

The slip of material masquerading itself as a dress was definitely not a gift. It was another way to control her. To see how compliant she could be.

"Come now," Vienne said disapprovingly, as she brushed her beautiful hair that was so like her sister's into an elegant knot at the base of her neck, "there's no time to waste. Get dressed. Idril has requested you keep your hair loose, so make sure it really shines."

"Idril, is it? So familiar, Aunt?"

Vienne scowled. "What are you getting at?"

"That you're groveling and it's beneath you."

Her aunt shook her head. "You have no idea what you speak of. Put on the dress."

"Why should I? I'm not wearing that!" Wren stated evenly. Where did the insidious elf get off on deciding what she should and shouldn't wear? Or what her hair should be like? "I will dress as I please."

For a moment, it looked as if her aunt would shout at her, but then her expression softened. "I'm wearing something very similar to you, niece, and you can trust I did not choose it either. But in these situations, we women have to use every asset we have in our arsenal to gain the upper hand in a world dominated by men. Think of this dress as armor and you will be fine."

Wren flinched.

Queen Astrid had said something very similar on her wedding day. She had been the only one to show Wren any kindness in the palace, since she was still unsure as to whether Kalles gifting her a knife to dispatch her new husband counted as kindness, cruelty, or something else entirely. And the way Arrik had begun to treat Wren before she ran away didn't count. It was all a lie.

Was it really, though?

He'd wanted something from her. Something she hadn't wanted to give. Her trust, her kingdom, herself. Even now, when she had more perspective on what the prince might be planning, Wren couldn't say that she'd actively help him the way he wanted her to.

For how *could* she trust him? But if that were the case, why didn't she kill him when she had the chance? Why did she let herself think on him without disgust? Why did she seem to trust his motives more than whatever the rebellion was doing by pairing up with Lord Idril?

She looked at the dress once more and scowled. A dress was a small concession. There were bigger battles to be fought.

"Fine. You win this round, Aunt."

Vienne grimaced. "I'm not your enemy."

Wren looked at her aunt. "It doesn't seem that way most days."

"I'm sorry you feel that way. I'm not trying to be hard on you, but war is upon us. We can't be soft."

"No one can accuse you of that."

Vienne's lips thinned. "I'll see you at dinner." She turned and left, closing the door softly behind her.

Wren walked to the door, locked it, and then leaned against the wood. She closed her eyes for a moment as she steeled herself for what was to come. Surely, it would be another night of revelries. She opened her eyes and stared at the dress once more and smiled. She'd wear the dress but add her own touches as well.

Rushing across the room, she dug out the strapless black silk nightgown that hugged all her curves, and held it up in the air. It had been a gift from Idril that she'd never planned to wear but tonight it would do just the trick.

Wren discarded her clothes and slid on the slip before donning the dress Idril had sent as a gift. She even wore all of the jewelry, including the Dragon Isles diamond earrings; they flashed through her hair, alluring and entrancing. She touched the cool surface of them, fingertips tracing a line along her ears to feel the barely discernible scars that sat along the edge of her skin there. She hadn't thought about the scars in a long time—she didn't even know how she'd gotten them—but now she was wearing such outlandish earrings adorned with the spoils of her homeland it got her wondering why the scars were there. But she pushed the thought to the side to scrutinize her reflection. Wren had to admit she made quite a sight dressed this way, especially now that her skin had taken on the barest hint of a tan from the Verlanti sun.

She hated that she looked good.

Wren grinned as she pinned up a couple sections of hair with simple bronze clips Ever had loaned her weeks ago. Her lips lifted. Not only had she preserved her modesty, she'd also complied with Idril's request.

Well, mostly.

She ran her fingers through her hair once more before

moving to the door, the bangles around her wrists and ankles tinkling merrily. She unlocked the door and stepped out into the hallway.

Her aunt scanned Wren from head to toe and pursed her lips.

Wren arched a brow. "What do you think?"

Vienne shook her head, but a ghost of a smile touched her lips. "You look lovely, although I'm glad I didn't have any children. You all are so contrary."

A small chuckle escaped Wren. "Perhaps."

"Let's be off. We mustn't be late."

Vienne directed her to one of the larger banquet halls. Wren had imagined a long table covered in an excessive number of dishes from all across the world, along with a dozen wines in different colors, but Idril's idea of a dinner party included none of that.

It was more akin to a full-on party.

At first Wren didn't see any food, but then she noticed servants discreetly carrying trays of bite-size morsels through the horde of people attending the event. Even more servants were ensuring everyone had full glasses—or providing thimblefuls of white powder when it was requested.

Drugs.

She hated the stuff.

Stomach churning, she observed the room once more.

"Is it just me or is everyone a man?" Wren muttered through her teeth toward her aunt, who held an easy smile on her face. She didn't seem fazed in the slightest by the leering, hungry looks thrown their way. Some of the men were old enough to be Wren's grandfather—or even Vienne's. At least from what she could spy from beneath the half masks all the men wore.

A shudder ran down her spine.

These were the people they were trusting with the future of the Dragon Isles?

"This is the way of things, Wren," Vienne said mildly as they wound their way toward Lord Idril—the only unmasked man in the room. "You have been spoiled, living in Lorne and being treated like a firstborn son. Verlanti is not kind to women. Even women who find high status—like Queen Astrid—do not truly have their freedom, so long as there's a man like Soren keeping her under his thumb."

"But that doesn't have to be the way things are," Wren shot back, upset to discover that her aunt thought this way. Her mother—Vienne's sister—had been forced into slavery before escaping to the Dragon Isles. How could she simply accept that the world was not fair to women? Why wasn't she angry? Why wasn't she fighting back?

Maybe Vienne leading the rebellion *was* her way of fighting back. She simply had to dance with the devils who enslaved her sister first.

Vienne did not respond to Wren's protest, instead placing a finger to her lips to subtly silence her as they approached Lord Idril. The elf took them both in with obvious approval.

"I am glad to see the two of you accepted my gifts." He beamed, gaze lingering on Wren for far too long. She could feel all eyes on her, creepy and lecherous, but she kept her head held high to retain what little shred of dignity she possibly had left. The dark elf smirked. "I see that you made alterations to your dress, my dear."

Wren dipped her head and spun in a slow circle so he could see the full effect of what she'd done. She faced him once more. "I'd say it is an improvement, don't you think, my lord?"

He smiled thinly. "Quite fetching. The silk is a nice touch."

"I thought so." Wren touched the jewels at her ears and neck. "Thank you for the jewelry. They're quite stunning."

"I thought you might like it."

"The diamonds are from the isles, are they not?"

He cocked his head. "I thought you might like something from your homeland."

"So thoughtful," she murmured, holding his assessing gaze.

Idril broke the moment and waved a lazy hand to a servant who held a tray full of goblets. "Won't you have some wine?"

"Graciously so," Vienne said, taking a cup when a servant proffered one to her.

But Wren shook her head. "No thank you, my lord."

"We can add honey to the wine, to make it more palatable for you."

"No thank you," she said, firmer this time. "Forgive me. I am in an unfamiliar place with unfamiliar people. I wouldn't want to make a fool of myself or of your great house by drinking too much."

Idril's dazzling smile remained, but there was an iciness

to his blue eyes that hadn't been there before. He'd seen right through her flattery. "Very well. Then we shall begin."

The men around Wren and her aunt began to listen intently as Idril spoke. "We are all gathered here today for one common cause: to overthrow our dear king and take Verlanti for ourselves."

Wren froze as she gazed around the room. *They are* all *in on this?* She took note of as many faces as she could, although the golden masks covered up too much for her to really remember them. There was not a single soul she recognized, not even the small handful of Vadonese men who were standing at the back of the room. Regardless, she couldn't believe that Lord Idril was happy to so openly discuss treason against the crown. How could he possibly trust everyone in the room?

This is dangerous.

"Talk of usurpation can wait for tomorrow, Idril," a man of a similar age to Vienne complained. Most of the people around him nodded in agreement. "We did not come all the way to your most esteemed residence to *talk*." That had even more people agreeing. A murmur was going through the room, on the edge of turning rowdy.

Then what were they there for?

Why wasn't the rest of the rebellion arguing against them? Surely all there *was* to do tonight was talk about overthrowing King Soren.

Speaking of, Wren thought, casting her gaze around the room, *just where are Bram and Leif? And Ever?*

The older woman hadn't wanted to work with Idril, but

Wren thought that, at the very least, she would still come to support Vienne during such important talks as this.

But if no talking was going on, then…

Lord Idril held up a hand to silence the room. "My apologies," he said, acting every inch the gracious host. "Where are my manners? Of course, there should be entertainment first. After all, you came all the way to my *most esteemed residence,* as you so aptly put it. Bring them in." Idril clapped his hands and the doors to the banquet hall swung open.

Two dozen men, women, and adolescents barely on the cusp of puberty were corralled inside, all dressed in the same flimsy nude material as Wren—but without the jewels and jewelry. Some had the dark skin of Vadon, whilst others looked disconcertingly like Leif. None looked like they came from the Dragon Isles, which Wren felt relieved about for the briefest of moments.

The children looked fearful, though the men and women looked merely resigned as Lord Idril's supporters smiled in approval and began choosing who they wanted amongst the crowd. Who they *wanted.*

Her stomach dropped.

In that moment, Wren realized that all of them were slaves.

"I'm sure you'll find someone to your tastes," Lord Idril purred, eyes gleaming as his supporters began pawing at their chosen slaves to remove their clothes. Right here and there, in front of everyone.

Wren saw red.

They were men and women and *children* that were here against their will. Performing against their will.

It was horrifying.

Disgusting.

Savage.

The reason Ever hadn't shown up at the party was painfully loud and clear to Wren.

Lord Idril was a hedonistic monster.

How could my aunt ever agree to work with him? To work with him makes the rebellion no better than Soren himself.

Her fingers curled into fists and she took a step toward the nearest child who'd been leashed like an animal.

Wren had to stop it.

She had to stop it all.

CHAPTER TWENTY

WREN

"Stop this." Her voice was a hiss.

Nobody listened to her.

Wren had spoken too quietly and there was too much going on around her. But when she repeated the words, hands curled into fists at her side, Vienne caught on to what she was saying and fired Wren a warning glare.

As if that will stop me.

Her aunt pushed through the crowd, shaking her head.

Wren was past caring about Vienne. Someone who stayed silent while others were abused was not family or friend of hers.

"*Stop this*!" she bellowed over the masked crowd, her protest echoing off the walls of the banquet hall for all to hear. All at once, the motion around her seemed to freeze. Her skin crawled as all eyes turned to her, pinning her to the spot. She attempted to regulate her breathing even as her pulse thundered in her ears.

Lord Idril's easy smile wavered. "What sort of ruckus are you causing in my home? I'm all for screams, but not that sort."

The crowd laughed uneasily.

Her aunt reached Wren's side.

"Just stay quiet," Vienne hissed, making to grab Wren's arm.

"No."

She wrenched herself out of reach, pointing at the nearest slave woman being forcibly undressed by two elderly elves with ruddy faces.

"You cannot expect me to abide by this," Wren yelled out, though it was largely aimed at her aunt. "I refuse to cooperate with you if we allow *this* to happen before our very eyes! Wasn't the whole point of what we're doing to free—"

"It seems our guest is overwrought," Lord Idril commented with an icy smile.

Wren snarled when his warriors converged on her. A hand clamped around her arm, then another, then another and another. Through the crowd, two of Vienne's men joined the fray and shook off two of Idril's men.

It was a complete betrayal. How could they let this happen?

"Let go of me!" she demanded, turning on them. Her aunt's men didn't dare look her in the eyes while Idril's smirked. "You cannot be all right with this. You *can't*, you—"

"It seems the Dragon Princess has truly been tainted by her upbringing," Lord Idril drawled, all at once confirming—though Wren knew in her heart he had to have known—that he was aware of who she was. He waved toward the door.

"Return her to her room. We can't be having such barbaric behavior ruining the evening."

He wouldn't get the last word.

"The only *barbaric behavior* I can see tainting the evening is yours, you beast," Wren growled. Lord Idril's smile wavered for a moment when she bared her teeth at him. "You're disgusting."

He stared hard at her before turning to the pretty woman kneeling at his feet. He pulled her into his lap and then met Wren's gaze as he petted the woman's arm. Wren blinked as she caught sight of the woman's profile and frizzy orange hair.

Bile burned the back of her throat.

Clara, her cousin.

"Clara!" she yelled, fighting harder.

Idril licked his lips and placed a kiss on Clara's neck. Wren's cousin didn't flinch. She didn't do much of anything but stare blanky across the room. How did the dark elf have her cousin? How long had Clara been here?

"Clara?" she screamed, seething down to her very core as she was unceremoniously dragged from the banquet hall. Lord Idril's supporters sneered at her when she passed them, their wanton and disgusting gazes still upon her. The slaves Wren passed, by contrast, merely shook their heads at her, as if telling her that her protests were pointless.

She didn't stop struggling or hollering the entire way back to her room. It was only when she was shoved inside, the heavy door locked behind her, that she finally stopped.

Pacing across the room like a tiger draped in silk, Wren

sank her fingers into her hair. How the devil had Idril gotten his hands on Clara? Was it mere chance? Or was it a power play to keep her in line?

She grabbed a vase on the nearby dresser and threw it against the far stone wall. It shattered into a million little pieces but it didn't make Wren feel any better. Her stomach lurched and she stumbled to the window and emptied her belly over the ledge. Tears blurred her eyes.

Wren slammed her hands against the stone balcony and screamed as if it could block out the party below. She cried and railed against the stars until her throat went hoarse and raw. Could nothing possibly go her way? Was everyone a villain? Were there no good people left in the world?

Angrily, she wiped at her cheeks with the back of her hand and moved deeper into the room. Her hand shaking, she poured herself a drink. Water sloshed over the edge as she took deep gulps to soothe her parched throat.

How could her aunt accept anything from Idril?

Wren slammed the goblet down on the side table and began pacing the room once more.

It was large and sumptuously furnished—a four-poster bed, ornately carved stone fireplace, tapestries woven in fine, expensive threads, a long velvet couch made for lounging and sleeping, and lush carpets that absorbed Wren's every barefooted step—but it felt more like a prison than the Verlantian dungeon ever had.

At least in the dungeon there was a way out, even if it meant risking almost certain death.

Her gaze darted to the window. Getting down would pose

a challenge. She was four stories up. Even if she was to tear up the bed and braid it into a rope, it wouldn't reach the ground.

The night breeze blew through the window and she shivered, goosebumps breaking out across her arms. Wren scowled at her dress. It did nothing to keep her warm. Panic began to claw its way up her throat as she swore the jewelry around her neck tightened.

Wren tore the necklaces from her throat and the bangles from her wrists and ankles, tossing them onto the bed. Next, she yanked off the dress and slip and kicked them into the corner like rags. She reached for her ears, but something stopped her from removing the Dragon Isle diamond earrings. A sense that they *should* be hers perhaps. They could come in handy if she ran.

Not without Clara.

Only once Wren had donned the clothes she'd ransacked from Gunn's ship did she feel more like herself. Men's clothes, but Wren had often worn men's clothes back in Lorne. She liked the feeling of the soft linen shirt and trousers. She liked them even more when she laced on a pair of boots as if she meant to kick the door down and run away.

But there *was* no running from this room. It was impenetrable—Wren had already scoped it out. Vienne had been smart enough to confiscate her sword, bow, and quiver when they arrived at Lord Idril's castle, and she'd lost a dagger to the trap in the forest, so she could not fight her way out.

Even so, she still had one dagger left. She moved to the

door and knelt, running her fingers over the lock. There was no way she'd be able to pick it. She climbed to her feet and walked to the other side of the room. The broken vase crunched beneath her boots, and she picked up a large piece that fit nicely in her hand.

Two weapons now.

She wished Lord Idril would materialize at her door so she could strike the blackguard down. The prince would want him to die.

For once, you'd agree on something.

It was bound to happen at some point, but it still disturbed Wren how right and honest the notion was. How was it that she knew so much about what her elvish husband wanted? What he believed in? And why was it that what he wanted and what Wren wanted kept aligning?

"Stop thinking about him," Wren berated herself, still pacing. She knew why he was on her mind so much. With nobody else to talk to, the last time she'd actually felt *heard* was when she and Arrik had fought—even if she had hardly spoken a word, not wishing to give the prince more leverage against her than he already had.

She'd shied away from recounting the interaction. Shame and guilt rose each time she remembered her failure. And yet...a small part of her had felt relief in the moment the prince had captured her. The look in his eyes as he allowed her to press her knives against his back...that's what got her. Arrik could have disabled Wren at any second and he *let* her have the upper hand. Why had he done that? A ploy to gain her trust?

It was working and she hated herself for it.

Wren needed to talk to someone. To plan something. To *do* something about the horrible situation she had found herself in. If Vienne and Bram were going to insist on keeping Leif away from her, then Wren had to make friends elsewhere...or simply do it all herself.

From inside Lord Idril's castle. With no outside help. Does Trove know where I am? Or did he return to the sea, as I wanted?

She sagged against the wrought iron mirror that took up much of the west wall. She couldn't do anything of importance by herself. Going off to hunt only to narrowly avoid being captured proved that. As had taking on the prince one-on-one back in Lorne. How was she supposed to get her cousin out of this purgatory? She couldn't even take care of herself.

She needed help.

Real help.

And if that help couldn't come in the form of *friends*, then perhaps it really was time to start looking at getting that help from the one person who'd asked it of her first.

Time to make a deal with the devil.

The lock clicking in the door caused Wren to jump to attention. She hated how her reflection in the mirror appeared startled, so she forced a level of calm onto her face that she absolutely did not feel. She slipped the shard of vase up her sleeve and waited.

Lord Idril stepped into her room like he belonged there.

She exhaled slowly and kept herself rooted to the spot,

beyond temped to gut him then and there.

Easy, dragoness. Easy.

He had promised they would talk, after all, and she had publicly insulted him by protesting the slaves. But even so, it took everything she had for Wren to stop herself from backing away as the elf approached, eyes slightly red from the effects of all the drugs and alcohol he'd already consumed that evening. There was the smallest of stains upon the collar of his frothy, unbuttoned shirt, but he didn't seem to care.

He ran a finger along her bedspread before meeting her gaze. "So what exactly was *that* display all about?" Lord Idril demanded, stepping right into Wren's personal space. "You dare step foot inside my home and disrespect me like that? Were you taught no manners from your mother whatsoever?"

"Keep my mother out of your mouth!" Wren lashed out, daring to shove Idril in the chest to push him away. Feeling his bare skin against her fingertips made Wren want to vomit.

Idril's pupils turned to slits, incensed.

She reached for her blade as he backhanded her. Her ears rang and her cheek throbbed. It stung like the dickens but she didn't care. If he could hit her, then *she* could hit him.

Wren swung and he caught her wrist in a surprisingly strong grip. She lashed out the other, managing to get a good hit to his gut. He wheezed but captured her other wrist. The elf lord locked them together between their bodies—his mouth all sharp-pointed teeth and rage.

"I may have enjoyed your mother's fiery temper," he breathed out, "but I will not abide any offspring of mine to get away with what you just tried to do. I will have obedience from you, *Princess Wren*, or you shall find yourself suffering far worse than Anneke ever did."

She stiffened, and a dull ringing filled her ears.

He lies.

But as her eyes locked on Lord Idril's, she could see he believed it to be true.

"Not possible," she murmured, her lips going numb.

"Oh, I assure you it is."

Wren trembled as she attempted to process what he'd just said. It couldn't be true. But the longer she stared into Idril's eyes, the more it was like looking in a mirror. Had Idril himself not pointed out that redheads had to stick together, and kept casting Wren undue attention when the rebellion arrived in his home?

Horror struck her.

She stomped her booted foot over Idril's bare toes and wrenched her wrists free from his grasp and brought them to her ears, to the tiny scars that were barely discernible against the pads of her fingertips when she ran them across the skin there. Had Wren's pointed ears been *cut* when she was too young to remember anything—to stop her from ever reaching the conclusion that her father had not, in fact, been a man, but instead an elf?

"That *hurt*," he growled. "It seems you're more like me than you realize. You're a little bloodthirsty thing, aren't you? The apple doesn't fall far from the tree."

Lord Idril was her true sire. She could see it not just in his familiar eyes and hair and other shadows of herself in his face, but in the way his rage turned into a grim smile of satisfaction when he saw Wren reach the horrible conclusion all on her own.

"How?" she gasped.

"The usual way, of course, but I'll spare you the details."

"I am no daughter of yours," she rasped, feeling like the floor was collapsing beneath her.

"You and I both know that's not true. You must get yourself together, daughter of mine," Idril said, finally stepping back from Wren. He sat down upon her bed as if he owned the place—because he did. Clearly, that extended to him believing he owned *her* too. "You must keep a clear head, otherwise you'll ruin everything we're working toward." He rolled his neck. "Plus, I'm sure you don't want anything happening to my pretty little plaything."

Clara.

"Leave her alone."

Idril grinned. "As long as you behave, dearest. You keep up your side and I'll keep up mine."

He was as trustworthy as a snake.

Wren didn't *want* to work with the vile creature. Idril forcing himself upon her mother—enslaving her, raping her, brutalizing her—gave him no right to possess Wren. Not as her father or in any other respect.

Nobody could have her. Wren had already lost the man she'd loved. There would be nobody else.

She ignored the fact Arrik flashed through her mind at the

mere thought of having a husband.

Wren equally knew, however, that screaming and fighting and struggling like a spoiled, angry child was all wasted energy. She had to remain pointed and focused on taking down what really mattered.

She smiled at Idril, the very picture of a woman who had finally worked out where her place was in the world, and he relaxed. It was so easy to make him believe what he wanted, because the elf was clearly used to getting everything he desired.

The night had been horrific thus far. Disturbing. Traumatic. But at least it had finally brought Wren something she never thought she'd be given in all her life: an opportunity to avenge her mother.

She was going to send Lord Idril straight to his grave.

Now.

CHAPTER TWENTY-ONE

Wren

Wren didn't give Idril an opportunity to see what she planned to do. He sat there on her bed, that greasy, commanding smile still on his face that meant he was certain of Wren's compliance.

It was a good thing she had been brought back to her own room when she'd kicked up a fuss. Her one remaining dagger lay beneath the pillow right by Idril's left hand; the vase shard was up her sleeve.

"I see you had a tantrum," Idril tsked. "So wasteful."

She lunged for the bed, slamming the shard of glass into his thigh. He yelled as she threw the pillow into the elf's face and grabbed the blade.

"You little piece of trash," he growled. Idril was quick to recover, twisting out of the way when Wren slashed at him, his leg bleeding. "You think you can face off against me with such a tiny thing?" he said, laughing like a maniac as Wren came after him again.

Idril dodged, as fluid as water, though there was a pattern to the way he moved that she was quick to pick up on.

"I think it is *you* who has the tiny thing," Wren shot back, an insult which sounded as if it came straight from Arrik's mouth.

It only caused Idril to laugh harder. He avoided another jab of Wren's dagger. "You think you are clever, my child, but insults and innuendo only get you so far."

"I find that blades get you further," Wren countered, deftly dropping her blade from her right hand to her left to position the tip of the dagger against the elf's groin. A vicious grin spread across her face. "We aren't kin. I hope this makes my point clear."

A flash of fear crossed Idril's face, but it disappeared in an instant. His proud face sneered at Wren. "So you kill me. What then, Dragon Princess? What do you think becomes of your precious rebellion and the war they're fighting? What do you think happens to your aunt, or that talented slip of a bard I have on good authority you consider a friend? You saved him from the Verlantian dungeons, I heard. He must really be dear to you. What about your Clara? I am the only thing standing between them and the wolves."

Wren was undeterred. "If you are dead, we'll survive."

"Do you really think that, or is that sheer naïveté speaking through your mouth? I truly hoped my own daughter would be smarter than that."

"*I am not your daughter.*"

"And yet you are. The facts of blood cannot be ignored, pretty child of mine, nor the position of power that gives me over you. Do I have to remind you that your mother was *my* slave? That makes you mine, no matter where she ran off to.

No matter who raised you. I own you."

"No one owns me."

Idril grabbed Wren's cheeks in a vise-like grip, completely ignoring the knife she still held firmly against him.

"Just try it," he urged, mad eyes shining. "See how far killing me gets you. My guards will crash into this room and drag you to the dungeon. You will bear witness to each and every member of the rebellion being tortured in the most despicable, wickedest of ways until they are begging for death. Then they'll endure some more, purely to make you suffer. Is that want you want? Can you really bear to have that on your head after you've lost so much?"

Wren faltered. There was no lie in Idril's threat. Her brain was running on overdrive, processing her options. If there were indeed guards right outside, then she couldn't escape after killing Idril. If she held him hostage to allow her safe passage to the castle doors, then the rest of the rebellion and Clara would still be subject to torture and death. And, even if they weren't, Idril would simply dissolve his deal with the rebellion, and all their hard work for change would have been for naught.

Wren couldn't even exact her vengeance successfully on one single target.

Her father would be ashamed once again.

Who had she become?

In anger and humiliation, she wrenched the blade up and slashed Idril across his cheek. He yowled in pain and placed a hand over his face, glaring at her.

"So you'll have a reminder of me every time you look in

the mirror," she spat, knowing she would pay for doing so but was unable to stop herself. She wanted to *hurt* him the way he'd hurt her mother.

Blood dripped through Idril's hand to the floor as he clutched his cheek, icy eyes venomous on Wren's. His thigh also bled, the vase shard still in the muscle.

For a moment, she thought he might strike her again. His grip on her chin had certainly tightened enough to bruise. But then the elf cackled—an ugly, foreboding sound—and he let go of her.

"You think I would be so foolish as to believe you'd behave immediately? You idiotic child. I'd have long-since been murdered if that were the case. It is people like *you* who are easily manipulated, not me. Just like your mother. But you *are* going to behave now, and we both know it. You're my pawn, Wren, but if you take my promises—" he meant threats "—to heart and rise to the station you should be *grateful* I'm giving you, then perhaps you might one day be something far more valuable." She jerked in shock as he ran a bloody finger down her cheek. "Thank you for the interesting visit."

Idril left, locking the door behind him as he went. Wren sagged to the floor, shaking from head to toe. She clutched her knife to her chest.

He'd been right; she *was* easily manipulated. At every turn she'd been manipulated—by Arrik, by Soren, by the rebellion. Wren hadn't been broken, no, but still she'd been made to do what everyone else wanted.

"Just what am I *doing*?" she cried, tears welling in her eyes that she did not want to shed. She pounded her fists against the carpeted floor, enraged that they barely made a sound, then scrubbed his blood from her face. Already it was swollen; when Wren moved her jaw from left to right, she winced in pain.

All she'd managed to do was give Lord Idril further leverage over her. Even escaping seemed impossible now, though all she wanted was to disappear, grab her cousin and sister, and flee to the sand lands in Vadon to live out the rest of their lives.

Her watery gaze strayed back to the jewels on her bed. It would be so easy to run.

That's not who you are.

When she heard a noise at the door, she braced for Idril's return. Perhaps he had thought better of leaving Wren in her room and had decided it would be better to throw her in the dungeons. Perhaps he wanted to hit her again.

Or worse.

She tightened her grip on her blade.

But whoever was unlocking the door clearly did not possess the key, if the clicking in the lock was anything to go by. Frowning, Wren got to her feet and readied to defend herself. The door swung open and she was met with a more than welcome sight.

"You look awful," Leif said, quietly easing the door closed before holding his arms open.

Wren cried out and flung herself into his embrace, shaking with anger, grief, and relief. Leif gently stroked her hair, hugging her back with the pressure she so desperately craved.

"Tell me what happened," Leif urged.

She pulled back and he frowned, gently touching her chin to turn her face so he could see her cheek better.

"He struck you?" His tone was deadly.

Wren's bottom lip quivered but she waved him away. "It's nothing, but..." A sob lodge in her throat but she managed to get out a tumble of words and sobs mumbled almost incoherently into Leif's shoulder: "He can't be my father," she cried, again and again, when she was finished explaining. "He can't, he—"

"Just because he sired you, that doesn't make him your father," Leif reassured softly, pulling Wren to sit in front of the fireplace with him. He grabbed a blanket from the long couch to place over her shoulders. Wren hadn't realized until that moment how very cold she was. He smiled reassuringly at her. "You must know that."

She did, but it was easier to believe it when someone else believed it too.

Hands still shaking, Wren rubbed away the rest of her godforsaken tears from her eyes. "Just who am I turning into, Leif?" she wondered aloud. "Having seen who—*what*—the rebellion is willing to work with, I can't...I can't keep following them. But I can't allow them to be murdered either. And my cousin..." She swallowed hard. "Gods, my mother would be ashamed of me."

"No, she would be proud. How could she not be? You have been through so much, yet still you did the right thing by standing up for those slaves."

Wren sniffled. "How can—how can *you* work with the rebellion, knowing what that *monster* does? How can you stand aside?"

"In truth, I didn't know we were working with Idril until the day you yourself were told," Leif admitted, clearly unhappy. "After you left the tent, I protested against it. It's why Bram and Vienne kept me separated from you."

"Why? What were they worried you would do?"

"Follow you instead of them," Leif said, as if it were obvious. But nothing was obvious to Wren anymore, not even having a friend who trusted her. He scratched his nose a little self-consciously. "Ever wasn't the only one who was a slave, remember. I don't want to work with Lord Idril. Bram doesn't either—he rallied against Vienne she first suggested working with Idril—but he won't go against her orders. They're bonded."

Wren held up a hand in disbelief. "Hold on. *Bram* doesn't want to work with Idril either?"

"He was also a slave. Most of the rebellion are former slaves. I thought you'd worked that out by now."

"So then *why* is everyone all right with working with...with—"

"Because all they can see now is the ends justifying the means," Leif said softly, squeezing Wren's hands. "You cannot blame them. If the only way to end slavery in Verlanti is to put up with evil people for a few days or weeks or months, then they'll do what needs to be done. A monster's gold is still valuable."

"But I can't..." Wren shook her head in despair. "I can't do that, Leif. There were children in there. *Children*. Barely older than Britta."

Leif frowned. "Who's Britta?"

It occurred to Wren then that not once had she mentioned her sister to Leif. She hadn't mentioned her to *anyone*. To protect Britta, herself, and the Dragon Isles. But she couldn't hold it in any longer. She couldn't do everything alone, and Leif had proven that she could trust him.

She sidled closer to Leif, who instinctively tilted his ear toward Wren's mouth. "I have a sister," she whispered. "A little sister."

Leif's eyes widened. "Is she—?"

"She's safe. She's the only reason I didn't fly off with Trove when he saved me in the forest."

"Hold on, when did *that* happen?"

"When I spoke to Arrik. He saved me."

Silence. Then, all at once, Leif erupted into laughter. Wren didn't know what was so funny, but the sound was infectious. After all the crying she'd done, it felt *right* to laugh, so she did.

"Your aunt was right to keep me away from you," Leif said, wiping away tears of mirth. "For how could I *not* follow you? I am humbled that you have trusted me."

"I am humbled by your friendship."

Leif pressed a kiss to her forehead. "We are bonded. Today, I claim you as kin."

"As kin?" she repeated.

Her friend smiled. "Aye. As I have no family, I must make my own. I claim you as my sister from this day forward."

Wren swallowed past the lump in her throat. She'd missed having a family so much. "I've never had a brother."

"Now you do." Leif clapped his hands together. "So, what are we doing, mad sister of the dragons?"

Wren thought about it, though in truth she knew what she had to do. She had to fulfill the rebellion's *actual* mission of freeing slaves, before her own people became the faces she saw being forced to serve the evil nobles of Verlanti.

Starting with the very ones trapped inside Lord Idril's castle.

"We free Clara and the slaves," she said, nodding toward the door. "Running won't solve anything. We need to play to our strengths. Can you help me free them without anyone knowing we did it?"

Leif gave her a conspiratorial grin. "Doing something beneath people's noses is my specialty."

CHAPTER TWENTY-TWO

ARRIK

Arrik rolled his neck and stifled a groan.

It was close to daybreak, and he had finally come upon Lord Idril's gaudy castle. It had been a punishing journey, delayed because a storm had hit two days into their ride. The terrible weather had closed the roads, slowed the horses, and felled several trees in the forest when they attempted to divert their path through it. It was therefore the morning of the ninth day, not the seventh, that Arrik found himself in front of the cavernous doors leading to Lord Idril's home.

He was in the worst of moods—bad enough to rival his father's—but Arrik knew he had to maintain a cool head if he was to succeed within the castle's dark stone walls. Lord Idril, after all, was a dangerous snake to cross paths with even for the quickest, cleverest of folk.

"Lord Idril is about to retire to his chambers for the day," a servant hurriedly informed Arrik when he crossed the threshold without bothering to announce his arrival. He wanted to catch the elf off guard. It was perfect to catch him just as he was about to sleep off one of his countless debauched nights.

"Take me to him," Arrik commanded, noting the music and drunken laughter from the ballroom. His nose wrinkled as he scented opium.

The servant nodded and beckoned him to follow her.

The lord was just as twisted as the king, but for all their similarities Arrik knew Idril hated Soren. He had it on good authority from Josenu that he was, in fact, working directly with the rebellion to unseat his father.

It definitely gave the rebellion some advantages. Idril had connections and power and influence to match High King Soren—perhaps more, if his slave routes to Vadon were anything to go by—but Arrik knew fine well that working with him was going to end up being a curse to the rebellion. Once Soren was cast from the throne, what then? The rebellion wanted to stop the slave trade. Idril *owned* the slave trade. He'd never agree to the abolishment of slavery, nor would he be willing to part with the power of the throne if he ever got his hands on it.

It just so happened that Arrik was fine with the rebellion working with the viper to get rid of his father. They were doing all the heavy lifting for him—keeping Soren too busy to truly see what his own son was planning until it was too late. The only hitch was that Arrik had no intention of seeing Lord Idril take the throne. That, at least, he had in common with the rebellion.

He had to find a way to ensure Idril—or no other highborn Verlantian lord, for that matter—ascended the throne. To do that required information. Leverage.

He was determined to find that leverage now.

It wouldn't do to just kill Idril. One of his sons would rise up in his place. It would be easier to keep an eye on the lord and use him.

Arrik followed a servant up the stairs to Idril's wing of the castle, the chains around her neck clinking together. Guards stood outside the lord's door.

"Open it," he commanded.

They didn't hesitate to obey as they spotted the sigil on his breastplate. The shorter of the guards scrambled to unlock the door.

The door creaked open.

"Who dares to disturb me?" Idril barked.

Arrik moved over the threshold. He was gratified to see Lord Idril weaponless and barely clothed, as expected. The elf's eyes widened when they took in Arrik—in full armor and armed to his ears in all manner of blades and arrows.

"I hope I'm not intruding," Arrik said even though he was.

Idril sized him up, his eyes narrowed. He was a couple of inches shorter than him, but his haughtiness more than made up for the height difference. A false smile that didn't meet his eyes curled his mouth.

They both knew fine well who would win a fight if the elf tried anything.

"Not at all," Idril murmured. "What a surprise to see you, my prince."

"Are you surprised?" Arrik asked, tone bland.

A ripple of emotion moved across Idril's face before his smile widened. "But of course. It's an honor to host our kingdom's most feared prince." The elf moved away from his bed and pulled a shirt from his closet, presenting his back to Arrik.

A blatant show that Idril didn't consider him a threat despite his pretty words.

His pride is out in full force. A boon for you.

Arrik leaned against the wall and crossed his arms as Lord Idril once again faced him. The elf had an enormous gash on his cheek that looked to be only a couple of days old. Arrik had one guess who'd caused the injury. There'd only be one brave enough to try.

Naughty, naughty, wife.

He resisted the urge to smirk with satisfaction. Idril was a vain creature. Many people—including himself—would surely have loved to see her attack the lord and bring him down a peg or two.

"To what do I owe this pleasure so late in the night?" Lord Idril asked. "Or early in the morning, I should say," he amended, glancing at the promise of sunrise outside the cavernous window that covered the north wall of his chambers. "I might have been retiring to bed, but the party is still going strong downstairs, my prince. Perhaps you might grant me a few hours of sleep while you can enjoy all that my castle has to offer you?"

"You and I both know by now that what your castle can *offer* is of no interest to me."

"Pray tell me, then, why are you here?"

"You know why I am here."

Idril cocked his head. "Is the king's beast here to kill me?"

Arrik allowed himself to smirk. "In not so many words. To *take care of you* was the order. How I proceed is up to you," he said without feeling. It gratified him to see the elf begin to squirm.

"I should have expected that. So what do you want from me this time in recompense for my actions? Gold? Women?" Idril studied him. "A kingdom?"

"A kingdom?" Arrik mused, touching his chin in thought. "Did I miss you becoming a king in the last few months?"

The elf arched a brow. "One doesn't have to be king to rule a kingdom."

Those were true words. Idril held much power in Verlanti because of his gold and the slave trade.

"Tread carefully. What you're saying could be construed as treason." A pause. "And treason always means death."

Lord Idril was hedging his bets and—being a clever, careful person—he more often than not *won* his bets. But he'd stepped over a line that needed to be punished or Soren would kill both Idril and Arrik.

Slowly, purposefully, he pulled out a dagger and pointed the tip of the blade to the cut on Idril's face. The elf blinked slowly but didn't move.

"Who gave you this?" Arrik asked, simply to see what Idril would say.

"...let's just say one of my revels got out of hand and leave it at that."

"Hmm. Daring of someone to do this to you. I know how much you value your pretty face. That will scar."

At this, Idril scowled, his pupils turning to slits in his

anger. "The woman got her punishment. Now get to the point of the matter, my prince. I hardly think you came all this way to mock me. What do you want? It's not my life or you would have already taken it."

"That's a bold gamble. You know I like to toy with my prey."

Fear flashed though the elf's eyes, but it was gone a second later. "I always win."

Not this time.

Arrik leaned into Idril's space. "Do you deserve to live?"

"You can't kill me."

"Why ever not?"

The elf lord smiled. "Because you need me."

"I don't think so. I'm sure if I dispatched you right now, my father would give me your lands if I asked."

"Do you do everything your father commands you? Are you really his pet?" A dark smile curled the elf's lips. "I don't think you're nearly as devoted as the court says you are. I think you hate your father as much as me."

An actual guess, or does he have a spy planted in your retinue?

That didn't seem right. Only Josenu, Shane, and Ronan knew how Arrik really felt toward his father. He'd kept that secret for years.

Your wife could have betrayed you.

His gaze strayed to the cut on the elf's face once again. He knew in his soul that Wren had given Idril that cut. There's no way she was allies with this snake.

Idril was just guessing.

Sheathing his dagger—Idril breathed out a small sigh of relief—Arrik said, "I happen to think it would be far more beneficial for the both of us for me to threaten you into doing what *I* want, rather than what my father wants."

"I knew I had a comrade in arms," Idril said, a glint in his eye. "What would you have me do, in order to save me from our dear king's wrath?"

"That remains to be seen. Consider it a debt to be repaid at a time I so wish."

Arrik so loved favors.

Idril nodded. "Consider it done with thanks. Will you stay the night? You must have traveled without sleep, if the shadows on your face are anything to go by. Let me—"

"I'd rather sleep with a pit of vipers if it's all the same to you," Arrik threw back, already on his way back to the door. He turned to point at the gash on Idril's cheek. "Though by the looks of things, your castle *is* a pit of vipers."

"You have no idea," Idril drawled as Arrik strode down the stone hallway.

He eyed the half-dressed servant who kept her eyes downcast. She even cringed into the walls as he passed. It disgusted him. No one should have that power over someone.

He ran over the interaction with Idril.

That went better than I thought it would.

He headed for the servants' entrance to the castle in order to make as discreet an exit as possible—and to snoop. He found that the servants were always happy to throw away seemingly innocuous scraps of gossip in exchange for a few coins.

He paused as he reached the corridor, catching a flash of red creeping toward the servants' entrance that most definitely did not belong to the lit torches on the wall. Several bodies all dressed in the same gauzy material followed the flash.

Arrik froze where he stood. He knew that flaming head of hair anywhere. The set of those shoulders. The curves of her body.

His wife.

Wren was sneaking out of Lord Idril's castle…with what appeared to be most of his slaves. When she cast a furtive glance left and right, she caught sight of Arrik lurking in the shadows and she, similarly, froze to the spot.

He could do nothing but stare at her staring at him. Just what was he supposed to do in this situation? Help her out? Drag her off?

He liked the idea of the last one.

But then he heard Lord Idril calling his name and Arrik's decision was made for him.

Time to grab his little wife so they could have a chat.

CHAPTER TWENTY-THREE

Wren

The plan had started out well.

Too well.

Wren and Leif had managed to convince most of the slaves to escape, and the ones who had chosen to remain behind swore not to tell a soul what had transpired. Leif was waiting on the outside to take the slaves to the closest port town, where he had assured Wren that Gunn would be waiting to transport them back to their respective homelands.

All Wren had to do was get the slaves out of the castle.

It had been a harrowing escape, with added stress from the fact that she was half carrying her cousin. Clara was lost to opium, her eyes glassy and blank, but at least she could walk. Sort of.

Their group had almost been caught by Lord Idril's guards when she'd liberated them from their cramped communal quarters and chains, but luck had been on their side. Everyone in the house was either inebriated or high. When a wavering man stumbled into the hall, spotting their procession, he'd only laughed and then promptly passed out.

Wren managed to sneak the frightened men, women, and children away toward the servants' entrance to the castle.

But their luck had run out.

So close to escape.

She stared at the prince, who almost blended in with the shadows.

Wren couldn't move. Couldn't breathe.

Any moment now, he'd call out and everything would go up in smoke.

He took a step closer into the soft light of the nearest lantern. Arrik was decked out in full, shining armor, reflecting the flaming torches littering the otherwise dark corridor. Her husband's eyes were unblinking, predatory, and calculating.

Clara moaned and leaned her cheek against Wren's shoulder. Yet she still didn't move.

How had her husband found her once again?

Questions for another time.

She glanced over her shoulder at the shivering people and back to the prince. Wren had a dagger and nothing else to defend them. Now there were slaves Arrik could use as leverage against her. And no dragon to save her now.

She took a step backward and the prince shook his head as if to say, "don't you run from me again."

"Prince Arrik!"

Her blood ran cold. That was *Lord Idril's* voice.

Down here, in the servants' quarters.

We need to move, now.

Behind her, one of the women whimpered in fright. Wren reached behind her for the woman's hand and squeezed it tightly, but she kept her eyes on Arrik. Lord Idril's voice had come from behind the prince. The moment the dark elf reached her husband, Idril would see what Wren was doing and everything would be so, so much worse.

She twisted and handed Clara off to a tall, lanky man with haunted eyes.

"Take care of her," she whispered.

He nodded and Wren pressed a kiss to her cousin's cheek. "See you soon." She scanned the group and jerked her chin toward the exit. "Run now! Leif will see you out. Tell him not to wait for me."

No one hesitated.

She yanked the dagger from her belt and faced the prince, who watched them in silence. Wren sank into a defensive position, daring him to try to stop their escape. Even when this came back on her, at least she'd done some good.

The prince cocked his head and then gave her the tiniest of nods.

She blinked and held her breath as he spun on his heel and rounded the corner, his boots thundering against the cobbled stone floors.

"What are you doing?" Arrik demanded, his voice echoing down the corridor. Wren flattened against the wall and listened in. "You said you were going to bed."

"The guards told me you headed into the servants' quarters and I—ah—was curious as to why. I'd be happy to supply you with whatever sort of flesh you desire."

Wren blanched. Was that why he was down here? To find a willing body to slake his lust on?

Her stomach rolled.

She'd heard enough.

By some miracle, he had let her get the slaves out to safety. But she had no false ideas of him doing so out of the goodness of his heart. She would likely pay for his act of grace with her own life.

It was time to go.

Feeling like her heart was about to burst from her chest, Wren rushed down the hallway and slipped outside on silent feet. She wove through the outbuildings until she reached the forest. It was only once she was well away from the castle that she dared stutter in a breath.

Leif had taken care of the patrol already, so there was nobody to stop them on their rushed journey deeper into the forest. He hadn't said *how* he'd taken care of the patrol of course, though Wren highly suspected it involved several bribes and charming words.

Wren spied Leif's dark hair through the dim early morning light of the forest. His shoulders dropped in relief as he spotted her heading his way. He held Clara to his side.

"How could you ask me to leave you?" he demanded.

"There were complications."

"Such as?"

"Arrik."

Leif's eyes rounded. "He's here?"

"Yes, and he spotted me."

"How in the blazes did he find us?" He shook his head. "It

doesn't matter. You need to come with me now."

"I can't. You'll be hunted." She gave him a weak smile. "We all have to make sacrifices and we both knew I wasn't going with you in the first place," Wren replied, squeezing his arm, and checking Clara's pulse. It was thready. "We need to get moving. She needs a doctor."

"They all do," he replied grimly.

"You're not wrong," she muttered into his ear.

"Will you be alright?"

"I'll be okay."

He patted her on the back and then scooped Clara into his arms, bridal style. "It will be close if you don't get back right now. I could only fob off the patrol for ten minutes, which leaves you with…two."

"They will know you did this when they see you gone," Wren said. There was no going back now.

Leif laughed very softly. "They will, and all the better for it. I'll help Gunn get everyone home safely, and then—if the rebellion doesn't kill me for insubordination—I'll see you after. Now *go*. Be safe, sister."

"And you, brother." She pressed a kiss to his cheek and then one to Clara's. "Take care of her for me."

"I will."

Not daring to look a gift horse in the mouth, Wren smiled reassuringly for the slaves. No, not slaves. Free men, women, and children, who would soon be reunited with their friends and families from the homes they were so unjustly plucked from. She focused on that thought as she bolted back to the castle, dewy plants brushing against her legs as she ran.

Wren slowed as the castle came into view. She snuck between the outbuildings, the servants' entrance enticingly in sight as she paused next to the stable. No one in sight. Time to go.

She took one step toward the door when hands roughly grabbed her and hauled her into the stables.

The scent of sage and citrus wrapped around her.

The prince.

Wren didn't struggle. There was no point in fighting him.

The only reason she'd achieved her goal had been because of him. Her husband had distracted Lord Idril. The question was why? Arrik wanted something from her and Wren wanted to know what it was.

He pulled her into an empty stall in the stable and she shoved him away, backing into the middle of the small room that smelled of horses and hay. Arrik locked the door and she fought a shiver.

She was well and truly caught now.

"Imagine meeting you here, my darling wife, and in such circumstances," he murmured, turning from the door to land his haughty, satisfied gaze firmly upon her. The prince cast his eyes from her head to her toes, crossing his arms as he began to circle her. "Freeing Lord Idril's slaves from beneath his very nose. A bold move."

"What do you want?" she gritted out, tracking his movements.

He smiled at the ground and touched his cheek. "The wound to his face was a nice touch. His vanity is a weak spot." He lifted his gaze, once again in front of her. Arrik stiffened and his eyes narrowed. "Did he hit you?" His voice was deadly. Sharp like steel.

"Does it matter?"

"More than you know," he murmured. "No one touches what is *mine*."

"I'm not yours," she bit out.

"We shall see." He began his pacing once more and her skin tingled. "So what next? Will you burn his castle to the ground?"

"If I could, then yes," Wren glowered, "The castle he's built has been from the blood and sweat of those he should have protected."

"On that we can agree." The blond prince chuckled softly, then indicated toward a torch gently flickering upon the stone wall with a jerk of his chin. "There's a flame. Burn it down."

"What is it that you want?" she questioned, too tired yet full of adrenaline to bother with his games. "Do you want me to destroy him? Do you seek to wield me like a blade? I will tell you now: I won't be your weapon. Ever."

"I don't need you to destroy my enemies for me."

"Then *what* do you want?" She lifted her chin. "Why did you help me? This is the second time we've met like this—and the third time you haven't immediately dragged me back to the palace. You swore to hunt me and yet you've let me go *twice*. What games are you playing?" Her chest heaved with feeling.

"Dangerous ones." A devilish grin lifted his lips. It sent a shiver down her spine that was anything but unpleasant. No matter how much she fought against him, Wren found herself drawn back. "Plus, I've always enjoyed the chase."

"I'm not playing your games."

"Oh, darling, you already have been. And I *like* it."

Wren darted forward and grabbed one of his daggers, but Arrik merely laughed again and grabbed her wrists and bodily pushed her against the wall. She gasped as he locked her hands above her head, forcing her to drop the knife. Why did he always make her feel so weak?

You're a warrior. Fight.

"Oh, I do love when you play hard to get," he murmured, lacing their fingers together like lovers.

Wren swallowed and held her head high. "Just *kill* me if that's what you want," she said, staring him down.

He leaned closer. "What makes you think I want you dead?"

"I don't think you want my life," she whispered, her eyes dipping to his lips that were far too close, and then back to his eyes. "You're after something else entirely. I think you're trying to steal your father's throne." He didn't react and she sighed. "I don't have time for this. Give me the truth of your intentions."

"Is that all?" he asked softly.

"I think you want to tell me."

For a long moment Arrik did nothing. His eyes flickered from Wren's hard gaze to her lips then back up again. Her throat ran dry; she desperately swallowed to fight against the confusing feelings roiling in her chest.

All traces of humor fell from his expression; his grip

tightened on her fingers.

"You want to know the truth?" he asked, brushing his nose against the tip of hers.

"I'm tired of being in the dark," she admitted. "You can trust me."

He chuckled, his minty breath puffing into her face. "I want to."

Wren held her breath. Maybe she'd gain the information she so desperately wanted.

Arrik shook his head. "You'll be the death of me."

"The feeling is mutual." It seemed they both were conflicted.

"You want the truth, wife?" She nodded, afraid to speak and break the moment. His expression hardened. "My mother—her name was Lorelai—refused Soren's advances time and time again when they were teenagers. Still years away from true adulthood. But he didn't like that. Of course he didn't." His jaw tightened. "So he forced her to bend to his will, and in doing so…drove her to her death." Wren's lips parted in surprise. Was he telling the truth? The prince cocked his head, still holding her gaze. "It's true I intend to take Soren's throne, but I want him to suffer for the crimes he's committed against my kin and our people."

Wren couldn't speak.

That wasn't what she expected him to say. She thought Arrik was just another warmongering, power hungry prince with an insatiable appetite for blood and power.

But it was something deeper. Truer.

It was the only reason he could have ever given that

would result in any sympathy from her. They had something in common.

It only made Wren hate herself more.

"What do you plan on doing now that you have me within your grasp?" Wren asked, changing the subject. Bonding with her enemy husband wasn't on her list of things to do that day.

He flexed his fingers. "There have been *three* other instances when I could have captured you. Including when you left Verlanti in the first place." A slow, dangerous smile crossed his face, entirely devoid of humor. "Surely you must have at least suspected that someone was planted within the rebellion?

"Who?" she demanded.

He gave her the same infuriating smile. "Josenu."

"I—" Of course Wren had thought it, at first, but that had been quickly extinguished when Arrik failed to stampede into the rebellion's base and recapture her. Josenu clearly worked *for* the rebellion. But if he was working there on behalf of Arrik...

"Why?" she breathed. "Why did you let me escape?"

"Because I wanted you to be safe."

Such a simple answer, but she couldn't trust it.

Can't you?

He released one of her hands and stroked her chin with a tenderness the huge elf should never have been capable of. Her free hand dropped to his chest.

"Why?" she pressed again. She badly wanted to know. *Needed* to know. "Why tell me?"

The tenderness from Arrik's touch met his eyes, softening them beyond compare. Her breath caught and her heart clenched. She'd never seen him look so vulnerable and sincere.

"You might believe me a monster, Wren. And I am, when it comes to many things. I've had to be. But if there is one thing I would have you believe to be true about me is that I never want to involve innocent people in the goings-on of my corrupt family. Of the high court. It's why I never wanted to marry, though my father insisted on it time and time again. The path I've chosen is a dangerous one. Treacherous." He paused. "I could never ask a woman to be part of it—least of all a woman I care about."

Wren believed him. She believed every word the barbaric man who'd murdered her family said. She believed him, and she respected him for it, because if she had walked down the path of a monster for pure vengeance, she expected she would have had a similar kind of moral compass to Arrik too.

People weren't just black and white.

Good and evil.

Her husband was both and yet neither.

He'd attacked her kingdom.

He'd protected her.

He'd imprisoned her.

He had let her free the slaves.

Wren flicked her gaze to her hand, still trapped beneath one of Arrik's gigantic palms, and he let her go. But he didn't move away. She could feel his breath fanning her face, hot and somehow desperate.

"What is it you want from *me*, then?" she asked, knowing that it was the only question she had left that needed answering.

When Arrik lifted his fingers from Wren's chin, the tenderness in his expression disappeared along with them. It was as if he had shaken back into the skin he'd worn *before* spilling his innermost secrets to Wren. She discovered that she was sad about it.

That was something for her to deal with another time, when sleep escaped her and all she'd be left with were thoughts of Arrik and his fingers on her cheek.

"Everything and nothing."

"What does that mean?"

"Your help," he said, straight and to the point. "Just as I told you back in the palace. I need your cooperation, and your position, and your skills. I need *you,* Princess Wren."

She wanted to refuse. But she'd be beyond stupid if she didn't acknowledge how powerful a player Arrik was in this dangerous pit of vipers she'd found her in. It would be to her utmost advantage to help him.

After all, hadn't Wren *already* come to that conclusion all on her own?

"I won't be your plaything," she said, slowly, "but I'll be your partner. No secrets. No manipulating me into doing something when it actually means another thing. Equals."

"That's all I ever wanted."

It sounded so genuine, Wren's heart hurt to hear it.

She couldn't trust it.

Keep your wits about you.

Arrik finally, inexorably, took a step away from her, then another and another. He nodded toward the dagger on the ground. "Keep that for protection against the men in Idril's court. I trust you know you must be careful in there." He paused again: "It was given to you in the first place anyway."

She picked up the dagger and peered at it, curious about what Arrik meant, only to realize it was the Vadonese blade the prince's brother, Kalles, had given her on her wedding day.

"I don't need this to protect me from the men in there," Wren assured Arrik softly, holding up the Vadonese blade to point it at him for emphasis. "I can handle myself just fine. All I ever needed protection from was the devil I married."

He smiled. "You need more protection from me than you know, wife."

CHAPTER TWENTY-FOUR

Wren

The week passed in a flurry of yelling, threats, and interrogations.

She kept expecting to be caught out for her duplicity, but **after it** was discovered that Leif had broken several of Lord Idril's slaves out of his castle and set them free, she remained free.

Vienne suspected Wren was in on Leif's plan, but she had no proof.

Idril was convinced that Wren had orchestrated the whole thing. He had no proof either and Vienne wasn't about to let him go after one of her people.

Arrik's appearance had rattled the lord, and despite his anger he kept his hands and threats to himself.

She hoped Leif made it to Gunn's ship safely. She hoped they could trust the pirate to actually get the people they'd freed to their homes. That was the only part that she worried about.

She prayed Leif would escape death at the hands of the rebellion and Lord Idril for betraying them. Not just so Wren had a comrade in arms whom she could confide in and trust, but because, first and foremost, Leif was her friend. Without him, there was only the prince, and he was as far from a friend.

Still, for the sake of remaining silent, it was good for Leif to be out of sight. Wren would catch him up on everything that had occurred when she saw him next.

Which meant he *had* to be all right.

"Something on your mind?"

Wren bolted upright from the log she was sitting on in the outskirts of the forest, just by Idril's castle. The prince had crept toward Wren as silent as a jungle cat. He wasn't wearing armor today—not even leather—but dressed in a simple black cotton shirt, thick black trousers, and knee-length lace-up boots. He was a massive man, but the far lowlier clothing made him seem, if not more approachable, less intimidating somehow.

"Was that necessary?" she barked, her tone sharper than was needed. Why did he feel the impulse to sneak up on her?

"I enjoyed it immensely."

Her gaze darted to the castle and then back to Arrik. She arched a brow. "Bold of you to come so close. Aren't you afraid of being caught?"

"Idril is never awake during daylight hours." He cocked his head. "You still didn't answer me."

Arrik slid a hand through his silvery blond hair, which was unbraided and loose for once, watching Wren with an expectant expression on his face, waiting for her to answer his question, though she had several dozen of her own—how had Arrik taken care of the guard stationed to watch Wren whilst she got some fresh air, for one?

He is a prince, and he is adept at blackmail.

"I'm worried about a friend," she admitted, choosing to be honest. She collapsed back onto the log with a huff of breath, trying not to show how much he'd rattled her. Though she sucked it back in when her husband easily sat himself down beside her.

Like they were friends.

Not enemies.

"The one from the dungeons?" he surmised, either oblivious to how uncomfortable his newfound proximity had made Wren or simply uncaring. "The mad boy?"

"He isn't mad. I think." Leif was different. Interesting. *Special.*

"You think?"

"He makes more sense than everyone else."

"Then perhaps he truly *is* mad," the prince said, plucking a leaf from a nearby bush and running his thumb over its wavy surface. Wren resisted the urge to laugh; his gaze softened when he saw the proof of it on her face. "It is good you have a friend. You need people you can trust."

She ignored that and how it warmed her slightly. "How did you know I meant Leif? It could have been anybody."

It was Arrik's turn to laugh. "Because something tells me there are not many within the rebellion who like the fact you are with them. But you saved the boy—Leif—from the dungeons. You could have left him, but you didn't. There's nothing quite like true selflessness in the face of danger to tie someone's affections to you forever."

"You...are unexpectedly shrewd," Wren said, adding it to the slowly growing bank of information she had concerning her husband. He grew more dangerous by the minute.

"Unexpectedly? You don't expect me to be this observant?"

"I don't think I expected much of anything from you other than being a bloodthirsty beast." Arrik didn't flinch at her assessment of him, and she shrugged. "Why would I think anything else? All that mattered to me was getting away from you. I never saved Leif so that he felt indebted to me. I saved him because it was the right thing to do. How could I leave him to you? To Soren?" Just the thought made her sick. The Verlanti king was a monster.

Arrik stiffened and dropped the leaf. It was clear from his body language that he didn't like being lumped in together with his father.

"That's true," he admitted, his tone dark. "If it hadn't been for the fact I *wanted* to get you out of the palace, I would have mercilessly interrogated the boy to find out anything you might have shared with him whilst you were both prisoners. That's why I thought you took him with you, if I'm being honest. It's why *I* would have risked my own escape to save him."

"And therein lies the difference between us, plain as day." Something about that reassured Wren—to know that she hadn't lost sight of what made her a good person. Yes, she had thrown her hat into the ring with her enemy husband, but that didn't mean she had stooped as low as he'd gone to achieve his goals.

She'd drawn lines that she would *never* cross.

She was not the same as Arrik.

There was still hope for her to get out of this with a shred of integrity left.

"What is it you need from me anyway?" Wren asked, when silence stretched out between them for a beat too long.

"Tell me about Lord Idril and Vienne. What have they been planning?"

She arched an eyebrow at him. "What do *you* know about Vienne?"

The smallest of smiles. "I know that she's your aunt, and I know that she's running the rebellion."

"Is she working for you as a spy, like Josenu?"

"No. But she does incredibly useful work that benefits me, nonetheless."

"So you have no plans to…" She squared her shoulders. "You have no plans to hurt her, do you?" She might not have seen eye to eye with the woman on many issues, but she was still, at the end of the day, her family. Vienne was the only one who could share stories about her mother's past, and would have Wren's best interests at heart outside of the rebellion.

Or, at least, Wren hoped that were the case.

For just a moment it looked as though Arrik might reach for her hand and squeeze it. Wren tensed and pulled her hand into her lap. His arm twitched but stilled when he noticed her observing him.

"I won't hurt your aunt, Wren. Do not worry about that."

That wasn't good enough. "And I'm supposed to trust you just like that?"

"No, but in time my actions will convince you. Vienne is safe unless she gives me cause. But if that were to occur, I will speak to you first. She's your kin after all."

That's all she could ask.

He tipped his head in the direction of the castle. "What are your thoughts on the rebellion and Idril's operations?"

She had many thoughts, but she'd only share a few.

"Lord Idril and Vienne seem to be in league with mostly all of the high court of Verlanti. It doesn't look like Soren has many allies even within his own ranks, if the number of people who visit Idril's castle is anything to go by."

Arrik nodded. "That's what I thought. Thank you for confirming my suspicions."

Her eyes narrowed. She hadn't told him anything he didn't know. "Was that a test?"

"Everything is a test."

That didn't make her feel any better.

"There's something I need you to do."

She arched a brow. "You think to command me?"

He mirrored her expression. "Never."

The word hovered between them. Whether truth or a lie, she didn't know. But it felt personal.

"I'm not going to like this *thing,* am I?" she said dryly, standing up to try to dispel some of the tension.

A slow grin crept across Arrik's face as he followed suit. She stepped back but paused when he brushed his fingertips across her wrist to stop her. Wren stared hard at his hand until he pulled away, his expression schooled.

"We are husband and wife in name only," she said lowly. "We are not friends. Keep your hands to yourself."

"Understood." He took two steps back, once again the beastly prince. "A masked ball is being held in Othos. It's a three-hour ride from Idril's castle. Everyone will be there—my father, Astrid, my brothers, mostly all of the high court of Verlanti. Idril, of course, will not be there, as he is being punished for complaining about Soren's hold over the country. I want you to attend. As my wife. As yourself."

Her jaw dropped. What the devil was he proposing? "You cannot be serious. That is...that's utter madness! How could you suggest such a thing? Your father would surely have me thrown in prison or killed."

"Exactly. We need to shake things up—to get things started. My father fully expects me to fail in my retrieval of the Dragon Princess, even though it's imperative to the Verlantian crown that I have a secure hold over the isles on his behalf. Seeing you there, with me, will be the last thing he expects. The last thing *anyone* expects. And when people are flustered—"

"They make mistakes," Wren finished for him. "But what of my aunt and Lord Idril? If I leave the castle to attend this ball with you, they'll believe I've turned traitor."

"It'll be easy. You'll have to sneak out." A wolfish grin. "You seem to be rather good at it, after all."

"But even if I successfully attend the party *and* return without suspicion," Wren said, unconvinced she could do even that much, "then they'll hear about the fact I attended the ball soon after. How will you explain that?"

"It will take a couple of days at least for them to hear about it. Attendees of the ball can't be seen visiting Idril so soon after the fact. They'll look like sympathizers. No one will want to earn the king's disfavor. By the time anyone hears about it, it will sound like mindless gossip. After all, you never left the castle, right? How could you have attended the ball? We can even send out a lie that it was a decoy. The only people who need to know it truly *is* you are my family."

"Sounds like you've thought of everything," Wren said slowly. "But what do I get out of this? Why should I help you secure the throne?"

"Because I will be better than Soren. I can give you the isles back."

She swallowed. "They were never yours to take in the first place."

"On that we can agree. If you help me take the Verlantian throne, I will give the Dragon Isles back to you."

"It sounds too good to be true. How can I trust you?"

"You don't have a choice."

She exhaled heavily and ran a hand through her hair. Everything was so muddled, but her uneasy alliance with the prince was the first true step to getting her younger sister Britta back on the throne and liberating the isles.

Arrik's plan was risky, but one with the chance of high reward. It certainly beat her sitting inside Lord Idril's castle doing absolutely nothing, waiting for her aunt to tell her what she was expected to do next.

But something bothered her about the plan, nonetheless.

She refused to be chained.

"I don't want to be locked up again," she said, turning to face Arrik with an abruptness he hadn't expected. It brought them almost toe-to-toe. "I won't be caged by your side because of this. If you are using this to trick me, I promise you won't survive the month."

He dipped his head toward Wren's. The sun was behind him, lining his pale hair in a halo of gold. It was almost too dazzling to look at, but still Wren kept her gaze on him. She wouldn't be cowed by him. Not anymore.

Never again.

"What would you have me do, then, to make you believe that I won't lock you up?" he murmured.

"Seal your promise in blood," she said, holding up a hand to cut it.

Arrik intertwined his fingers with hers. "How about sealing it with a kiss, instead?"

Her eyes widened and she gasped a moment before his lips descended on hers.

The feel of their mouths pressed against one another was familiar—Arrik had kissed Wren on their wedding day, after all—but it sent a thrill down her spine that the first kiss hadn't. His lips were powerful against Wren's, demanding her attention, but there was no violence or forcefulness to the action.

She broke away and slapped him hard across the face. His head turned from the blow. Wren's heart pounded in her chest as he slowly turned back, touching his red cheek.

"I told you not to touch me." Her words didn't hold as

much venom in them as she would have liked. She hated how heat swirled in her belly from just his kiss alone.

"No, you told me to keep my hands to myself. You never said anything about my lips. The devil's in the details, wife."

He was the devil alright.

She untangled her fingers from his, hating how flushed her cheeks were.

From anger, not passion.

That was the lie she told herself.

"Until the ball," he said, the faint outline of her hand on his cheek.

She nodded once and he turned on his heel, disappearing into the forest like he'd never been there. Wren stood there for too long staring into the dark woods. Her lips still tingled from the kiss. She touched them, a sickening sense of guilt trying to drown her. It was so easy to kiss him.

Enough.

She dropped her hand and returned to the castle, slipping in through the servants' entrance. The entire place was in an uproar.

"What's going on?" she asked a young servant.

The woman's eyes went wide. "Lord Idril has invited the queen to join him for a party tonight!" she exclaimed, before running off with her arms full of fresh linens.

Queen Astrid was coming? Surely she knew better.

Wren made her way back up to her room, not surprised to see her aunt waiting there. Vienne had taken to hovering the last few days.

She closed the door and faced her aunt. "To what do I owe

the pleasure?"

"No time for pleasantries." Vienne pulled her niece in to sit upon the bed. "I'm sure you've heard by now that Queen Astrid is expected tonight."

Wren nodded.

"Then you must know that you have to stay in here tonight. We can't afford for her to see you. She'll recognize you and it will put everything we've set in motion in danger."

Wren merely nodded again. "Of course. I've learned my lesson that going off on my own helps nobody." Her face still hurt from the last time she'd stepped out of line.

Relieved, Vienne squeezed Wren's hand before moving to the door. Her aunt paused and peered over her shoulder. "Much hinges on your obedience. Can I trust you?"

"Yes. But can I trust you?"

Her aunt jerked back. "What is that supposed to mean?"

Wren stared down Vienne. "You know what I mean. Did you know?"

"About what?"

"Stop playing coy. Did you know that Idril was my sire?" The words were bitter upon her tongue.

Vienne seemed to deflate a little bit. "I did."

"So you knew and yet you let me walk into this place to be ambushed by that degenerate?"

"I knew you wouldn't come if you knew."

As if that made things even better. "You are despicable."

Her aunt lifted her chin. "Just because you share blood doesn't mean a bloody thing. Plus, what I've done is in the best interest of all the people, not just you."

"Duly noted." Vienne was not to be trusted. Wren crossed her arms and nodded at the door. "Get out. I can't even look at you."

Vienne hesitated. "You will stay here?"

"Yes. Now be gone."

Vienne nodded and left, closing the door quietly behind her without another word.

Wren stared at the exit. Her aunt hadn't even apologized. No wonder Ever was so angry being here. Vienne cared only about her plans and no one else.

She exhaled heavily and focused on her plan. It had been easy to lie to her aunt.

Too easy.

Wren wouldn't blow things up like she'd done before. But there was no way she'd sit in her room when she could listen in on what was being said between the queen and Idril.

It was a good thing Leif had taught her a thing or two about disguises and subterfuge.

CHAPTER TWENTY-FIVE

Wren

Wren adjusted her wig—the same she'd worn to sneak into the gentleman's club several weeks before—and scanned the room. It was amazing what a change in hair color could do to one's look. She'd been tempted to toss it, but Leif had convinced her to keep it with her belongings, warning that a person never knew when they'd need a good disguise, even among allies.

She was thankful for his forethought. No one had recognized her.

Wren ran her hands along the front of her uniform that one of the slaves had gifted her. All traces of the Dragon Princess had disappeared, leaving a dark-haired servant in her place. She adjusted the golden veil that covered her eyes.

The servants always wore veils in Lord Idril's residence when he held revels; it helped to set them aside from the slaves on "offer" for guests. She was supremely grateful for this. Otherwise, sneaking into the party unnoticed would have been a lot more difficult. Not impossible, but not fun either.

Now she was ready to eavesdrop on Idril's meeting with Queen Astrid.

She had no idea what she'd discover once she was there.

A gentleman beckoned her closer and held out his goblet. Wren silently lifted a wine carafe from the table and filled his cup before retreating to her spot, carafe still in hand.

For the next hour or so Wren served food and drink to the group Idril was hosting. She recognized some of them from the Verlantian court: men and women who associated with Queen Astrid.

A courtier reached for her leg and she fended off his groping hand with a sweet smile and a regretful shake of her head for the fifth time in as many minutes.

It was odd. Wren's impression of the queen was somewhat positive. Why would she associate with such horrid people? The queen's courtly friends were indulging in just as many hedonistic activities as Idril's own retinue. It didn't make sense. Was this how they always acted? Or was it just in the absence of their queen?

She leaned against the wall once again, watching the occupants of the room. Where was the queen? Wren hadn't laid eyes on Astrid yet. Perhaps she was being entertained in another room? It was probably for the best. The queen would most likely be ashamed of her people. In any case, it was clear that Astrid was surrounded by as many vipers as Wren was.

A tap on her shoulder gave her pause.

She turned and came face to face with the chief of staff. The woman's face was haggard even through her mask.

"Delia can't handle the liquor Lord Idril keeps feeding her. We need you to step in and replace her, otherwise we'll end up with more vomit than I'd like to clean." She took the carafe of wine from Wren.

Step in?

Wren could do nothing but nod and stiffly follow the woman into a private antechamber. As she suspected, Queen Astrid was inside, away from the sight of her followers and their depraved activity. But something wasn't right.

Wren was given an ornate pitcher of wine and thrust into the room.

Bloody hell.

A man was chained to the sumptuous chair Queen Astrid was reclining on. He was feeding her by hand; she sucked his fingers whenever he brought them to her mouth. At her feet was another male slave—Wren's heart stuttered to a stop for a moment, because she thought at first it was Leif—acting as a footrest.

What the devil was going on?

Astrid was laughing. When her slip of a dress whispered off her shoulder to expose the curve of her breasts, she didn't bother fixing it. Her eyes were full of the same arrogant lust Wren had witnessed from every guest of Idril's thus far.

Stars, she was going to be sick.

This wasn't the Queen Astrid Wren knew. This was another creature altogether.

"Soren is being such a *bore*," Astrid drawled to Lord Idril, who Wren realized for the first time was sitting right beside her. Wren rushed forward to fill both of their goblets before they took any notice of her. "All he does is grouch about all the complaining the court is doing!"

"And we grouch with good reason," Idril replied, before yanking Wren onto his lap. She bit in a cry of surprise and fought to keep from doing anything stupid like slashing the monster's other cheek wide open.

Idril caressed the exposed bottom half of Wren's face, then trailed his fingers appreciatively down her collarbone to her waist. It sickened her.

"Take this beautiful morsel of a woman," he said, *licking* Wren's neck as he spoke. She pretended to giggle in surprised delight when inside she was screaming with disgust. "The Dragon Isles have plenty of them like this which I should be harvesting. But Soren is making things so difficult! Be off with you, girl," he sighed into Wren's ear, lifting her off his lap and slapping her backside in a way that suggested he'd find her later.

She retreated to the wall, feeling vulnerable and furious in equal measure at his assault. Her hands shook and she felt disgusting; she felt *used.* Her sire was a pig of a man.

Queen Astrid smirked at Idril. "Soren won't be a problem much longer, mark my words. Times are changing, Idril. For the better I believe."

Wren blanched, once again thankful for the veil. Did the queen know something about the rebellion's plans? Or did Astrid have her own plans to depose her husband? She sounded so certain, there was no doubt in Wren's mind that Astrid knew something.

Or was planning something.

Not wishing to hang around any longer in case Lord Idril decided he wanted her to sit in his lap once more, Wren filtered out of the antechamber and into the party proper. It took her a while to escape because of her disguise—people kept demanding her services—but eventually Wren made a blessed return to her room.

She closed the door and leaned heavily against it. The plot seemed to thicken at every turn.

Wren's brows furrowed as she spotted a package upon her bed. It was lustrous and glossy. Approaching it as if it were a poisonous snake, Wren gently lifted the lid to reveal vast swathes of black material.

A gown.

The bodice was strapless and low-backed, but it was solid, opaque, and promised to cinch in Wren's waist to within an inch of her life. She ran her fingers over the fabric. The skirt was far more Verlantian—flouncy and sheer, with tiers and tiers of gauze that swept to the floor and looked as if they'd trail behind the wearer. Perhaps it was because the dress was black, or perhaps the bodice was actually substantial, but Wren found herself admiring the dress rather than hating it. It was as fierce as it was beautiful.

The box also contained delicate-heeled shoes, gloves, and a hauntingly beautiful mask inlaid with black Dragon Isle diamonds. A creamy note fell out of the dress when Wren lifted it to inspect it further. She unfolded the thick paper and her breath caught in her throat when she saw the elegant script upon it.

A beautiful dress for my beautiful wife.

The prince.

Heat filled her cheeks and her heart traitorously quickened. She dropped the dress on her bed like it was a hot coal. Arrik was going to be the death of her. Irritated beyond measure, Wren replaced the contents inside the box, note and all, then stashed it beneath her bed.

The door creaked just as a familiar voice spoke from behind her. “Men are treacherous creatures, aren’t they?”

Astrid.

Wren spun around to face the queen, grateful beyond measure for her good sense in immediately hiding the box and not stripping out of her disguise.

“My queen,” Wren said, bowing low. “I do not know what you mean.”

Astrid laughed softly and sauntered farther into the room. “My dear, you cannot fool me, even with your clever disguise. I never forget a face—especially not the face of my daughter-in-law.”

Wren straightened, dread curling in the pit of her stomach. She stared at the queen, who motioned for Wren to come closer with a curled finger. She felt powerless but to obey, comforted only by the fact that her daggers were strapped to her forearms. If Astrid caused trouble, Wren would knock her out and escape to warn Vienne.

Gently, the queen removed Wren’s veil and her wig, satisfied to discover that she was indeed correct.

“My lovely Wren,” she purred, “how long you’ve been away.”

She said nothing.

The queen smiled. "You must have been surprised by what you saw back there. Idril makes Soren seem tame at times."

"What are you doing here, my lady?" Wren asked softly. "You shouldn't be here."

Astrid laughed and tossed the veil and wig onto the bed. "Neither should you. He has a way of destroying the women in his company."

"Then why are you talking with Lord Idril in private?"

"Sometimes we have to exploit specific expectations in order to lower someone's guard so we can get what we want." The queen's gaze sharpened. "I could ask the same thing of you, Wren. Why are you here? I half-expected that you were back in the isles, and yet I discover you here."

"Will you turn me over to your husband?" She needed to know how to proceed.

Astrid cupped Wren's cheek. "Never. It's been a long time since someone has gotten the best of my husband. I enjoy watching him struggle. He gets his way too much." She dropped her hand. "You still didn't answer *my* question. What are you doing here?"

What was she doing here? How much should she share with the queen? What had Idril told her?

Less is more.

"To get what I want," she admitted. "I'm tired of being at the mercy of others."

"Clever girl." Astrid gently touched Wren's bruised cheek, her lip curling. "I hope whoever damaged you suffered tenfold."

"He will never hit me again." Wren shared a smile with the queen, thinking of the scar Idril would carry for the rest of his life.

"Good." Her dark eyes warmed and glittered in the low light. "Never let them see you squirm. Also, you should not hide your beauty, lovely girl," she said. "It is one of your best weapons. Wield it whilst you have it, because before you know it, it'll be gone, and you'll regret never using it when you had the chance. What is the point of fighting if you don't use every tool in your arsenal?"

"Is that what you do?" The question was out before Wren could censor herself.

Astrid smirked. "I do what I must to survive. Something we both share, no?" Wren knew Queen Astrid was right. "Don't be ashamed of your femininity."

Had that been what she'd being doing?

Every time Wren had been uncomfortable in her femininity so far, it had been used against her. She had to swallow her nerves and her instincts to stab anyone who looked at her like she was an object and use her looks to her advantage. Tonight had been proof enough of that; she'd almost attacked Idril the moment he touched her.

Wren dipped her head in acknowledgement. "I'll take your advice to heart."

"Do." Astrid sauntered back to the exit. "For the record, I never saw you here and you never saw me here, correct?"

"Agreed. Safe travels, my lady."

The queen chuckled. "Happy hunting, little dragon."

CHAPTER TWENTY-SIX

Arrik

"Son."

Arrik didn't flinch. He'd learned years ago that at any sign of weakness his father would pounce. It had been several weeks since he'd seen Soren. Of course he'd choose the night of the ball to speak.

He turned from the window, bowed to the king, and then straightened. Soren was a few inches shorter than himself and the secret, petty part of Arrik liked that his evil sire had to look up to *him*.

"Yes, my lord?" His tone was even despite the dread that curled in his belly. Soren rarely used the term "son" when addressing Arrik. It was only used when the king was on the verge of striking out at him for some perceived threat, or when he wanted something.

"Walk with me." A command.

Arrik fell into place beside the king, noting the four guards trailing them. He could dispatch them in seconds. It would be easy to take out the king, but it wouldn't solve the rest of his problems.

It'll make you feel better.

Those kind of thoughts didn't help. He knew from personal experience that taking a life never really filled the hole carved in one's chest after a loved one died.

The king laced his fingers behind his back and sighed, his maroon silk robe dragging along the white marble floor with a soft hiss.

"I'm displeased."

Two simple words that could mean horror.

Arrik looked straight ahead, his expression one of a committed commander. "What can I do to ease your discomfort, my lord?"

"That's what I like about you. You're always willing and ready to do my bidding. You don't lounge around like my other useless sons. Kalles has some use for me as a spymaster when he's not drowning himself in opium. Then there's Cathal. He's lazy, entitled, and lives for pleasure, but he's my heir."

I'm your firstborn.

Soren slanted a look up at Arrik as if he heard his thoughts. "But out of all my children, you are the most like me, my most trusted."

"You honor me." It wasn't an honor. He wasn't anything like the king. He was *better*.

"And yet…you've betrayed me."

Unease trickled down Arrik's spine but he kept his calm. His father had no way of knowing what he was up to. He'd been too careful. "My lord?"

Soren narrowed his blue eyes, his countenance icy. "Did I

not ask you to take care of Idril?"

The knot inside Arrik loosened. So this whole charade was about the other elf lord. The situation could be salvaged.

"I handled it."

The king slowed to a stop and arched a haughty brow. "Then why is he still breathing?"

"You asked me to take care of him and I did." He was pushing his sire's temper if he judged how Soren's eyes flared.

"How do you figure that?" the king snapped.

"I sent the queen to him." A calculated risk.

His father stilled, like a serpent before it strikes. "And?"

"Idril took the bait. Within weeks, Astrid will own the slave trade and the elf lord will believe it was all his idea. None of his sycophants will try to rise up against the queen. You will own his trade without a civil war through your lovely wife."

The idea had come to Arrik as soon as Soren had sent him to take care of Idril. It would have been easy to kill him as the king expected, or to expose him for his dealings with the rebellion, but neither suited Arrik. He needed to distract the queen with a new conquest and to keep his sire happy with the outcome.

It was perfect.

The king slowly smiled. "You are a clever fox, my son. And my wife? How did you get her to agree?"

"I didn't. I just mentioned that you were unhappy with his murmurings and that I'd be dealing with him soon. I arrived first and put him on edge, then all I had to do was wait. My queen swooped in afterward as I expected, and insinuated herself into his business. You and I both know that she likes to collect valuable things."

Soren chuckled, the sound sinister. "That she does." He began walking forward once again and Arrik followed suit. "It seems I shouldn't have been planning your punishment but your exultation. What do you wish for?"

"Nothing. I am content serving as your shield." Another lie. He'd be much more, but not because his sire deigned to give it to him. But by his own merits.

"Such modesty. Maybe I'll find you another wife if yours never shows up."

A backhanded compliment veiled as a threat?

Arrik's jaw tightened. "My men are close. I'll have the dragon princess within my grasp in a few days." How would his father react when he saw Wren in a few short hours?

"Good. She's stirred up too much trouble. It's your job to break her before you return to the isles. We need her to control the people. She's the key."

Wren was the key. Just not Soren's key.

His.

CHAPTER TWENTY-SEVEN

WREN

It was easier than Wren had thought it would be to sneak away from the rebellion to get ready for the masked ball and spirit away into the forest. She had a servant slip her something at lunch that made it appear as if she had food poisoning, which was sufficient for Vienne and Idril. They'd sent Wren to her room to be left well alone until at least the next morning. After vomiting up the drug, Wren easily recovered.

Arrik had sent Josenu upon horseback to collect her from the forest just before sundown, a starlight-colored mare waiting for Wren to ride to the ball. In any other circumstance, Wren would have found it highly amusing to be riding a horse dressed in such splendor.

Josenu blinked slowly as she approached him, his eyes running down her frame. "You look stunning." A pause. "Although not very suitable for a ride, no?"

Wren gave him a wry smile. "My thoughts exactly." She gestured to the gauzy train of her dress. "Not sure how I'm supposed to get on the horse in the first place with all of this."

The spy grinned and beckoned Wren to his side. He whispered to the mare and the majestic animal gently folded its front legs until it was lying on the ground. Josenu held his hand out and helped Wren to settle. Her bare thighs clamped against the horse as it stood back up. Wren ran her hand along the mare's neck and crooned softly.

Josenu gathered up the train of Wren's dress and haphazardly tucked it around her. He grimaced. "That will have to do." He strode over to his own mount and swung into the saddle. "You ready?"

"As I'll ever be." Her fingers tightened on the reins and she nudged the mare forward. They reached a road and they began trotting. Her dress slowly slipped out of its confines and waved in the breeze behind her.

It had been a long time since she'd ridden a horse. It was jarring compared to a dragon. Wren laughed, imagining that she looked like the mistress of death with a liquid black dress and riding upon a pale horse.

Josenu broke to the left, taking a small trail through the woods. Wren followed him.

Rowen would have gotten a kick out of this.

Her chest tightened. He had always been more adventurous than Wren. She hadn't seen his ghost since Delansh. Clearly she had imagined him, otherwise she was sure she would have spied him again.

Stop thinking on the past. You need to focus on the future.

Butterflies filled her stomach; tonight was going to be beyond dangerous. Not just Arrik but his brothers, too, would be in attendance, as well as High King Soren and Queen Astrid. She had to play the perfect, compliant wife, returned to Arrik's side after deciding that being with him was far more agreeable than being on the run.

So much could go wrong.

The queen could have ruined everything already.

Wren couldn't afford to mess anything up.

Her mind wandered as the sun sank farther in the sky.

"You're nervous," Josenu remarked, picking up the pace when they exited the thick underbrush of the deep forest for a reasonably well-maintained dirt track. They had been riding for two hours; soon they would come upon the palace for the masked ball. Already Wren could see the signs of torches and stone walls upon the horizon: the city of Othos.

She winced at the observation. "Wouldn't *you* be? All things considered, I think I'm composing myself rather well." She slanted a glance his way. "I'm trusting him with everything."

"Nerves aren't a bad thing. They mean that you care about the outcome of the evening." He didn't assuage her trust issues.

"That's an interesting perspective," she admitted, shifting upon the back of her horse with as much grace as she could considering she was dressed in copious swathes of no doubt expensive black gauze. "Does that mean you're nervous too, Josenu?"

He laughed softly, glancing at her before speeding up their horses a little more. "If you aren't nervous when Arrik has planned something, then you've messed up somewhere."

"How did you become acquainted with the prince?"

Josenu sobered. "He saved my life. I owe him everything." Wren waved a hand for him to continue but he shook his head. "You may be pretty but you're not getting anything else out of me, Princess. Now, let's ride. We don't want to be late!"

With a kick of Josenu's heels, his mare flew forward, forcing Wren to let go of any sense of feminine dignity she still possessed to match his speed. In all honesty, this was the kind of riding she enjoyed—the kind she missed. It reminded her of riding Aurora through the skies—the wind upon her face and the rush of adrenaline.

As they pounded through the city gates and closed in on the venue of the masked ball, Wren thought about how devoted Josenu seemed to Arrik. It was clear he did not follow him blindly but did as the prince asked through a mixture of respect, affection, and shared goals.

How I ever thought he could betray Arrik is beyond me.

Having now had two meetings with Arrik where he showed a completely different side to himself—where he confided in her, and allowed himself to be vulnerable—she felt like she understood a whole lot more about him, and why he could possibly be a great leader. She still didn't trust him, but the devil you knew was better than the devil you didn't.

You like that devil way too much.

That was the problem.

She wished her bloody heart would stop throbbing whenever she thought about the prince's lips on hers, or his touch on her face, or the tension that crackled between them as he pinned her to the stable wall and—

"We're here."

Wren blinked. She had taken none of Othos in during their ride.

Idiot. Time to get your head out of the clouds.

Josenu dismounted his horse and moved to her side. He reached up and helped Wren off her mount and led her to the back entrance of a grand building constructed of vast stone columns the color of golden sand. It was as if she was having an out-of-body experience.

How was such a feat of architecture built?

"On the backs of slaves," Josenu growled.

Wren blinked. She'd asked that out loud?

The spy paused and pulled her into a dark alcove. Wren flinched as he ensured her mask was secured to her face, then fussed with her hair for a few moments.

She resisted the urge to laugh after she'd gotten over her surprise. "What are you, my handmaid?"

"No, but Arrik will have my head if you enter the ball looking as if you rode at full speed on horseback through the city to reach it in time. You must look perfect. You are a representation of the prince."

"That...seems fair." Though she was nervous, she forced herself to spin on the spot. "How do I look?"

"Like the Dragon Princess." Josenu bowed graciously, waving a hand in front of him toward the door. "Try to sneak into the ball proper with as little fanfare as possible. Better for Arrik to find you *before* anyone else realizes who you are."

Wren understood the hidden meaning behind the spy's words: if anyone else discovered her first, she might not ever make it to Arrik's side, and all would be lost before it began.

"My hair will be a dead giveaway."

"Then be quick."

She nodded her assent. "I understand. Thank you, Josenu. For...well, for everything, I guess."

His expression softened into a smile, and Wren for a moment saw a striking resemblance between Josenu and Arrik—or, at least, the version of Arrik Wren had been discovering over the last few weeks. Was she seeing things again? Was her mind truly broken?

Wren shook her head and pushed out of the alcove. She slipped down the corridor toward the ballroom. Music filtered through the open doors; a set of elven warriors bracketed the entrance. Her palms began to sweat as they tracked her approach. Everyone in the high court of Verlanti had varying shades of blond, brown, and black hair. They were tall and willowy and had pointed ears.

Between her flaming red hair, short stature, and round ears, she was sure to stick out like a sore thumb.

Wren held her breath while she surreptitiously followed a group of servants into the ball and the elven warriors didn't detain her.

One challenge down, a hundred to go.

Her eyes rounded. If she'd thought Idril's banquet halls or the Verlantian palace had been lavishly decorated, then the stone hall of Othos put them both to shame.

Wren grabbed a glass of wine from the tray the servants

were holding, taking a large gulp of the rich liquid as she took in every inch of her surroundings while skirting along the back wall, clinging to the shadows.

The stone columns from the exterior of the building also lined the interior, and held up a high, sweeping, vaulted ceiling at set intervals. Vines of roses in purple and crimson scaled these columns. From the ceiling hung several gigantic, glittering chandeliers, casting the entire hall in a low but glimmering light.

Between the columns were recessed pits filled either with pillows or upholstered seats surrounding tables laden with food and drink. Lord Idril's castle had contained something similar, though his had been at least half the size.

In the center of the room was a raised dais upon which a twelve-man band dressed all in white played upon equally white-stringed instruments, filling the air with lively, uplifting music.

All around them were at least a hundred guests dressed in lavish gowns and bold jackets, sweeping skirts in cerulean blue that moved like the sea, shirts of such insubstantial material they seemed likely to dissolve. Everyone was masked in one form or another, adorned in horns or scales or feathers or long fake ears that exaggerated their own, naturally pointed ears. Most were inlaid with some kind of gemstone to indicate wealth and social standing.

Wren gritted her teeth, her fingers tightening on her glass. No one was dressed in black.

No one but herself.

You can't hide all night. Get moving.

She blew out a breath and departed from the shadows.

Wren swept through the crowd, drawing attention that made her skin prickle.

Though nobody save Arrik's family could *really* know it was indeed the Dragon Princess, the image of her dressed in Dragon Isle black diamonds, with her scarlet hair softly curling down her back, was going to be the topic of every single conversation.

She could already hear the whispers as she trailed through the crowd.

They'd have a dozen different accounts of who or what she was. It would quickly become gossip. Nobody but Arrik and his family would know for sure that it was Wren, so her presence at the ball would be protected from Lord Idril and Vienne's knowledge.

Josenu's warning hung in Wren's ears. She had to find Arrik before anyone else thought it wise to try to steal her away. Such as...

Soren.

She froze to the spot when she noticed him dancing with three sumptuously dressed women. He had not yet noticed Wren. She moved away from him, making sure to keep the king within her sight.

The hair at her nape rose.

Wren scanned the crowd and she spied Queen Astrid, who was sitting in a pit of cushions close to where Soren was dancing. She was staring straight at her. When she noticed that Wren had spotted her, she saluted her with her goblet of wine.

Wren's pulse thundered in her ears. How did she think she could do this?

You're a dragon warrior. Hold your head high.

All eyes were on her as she forced herself to keep moving through the crowd. She took another sip of her wine, searching the sea of masked faces. Where was the prince?

The music changed to a heartbreakingly melancholic tune made for slow dancing. She watched as couples paired off.

"Might I have this dance?" Arrik asked from behind Wren, his voice smooth as silk over her skin. She turned to face him and was immediately glad for the mask obscuring half of her face, for her cheeks flushed as red as her hair as she took him in.

Her husband was dressed all in black; his horned mask inlaid with Dragon Isle diamonds was a perfect pair for Wren's own. His long, pale hair was braided away from his face, though it was shot through with fine silver threads. The black velvet waistcoat he wore over a dark frothy shirt was also shot through with silver, which complemented the silver buckles that ran up his black boots.

His perfect lips curved into a genuine smile as he took in Wren, too busy with his own observations to realize she was doing the same to him. "I am glad to see the dress I chose fits you so well," he said, his voice holding a slight growl that caused her to shiver. He held out his hand and the whispering around them increased. "How lovely you are in my colors, wife."

She took his hand and he led her to the dance floor, skirts swishing around her bare legs. He pressed her close to him, arm snaking around her waist, and began dancing.

"Where did you get these diamonds?" Wren asked, though it wasn't what she'd wanted to ask at all. "The ones in the masks, I mean."

"They may have been seized when we raided Lorne," Arrik replied, so easily that Wren winced. "You will be reassured to know that each and every one of them is accounted for between the two masks we're wearing though. Soren did not get his hands on a single one. Idril, either. They're mine."

"Ours," she corrected.

He smiled. "*Ours.*"

He made the word sounds sinful.

Wren didn't want that to mollify her, but it did. It should have incensed her that Arrik had the audacity to take her kingdom's own gemstones to decorate himself.

But the diamonds suited him.

Too well.

"I was getting worried you had been held up," Wren muttered, when Arrik twirled her elegantly beneath his arm before pulling her back to his chest once more. To their left, Wren spied Kalles without a mask. He waved his hands above his head like a reed in the breeze.

"Is your brother high?"

Arrik's lips thinned. "When is he not?"

As if Kalles heard their conversation, his attention latched on to them. Despite his stupor, he was scrutinizing Wren with absolute precision.

She tensed. People overcome by drugs were

unpredictable.

"Do not feel concerned," he reassured her. "So long as you remain by my side, you'll remain safe." His hands tightened around her. He lowered his mouth to Wren's ear. "Make my father believe that you've become my complicit wife and all will be fine. He is losing his mind over the dissent in the isles. Your people are holding up against him with commendable strength."

A surge of pride filled Wren's body. Arrik seemed proud, too, or at the very least impressed. He was not frustrated by the Dragon Isles refusing to cooperate—not in the least.

Why did she find that attractive?

"My people ride dragons for fun," she whispered back, sliding her hand from Arrik's shoulder to the back of his neck without quite knowing what she was doing, her fingers tangling in his hair. "I thought you knew by now that we were not so easily conquered."

Arrik's eyes gleamed when he pulled away just enough to gaze at Wren's face. "Not conquered, no. Conspirers though…"

"Conspirers?" Wren raised a sharp brow. "I quite like the sound of that."

The two of them exchanged a look, then, and time seemed to pause. They stopped dancing, though the orchestra's song was yet to draw to a close and there were people all around them still twirling and moving.

He brushed a lock of hair from her cheek. "I hoped so. You're going to make an incredible queen."

"A queen?" She laughed.

His eyes were intense as he leaned closer. "Mark my words, Wren. You will become a queen of legend."

"Such pretty words," she whispered, tipping her head back.

She knew Arrik was going to kiss her. She knew she was going to let him. For appearances of course. Wren had a part to play.

Liar.

She *wanted* him to kiss her.

A scream rent through the air.

The music cut off.

"The prince is dead! The crown prince—*the crown prince is dead!*"

CHAPTER TWENTY-EIGHT

Wren

Astrid's scream pierced the air a moment before she passed out.

Wren froze in Arrik's arms, eyes wide.

Cathal is dead?

Pandemonium had erupted all around them in response to the announcement.

Her husband's grip tightened on her as he observed the room. Gone was the heat from his eyes—only calculation and predatory intent left. She dug her nails into his shirt and whipped her head around to try and see what was going on.

Where was Cathal? How had he been killed?

Soren powered through the crowd toward the entrance. The courtiers parted for him, creating a human-lined corridor to the pale warrior who was covered in blood.

"Speak," the king barked.

The eleven-warrior paled further but spoke. "The crown prince and all his men were slaughtered at the entrance to the city! An ambush was waiting for them. I barely escaped with my life to bring you the news." The words cut through the crowd like a hot knife through butter, temporarily silencing everyone.

Soren seemed to swell in size. "You left my son to die?"

The warrior shook his head and dropped to his knees, head bowed. "He was gone before I even arrived."

"Don't look," Arrik murmured, pulling Wren closer.

But she couldn't look away.

Soren tore away the warrior's sword and beheaded the man on the spot.

She squeezed her eyes shut and fought against the urge to vomit. The king had murdered one of his innocent men.

Men and women began to scream, even louder than before, and she opened her eyes as people began bustling into Wren and Arrik in their attempt to leave the ball. No one wanted to stay for more of Soren's anger.

They wanted to escape before suspicion was wrought against them.

Arrik began pushing through the crowd, his hands wrapped around Wren's forearms in an iron-tight grip as he towed her away.

"You need to leave. *Now*."

She nodded, stumbling after him, but then frowned. "But we didn't accomplish our mission."

"The plan has changed. You can't be discovered here."

"But—"

"That wasn't a suggestion," he cut in, holding her hand before ripping through the crowd in the direction of the back entrance Wren had come through in the first place. They rushed through the shadows, dodging terrified servants cowering against the walls.

"I can help you."

Arrik jerked to a halt and peered down at her. "No, you cannot. Who do you think they're going to blame if my brother is truly dead? *You.*"

"Me?" Her brows furrowed. "How could I possible orchestrate something like that?"

"Do you think rationality is something my father possesses right now? He killed the messenger, and you have been a thorn in his side for weeks." He led her out the doors and out of the palace.

Fearful elves were fleeing the palace in droves.

Wren flinched as a group of elven soldiers forced two men and women down into the dirt, dragging them back into the building kicking and screaming.

"Hurry up."

They picked up their speed, managing to make it to the stables.

Josenu was waiting inside, lips firmly pressed into a line. "I heard shouts that Cathal is dead."

"I'll confirm it with my own eyes. Get her back without notice," Arrik ordered, lifting Wren onto the back of the beautiful mare she had ridden from Lord Idril's castle. "She cannot be seen or he'll execute her."

She gathered up the end of her dress, shivering as screams continued to cut through the air. Her breathing became labored as images of the attack on the isles flashed through her mind.

"Wren."

Arrik's voice cut through the panic; she focused on his face, sweat dripping between her breasts. He studied her a moment before pulling a knife from his waist and cutting off the train of her dress.

"Ride hard and fast, wife. Stop for no one and nothing. Do you understand?" His voice brooked no argument.

"You can't honestly expect me to leave," Wren rasped. "You need help. It's not safe here."

"Are you concerned for my safety?"

She was, but wouldn't admit it.

He stroked the length of her calf through the gauzy material of her dress. Tingles ran up her leg.

"It's never been safe, darling. Nothing will be until Soren's dealt with." He turned his attention to Josenu. "Your life is tied to hers. Do you understand me?"

"Understood."

Wren gasped. "You can't put that on him. Accidents happen."

Her husband looked up at her, expression fierce. "I'm entrusting him with my everything. No accidents will be happening this night." Wren's mouth ran dry as he held her gaze, daring her to argue with him. "I'll meet you when it's safe once more. We didn't anticipate whatever...*this*...is. I won't be able to formulate a new plan unless I *know* you're safe."

He spoke with such sincerity and heat that Wren could do nothing but nod in silence.

Why did this feel like goodbye? And why did that scare her?

"Don't die," she murmured as Josenu urged his mount out of the stable.

"I won't. Believe me. I'll come for you, wife."

His words were a promise and a threat.

Wren kicked her mare to follow the spy away from the ball and onto the streets of Othos as quickly as they dared.

Adrenaline pounded through her veins as they crept through the city on horseback. Soldiers were everywhere, and several fires had broken out. She glanced over her shoulder more than once toward the palace. It was high time she admitted the truth to herself. The devil prince had grown on her. Somehow, they'd formed a bond. She wasn't sure what that was or what it entailed, but Wren knew she didn't want him to die. At least by anyone else's hand.

You couldn't do it even if you wanted to.

What concerned her was the succession.

Arrik had been claimed by Soren. He was second in line to the throne. If Cathal was really dead, then Arrik would be next up for the throne, painting a larger target on his back and her own.

Her chest constricted painfully as she tried to draw in another breath. Memories of the attack on her wedding day kept assaulting her to the point she felt like she was going to pass out. It was as if her organs weren't getting enough blood to function.

Get yourself together.

Wren scrubbed a hand over her face, trying to refocus on the cobbled streets as they tore along them. Arrik could handle himself. It was ridiculous for her to worry about him.

They neared the city limits and Josenu slowed. She followed suit and watched the people attempting to flee.

Ice dripped down her spine as she spotted a familiar face.

A ghost.

Rowen.

"*No*," she mouthed, shaking her head.

He's not real.

"We have to go now. Keep close," Josenu ordered.

She followed the spy, her eyes glued to the stunning dark-skinned man dressed in midnight blue as they galloped past. They moved too quickly for Wren to discern his face. She cursed underneath her breath. What was happening to her? Had she lost her mind? Why did she keeping seeing Rowen at the most inopportune times? What was her subconscious trying to tell her?

Put it from your mind.

She had to get back to Lord Idril's castle as fast as possible. No doubt a messenger was already on the way to inform him about the death of Prince Cathal. If Wren didn't make it back before then, the castle would be on high alert, and Wren would never make it back inside unnoticed.

The journey was punishing and chilly.

By the time she came upon the castle, both Wren's and Josenu's mares were frothing with exhaustion. She slipped down off the creature's back, patting its nose before asking the elf, "What will you do now? The horses can't manage another journey like that."

He smiled grimly. "I'll camp out in the forest with them so they can recover. Do not worry. I have plenty of food and water for them." Gratitude overwhelmed Wren at his reassurances, for she could not abide the cruelty of men, for dragons or horses alike. Animals deserved to be treated with respect, especially when they enabled you to escape certain death.

"Be careful," Wren said.

"You as well, Princess. Now run."

Wren turned and did just that.

She tripped on her ragged dress as she made her way through the servants' entrance, then quickly pushed herself into the shadows against the stony corridor wall when the silhouette of two patrolmen came into sight. Hardly daring to breathe, Wren counted: one, two, three, then rushed from her hiding place to steal up to her bedroom.

When she entered the room, it became clear that nobody had searched through her things or torn the place apart in their attempt to find a missing Dragon Princess, which Wren took as a good sign. Most days they left her to her own diversions.

She released a relieved breath and wasted no time in shedding her gown and all its accessories, though she spared a minute to carefully place the mask and jewelry back into their shiny box and tuck it beneath her mattress. Next, she stoked the fire and tossed the dress and gloves into the flames. She watched it burn, erasing some of the evidence of her night.

Then she dressed in a simple nightgown, making sure to strap her daggers to her thighs, before she headed toward the kitchen, on the lookout for something that might help the pounding headache building behind her eyes that was threatening to make her vomit. She needed to be able to *think*; otherwise panic and memories would overwhelm her.

Besides, considering she was supposed to have food poisoning, her current ashy appearance and search for medicine would only lend credence to her alibi.

"...they may help us," a familiar voice murmured from the kitchen when Wren crept up to the door.

Her brows furrowed.

Vienne?

Wren slowed and paused by the door, out of sight. She peeked around the corner. Vienne and Ever were sitting by the gargantuan fireplace within the kitchen, wine in hand as they conversed with each other.

Ever nodded, her graying hair shining like silver in the light of the fire. "Anything would be better than *him*," she said, inclining her chin to take in the castle in general. Wren knew she meant Lord Idril.

Wren didn't know what they were talking about, but she agreed with Ever. Anything was better than Idril.

"This new power would vastly overshadow his," Vienne reassured her friend. She touched Ever's hand tenderly. "I know this has been tough on you, but it needn't be that way for much longer. Once—"

The woman paused, her gaze flickering to the door.

Wren bit her lip.

If she hung around, she'd be caught. She silently backpedaled and rushed back up to her room, and didn't stop until she had locked her door and buried herself beneath the covers on her bed, fatigue riding her hard.

Just what the devil is going on?

She settled against the mattress and pulled her weapons from her thighs, stashing them beneath her pillows. Her hands shook and she found herself humming an age-old dragon song in an attempt to settle her nerves. People were making decisions on her behalf and expecting her to follow them, all the while changing the game behind her back.

Who was this new power that would render Lord Idril disposable?

Who killed Prince Cathal and all his men?

Was Rowen haunting her because of her attraction to Arrik?

Wren clutched at her chest as tears began to fall. Was she losing her mind? Or was she seeing Rowen because, for the briefest of moments within the magic of the masked ball, Wren hadn't minded being in Arrik's arms?

But it was more than not minding. She'd *wanted* to be there despite herself.

A shadow passed by Wren's window, then again a minute or so later. Wren pulled one of the daggers from beneath her pillow and sat up in bed before creeping over to the window.

She jerked as Trove flew by the glass, almost blending into the darkness.

He'd come for her.

"You foolish, beautiful creature," Wren murmured, beside herself with gratitude and relief. Fearlessly—because this wasn't the first time she'd done so—Wren opened the window and stepped up onto the balcony, dropping her weapon onto the floor.

Trove dove again and she jumped into thin air, biting back a laugh of delight when the dragon swooped to catch her on his back. Her breath fled as she landed, clutching at his spines to keep from slipping off.

The wind whipped at her hair and nightgown as he flew low over the forest. She peered over her shoulder at Idril's castle, almost breaking down and going back. News of Cathal's death would soon be spread everywhere.

Wren continued flying. She had time to live her life on her own terms for a short while.

Her fingers squeezed Trove's frills tightly when they descended by the mouth of a sizeable cave protected by a waterfall. She squealed as he moved through the cold water. She was soaked from head to toe, but it felt as if it cleansed her soul. He lowered to the floor and she wasted no time sliding off his back to wring out her nightgown and hair.

"Thank you for the bath," she said with a small laugh.

The dragon blinked at her and laid his head on the floor. He moved his tail and exposed his belly to her.

Wren stilled and stared down Trove.

An act of trust and submission.

He wanted to claim her.

Heat pressed to the back of her eyes as she entered the cocoon his body and tail created. Wren curled against the dragon's warm belly, leaning her chest on his smooth scales, listening to his hearts beat.

"How did I get here?" she asked after a while. The crash of the waterfall was soothing, and loud enough to block out her thoughts and lull her toward drowsiness and the promise of sleep. "What has my life become? Why can't I just—just run away for good?"

But Wren knew why.

So long as there were people she needed to protect—so long as her sister still lived, and her kingdom was valiantly fighting in her place against the Verlantians—Wren could not run. The thought had haunted her for months on end, taunting her, scaring her with how enticing it was, but Wren knew to run away was to surrender.

And a dragon never surrendered.

Trove purred, curling in tighter around her until Wren was suffused with heat.

But a dragon still had to sleep, so Wren slept.

CHAPTER TWENTY-NINE

Wren

Wren's entire body ached when she woke the next morning in the cave just before sunrise.

She'd spent too long with the dragon. It was time to go home.

"Trove," she murmured to the still-sleeping dragon, immediately alert and filled with urgency despite her fatigued muscles. "Trove, you must return me before I am noticed missing."

The dragon huffed his dissatisfaction and cracked open an eye to look at her with disdain as if he loathed the mornings as much as she did.

"Please," Wren whispered.

His other eye snapped open and the spines along his back rose, sensing her urgency. He heaved to his feet and ambled over to the waterfall and lapped at the small pool at the bottom. She followed him and drank from the crystal-clear water before clambering onto his back, right in front of his haunches. She once again grabbed the frills along his head and braced herself.

He spread his wings and launched through the waterfall.

Wren squeaked as the freezing water drenched her once again.

The sky in the east had just begun to color as they flew over the trees. She shivered, her teeth clacking together at the chill in the air. With winter on the horizon, Verlanti was finally beginning to cool down. It was to her advantage that it was getting later in the year, for the sky was dark and the grounds around Lord Idril's castle empty when they arrived.

She scanned the castle, noting a large fire where several guards were warming themselves, completely ignorant to her arrival. She hated the wind but was thankful for the sound cover it provided. Trove flew lower and hovered by Wren's window.

This was where it got tricky.

She slowly climbed to her feet and balanced on his back. Wren prepared herself and dove for her window. She cleared the balcony and rolled to her feet. Her heart pounded in her chest and she spun around with a grin. It wasn't her best dismount but at least she hadn't lost all of her skills.

"Thank you," she said to Trove, leaning out her window to caress his neck. She kissed his snout when he pressed closer. "Now I know it is useless to chase you away, I shall be sure to ask for your help or company the next time I need it." She chirped softly to him in farewell and stepped back.

Trove trilled in assent, then retreated from the window and flew across the forest at breakneck speeds. She watched him until he disappeared from sight.

A shiver wracked her body.

It was bloody cold.

Wren stripped out of her wet nightgown and wrung it out over the balcony before hanging it over the edge to dry. She tiptoed to the bed and yanked the coverlet around her shaking body. The blanket was freezing to the touch, and the fire in her hearth had burned down to mere embers.

Lovely.

You only have yourself to blame.

It had been worth it.

She rubbed the blanket against her arms to create friction and heat. In no time she'd warmed up enough to put on new clothes and somewhat dry her hair. Her eyes burned from fatigue as she climbed back in bed.

She huddled beneath the covers and sighed as her head hit the pillow. At least she'd get another few hours of sleep before she had to face the new day, and the fallout of everything that had occurred the night before. No one would be awake for hours unless a messenger arrived with news about Cathal.

She closed her eyes and dosed almost immediately.

A sharp knock raised her much too soon.

Wren rubbed at her bleary eyes and stumbled out of bed, grabbing her daggers before approaching the door. She hesitated to unlock it.

"Who is it?" she called softly, voice rough from sleep.

"It's Vienne. Let me in."

Wren tucked away her weapons and unlocked the door. Vienne pushed into the room and then frowned. "You look pale."

"I'm tired," she muttered, moving back to the bed and plopping down.

Her aunt sat beside Wren and placed a warm, dry hand on her niece's forehead. Vienne clucked her tongue. "If you had a fever, then it's broken. That's good news."

"Is there a reason you're here so early?"

Vienne nodded and dropped her hand. "Will you be able to suffer on horseback?"

"We're leaving?"

"For a time. Can you ride?"

"Yes." Wren ran a hand down her face. "Where are we going?"

"There's a new player in the game I wish for you to meet," Vienne explained in hushed tones.

"And who is this *new player*?"

Was it the queen?

Vienne shook her head. "Not here. Later. Come, we must leave now while Idril is busy."

Interesting. Her aunt was keeping secrets from the elf lord. Wren was intrigued.

"Am I still being treated as a prisoner, or will I be allowed my weapons for this journey?" she asked softly.

"You will have them returned." Vienne smiled. "This will please you far more than your current situation. Trust me."

Trust her? What a joke.

"What should I pack? How long shall we be gone?"

"Pack lightly," her aunt commented. "Then meet me down at the stables."

Wren watched Vienne leave, and then packed a change of

clothes, a waterskin, and her two daggers. She pulled the black box out and ran her fingers over Arrik's gifts. She took the mask out and cut the black diamonds from fabric and stowed them in a hidden pocket she'd sewn into her trousers. She never knew when she'd need funds.

Or escape.

Wren hid the heels once again, tossed the remnants of the mask into the embers, and stole down to the stables as quickly and as silently as she could. They mounted two mares and journeyed into the forest. Vienne urged her horse to a canter and Wren followed suit. She winced, hating how sore she was from the prior night's escapades.

It was only once she and her aunt had been riding beneath the trees for an hour that Wren realized she recognized the path they were taking.

"We are going to Othos," she remarked.

"Been reading up on your Verlantian geography, Wren?"

"I hardly have much else to do in my room other than read."

The older woman chuckled into her hand, looking for a moment exactly like her sister. It made Wren want to cry. Why had it taken so long for her to witness her aunt's laughter? When would they be able to simply be family, not fighters?

"I suppose I owe you an apology on that front," Vienne said, as they continued through the slowly brightening forest. "But you are too impulsive and virtuous for your own good. It gets you into too much trouble, Wren. I had no choice but to keep you restrained for the sake of the rebellion.

Verlanti has gained too much power in the last few years. There needs to be a balance."

"And here I thought you only cared for the elves."

Her aunt frowned. "While I was born here, my duty is to the Kingdom of Myths."

"You don't talk much about your guild," Wren drawled, hoping Vienne would speak more on the secret organization that pulled the world's strings from the shadows.

"Information is dangerous."

"True. Are all your advisers part of the Kingdom of Myths?"

Vienne smiled. "Some, but not all." An answer without really answering.

They lapsed into silence as they rode for a time.

"It was foolish to attack Lord Idril," Vienne added after a while.

Wren shifted in her saddle. "He told you it was me?"

"Of course not. He's much too proud to admit to such a thing. But I knew it had to be you. No one else would dare do such a thing." Her aunt paused, looking uncomfortable. "Anneke would have been proud." Her voice was gruff.

Wren badly wanted to talk to her aunt about her mother—and about how she could bear to work with the monster who had enslaved and destroyed her—but she didn't know which words to say. Which questions to ask.

As if sensing Wren's accusations, Vienne's gaze shuttered and her lips pressed into a thin line.

The rest of their journey was silent, and by the time they reached Othos the streets were bustling with morning markets, but everyone seemed to be on edge.

Wren made sure her hair was covered and cast her gaze around to try to work out where Prince Cathal had been murdered. She looked for blood upon the cobblestones, or a section cordoned off with soldiers. But there was nothing.

Since Vienne hadn't mentioned the prince's death to her, Wren kept her question to herself. No need to reveal more than she should.

They arrived at a nearby inn and handed their horses to a stableboy. They didn't enter the building but walked down the alley to a house of worship that hosted a tall stone tower. Her nose twitched and she suppressed a sneeze as they entered the building. The sweet incense was a bit much.

Vienne led her through the columns that circled the main cathedral to a small doorway that opened onto stairs. She suppressed a groan as they began their climb. Their steps echoed around them. Wren almost dropped down on her knees and said a prayer of thanks as they reached the landing.

Her aunt opened the door and Wren followed, glancing over her shoulder. The place gave her the creeps. It felt too confining. Like a trap.

"Tell me what's going on," she said, closing the door behind them. She glanced around the room. There were several chairs, a table between them, and a full bed to her right covered in brightly colored linens.

No one else was there.

Dread crept down Wren's spine. Did Vienne intend to imprison her here?

"No more excuses," Wren growled. "I'm done being left in the dark."

"I agree." Her aunt wandered over to the narrow window, peering down at the street below as if looking for someone. Then she turned her sharp gaze to Wren. She leaned a hip against the white stone wall and crossed her arms. "Vadon have agreed to ally with us against Verlanti."

Wren froze. *Vadon?* The southern kingdom?

"They're just as bad as the Verlantians," Wren muttered, disbelief and anger rising in her throat like bile. Rowen had been Vadonese, but he'd been raised by his grandparents on Lorne. Cal and Aileen had been forbidden to marry back when they were younger because of the prejudice of cross caste marriages, so they'd fled to the isles seeking refuge.

"They're bigots," she hissed.

"Not any more than Verlanti or the isles," Vienne retorted.

"That's not true! We would never treat people the way Vadon does. Plus, we would never sanction slavery. Vadon deals in slavery as much as Verlanti. What makes them worse is the opium trade. I refuse to let them have free rein to spread their poison."

"Do not say that," Vienne said, pointing a finger at Wren. "You've grown up on horror stories and know nothing of the real world. Vadon isn't as bad as you think. This union is to be celebrated. Many lives will be saved."

"I will not abide the Dragon Isles being used as a *bargaining chip* for another nation seeking to use our geographic position and our navy as a means to transport slaves across the sea!" Her parents would've never allowed such a thing. Wren wouldn't let their legacy be tainted by anyone.

"Wren—"

"I don't want to hear it!" Wren exploded. This was it; she'd had it. "Do you mean to tell me that your wonderful solution is for us to trade one tyrant for another? Soren for Idril, then Idril for—for—for whoever Vadon decides to represent them! I won't stand around and agree to this!" She glared at her aunt. "My mother would be *ashamed* of you."

Her aunt took a step toward her, but Wren backed away for the door. "You will agree with this if you would only stay and listen to what they have to say. Don't be rash."

"*They* can say whatever they damn well please. I won't be around to listen."

Enough was enough.

Wren turned around, yanked open the door, and walked straight into a body.

She stumbled back as the man clutched her biceps to keep her from falling.

"Sorry," she muttered, and then frowned at the hands that were holding her. They were familiar. Too familiar.

Her gaze darted to his swarthy face and her breath hitched.

A face that had been bloody and broken, plaguing her nightmares and her waking moments.

Rowen.

Rowen was standing there before her very eyes.

CHAPTER THIRTY

Wren

Impossible.

She began to shake, and squeezed her eyes shut.

Not now. Not today.

Had she finally lost her mind?

Wren forced herself to face the truth and opened her eyes.

Rowen still stood before her.

Wren couldn't believe what she was seeing. She'd spent the last few weeks convincing herself that whenever she had seen Rowen it had been her mind playing tricks on her. But here he was, solid and unyielding beneath Wren's fingertips.

"Please tell me you're real," she whispered, terrified her words would make him disappear. She crept her trembling fingers from Rowen's chest to his face just as her eyes found his. Soft, dark, fond eyes.

"It's me," he soothed, squeezing her tightly. "I'm real. I've missed you more than you could possibly know."

Her knees buckled, but then Rowen's powerful arms encircled her and held her close.

Protecting her. Supporting her.

Wren cracked.

Ugly sobs wracked her body, making a mess of Rowen's lovely tunic as she clung to him. It was part relief and disbelief. Relief that she hadn't descended into madness, and disbelief that her best friend stood before her alive.

He smoothed a hand over her hair, pressing her cheek to his chest. "It's okay. Let it out. I'm here. Everything is going to be okay."

They stood like that until her sobs became hiccups. Wren pulled back and ran her fingers over the buttons of his tunic while she tried to pull herself together. A memory niggled in the back of her mind, and she frowned at his chest, staring at his blue tunic. There was something familiar about it.

Midnight blue...

Her gaze flew to his face. These were the same clothes that she'd seen his ghost wear the night before.

Abruptly, she pushed against Rowen's chest, forcing him to let her go. Wren missed the security of his arms immediately, but that sensation was quickly overwritten by cold, heartbroken fury.

She placed a hand over her heart as if it would stop the pain.

"I saw you," she murmured, trying to make sense of the situation. "I *saw* you. You've been alive all this time." Shaking now from rage rather than disbelief, she glared at Rowen. "Tell me the truth right now. Have you been following me this whole time?"

"Yes."

Wren ran a shaking hand through her hair and stabbed a

finger at him. "You let me believe you were dead. I mourned you!"

Rowen held up his hands in a placating gesture. "Wren, let me explain. I didn't mean to hurt—"

She stepped into his space and slapped him. Hard.

"I deserve that," Rowen muttered, rubbing at the stinging mark Wren had left on his cheek. He glanced at Vienne over Wren's shoulder, then turned his attention back to her. "But we have a lot to talk about. You can leave your anger for later."

She shook her head. "I'm not talking to you about anything."

He squared his shoulders. "I see your temper hasn't lessened."

"Don't you dare—*Rowen, put me down*!"

She yelled as he tossed her over his shoulder and carried her out of the tower room. Wren fired a betrayed glare at her aunt, though the older woman merely sighed and mouthed, *See you later.*

Like she'd ever trust Vienne again. The rebellion leader had kept this from Wren. She'd known about Rowen the entire time. She'd kept the fact that the man Wren had loved deeply and grieved immensely had survived the attack.

Angry tears ran down her cheeks; she pounded her fists against Rowen's back as he carried her down the tower stairs to a new landing and into a smaller, more intimate room. All at once she wanted to run away and to cling to Rowen. Why did he pretend to be dead? How had he survived? Why hadn't he come to her?

"I saw you," Wren said, moments away from losing her mind entirely once more. Gently, Rowen put her down on a long, comfortable couch that reminded her of the one in her room in Lord Idril's castle. A couch made for lounging in peace and quiet. Wren sat on it, stock-straight, and shifted away from Rowen when he sat down beside her. "I saw you dying. So how are you *here*?"

At this Rowen smiled grimly. He rolled his shoulders forward, hunching slightly to make himself smaller and less threatening. It was such an achingly familiar gesture that Wren found herself crying once more.

"It's funny what an excess of adrenaline can do," he explained, voice calm and soothing. "Immediately after I made you and Britta leave me, your cousin appeared at my side."

Wren blinked. "Clara helped you?"

"Yes. You knew she was training to be a surgeon, didn't you? To work out at sea with the navy. If it weren't for her...well, I wouldn't be here."

For a long moment, Wren let that sink in. "How is that possible? She was a slave in Idril's castle."

"She got me patched up and we were on our way to my grandparents' when a patrol found us. She gagged and hid me. The soldiers took her."

His grandparents.

Wren paled.

Britta.

"My sister," Wren urged, forgetting her fury at Rowen not revealing himself sooner in the face of panic. She leaned toward him and gripped the front of his tunic in desperation. "Britta, is she—?"

"She's safe, don't worry," Rowen was quick to reassure her. He smiled broadly then, all white teeth, affection, and no trace of a lie. "My grandparents still have her."

Wren cast a sidelong glance out of the window, as if someone was somehow spying on them. "So the truth about Britta hasn't gotten out?" It was one of Wren's greatest fears that the Verlantians would get their hands on her little sister.

"No. Our people have been loyal."

"How bad is it at home?" She hadn't had any real word since she'd been captured. She was starved for information.

"The fighting has calmed. The elves can't raze the isles to the ground and expect the place to function," Rowen pointed out, though his expression darkened. "They *have* captured some of the...prettier...women. To bring them over here, as you've seen with Clara."

She felt sick, but at least her people hadn't been decimated in the invasion.

How would they make things right? Would Arrik stop the slaving if Soren was dethroned? Could she trust him to keep his word?

Focus. One thing at a time.

She blinked slowly and met Rowen's dark gaze. He was examining her.

"You've changed," he said. It wasn't quite an accusation but it felt like one.

Wren bristled, remembering why her aunt had brought her to Othos in the first place. "Why are you here, Rowen?"

she demanded, moving away from him once more to maintain some distance.

His eyes narrowed and his lips thinned. He didn't like that she was putting distance between them. Rowen huffed out a breath.

"How much do you remember of my upbringing?" he asked.

She cocked her head. That wasn't what she was expecting him to say.

"Your father had a falling out with his parents and moved to Vadon in his teens. He married but brought you over to live in the Dragon Isles when you were young after your mother died, though he hadn't been on speaking terms with your grandparents," Wren said, frowning as she remembered the hazy details. "You returned to Vadon for a year, though, when you were fifteen or sixteen. What does this have to do with anything?"

Rowen winced. "When I returned to Vadon that year, the country was in quite a state of upheaval because of Verlanti. Things were fraught between the nations at best." He ran a hand over his face. "The king wanted a spy placed in the Dragon Isles—it was imperative Vadon keep a better hold on the place than the Verlantians. Since I already lived there, it made sense for the responsibility to fall onto my shoulders."

Ice trickled down her spine as she tried to make sense of his words.

Spy. Vadon. Rowen.

"Why would the king reach out to you?" she rasped, her mouth dry.

"Because he's a distant relation," Rowen said, his voice gruff.

All at once Wren flashed hot and cold.

Everything she ever knew about her life—her feelings, her choices—seemed altogether false. Predetermined. It was as if her entire world were unraveling before her very eyes.

She rose to her feet and backed away from Rowen, though he was quick to follow suit. "So when you started showing interest in me... Does that mean...does that mean—gods, Rowen, our entire relationship...?" She was going to be sick. "Was it all a job to you? Did you ever love me? Do I even *know* the real you?"

"Wren, of course you do. Don't be ridiculous—"

"Don't tell me how to feel!" she screamed, shaking once more. She sliced a hand through the air, staring down her first love. *You never knew him.* "I was ready to give you everything. All of me. We were supposed to be happy together. But it was all an act to you." Her mother had been worried about Wren traveling and being used for her position. She should have been worried about the boy closest to her.

"Will you please just let me explain myself!?" Rowen bit back, reaching for Wren's hand. She slapped his hand away, her skin crawling. "Everything I felt for you—feel for you—is real. What we *have* is real. You have to understand that if I hadn't accepted the position, the Vadonese king would have sent someone else in my place. They might have even killed me for turning my back on my country. The best way for me to protect you, to protect your entire family, was for me to take the position. I already loved you before I visited my homeland. You were my childhood sweetheart. I already planned to marry you as soon as we were old enough. You must believe me, Wren. Please."

She could hardly look at him. Numbness began creeping into her chest.

All she saw was a stranger who had lied for *years*.

"I trusted you," she said, feeling hollow. Wren locked on to his pleading eyes. "You're right, you know. I've changed. I'm not the girl you used to know."

Wren couldn't believe a word Rowen said, even if she wanted to. After all of the lies, the treachery, the secrets, she couldn't find it in her to trust him.

He'd betrayed her.

"Don't leave," he pleaded. "Please."

She shook her head and spun on her heel, leaving without another word.

"I love you," he called after her.

One tear dripped down Wren's cheek.

His love was a lie.

She rushed down the stairs, leaving the stranger she'd once so desperately loved in a small room alone with part of her broken heart.

CHAPTER THIRTY-ONE

Wren

Wren raced down the stairs.

Rowen was alive. Alive.

And he'd been playing her from the beginning.

You still care for him.

Angry tears tracked down Wren's cheeks and she slipped, letting out a little scream. She clawed at the wall and caught her balance, heart pounding as she swiped at her traitorous tears, and hiccupped as she heard the telltale sound of someone coming down the staircase.

Rowen no doubt.

If he grabbed her and begged for her to stay and talk—if he embraced her, if he kissed her—then her fury was sure to dissolve as easily as seafoam. But she didn't *want* her rage to dissipate.

Her entire life had been controlled and dictated by everyone but her. She was tired of it. Sick of being manipulated. Wren pushed away from the wall and started her descent once again. She didn't know where she was going, only that she needed out.

Her footsteps rang through the quiet temple as she sprinted for the door, heart in her throat. Her mind shut down as she inhaled the clean air of Othos and entered the mass of people flowing through the streets.

Before she knew it, she had stolen through the streets of Othos toward their port. It wasn't as large as the capital city's port, nor as chaotic as Delansh, but it was still large and sprawling. The sound of the waves lapping against the docks soothed some of the ache within her soul. The ocean had always been a balm for her wounds.

Workers, fishermen, merchants, and sailors moved freely between ships—like ants on a log. It would be easy to get lost within the madness.

To hide away from everyone who would be looking for her.

Wren shoved her hands into her pockets as she decided which direction to go. Her right hand curled over the cool loose black diamonds from the mask Arrik had gifted her. Thank the stars for her good sense in packing them and that her aunt had returned Wren's weapons.

Time to find a friend who could help.

She crept from pier to pier on the lookout for a quiet place to gather her thoughts and hum a gentle song.

To summon a dragon.

She spied an abandoned, dilapidated pier and made for the end of it. She carefully walked down the length of it, making sure to avoid the potholes along the way. Once she reached the end, she closed her eyes and began to sing. Pain along with loneliness and betrayal turned the melody sad and broken. It was a lament.

Wren didn't know when her eyes had closed, but she opened them slowly. The water rippled gentle below her. It didn't take long for Wren to recognize the dragon lurking beneath the surface. She glanced over her shoulder, scanning the area. Luckily, because it was now late morning and the fish market had long since packed up, the port wasn't nearly as busy as it could have been. Nobody spared a moment for the lone person at the end of the pier. A drunk swayed and plopped himself at the entrance of the dock, his legs dangling over the edge of the sea.

Wren turned back to Trove, admiring how his scales shone beneath the waves. "Hello, friend," she murmured.

The dragon stayed beneath the waves watching her with fathomless eyes.

Here was her escape. She didn't need anyone else but her sister, Clara, and Leif.

A melancholy smile curled her lips as she reached over the wooden banister of the jetty, ready to abandon everything, fly back to Britta and—

"I thought I recognized a familiar head of hair," came a voice from behind Wren.

She turned; a very familiar merchant-turned pirate stood there, proffering Wren a silken cloth with which to clean her face. She had no doubt she looked like a complete and utter puffy mess of tears.

Gunn.

How the blazes had he snuck up on her?

Wren yanked up her hood and cursed herself for being so

careless in her escape. Her hair stood out like a bloody beacon. She'd basically waved a flag saying that she was in Othos.

She narrowed her eyes as she spotted a bottle tied to his hip, and his clothing registered. He was the drunk she'd spotted.

"Were the games really necessary?" she asked.

"If I approached you, Princess, would you have stayed or ran?"

A fair question. One they both knew the answer to.

"What are you doing here? Aren't you...shouldn't you be out at sea, returning former slaves to their rightful homes?" The fact he wasn't immediately raised Wren's hackles. Had he betrayed Leif?

Sensing where her thoughts had gone, Gunn laughed wildly. "Oh ye of little faith, Dragon Princess. Do you think I could possibly do such a thing in a ship High King Soren recognizes? Don't be so foolish. I smuggled Leif and the slaves to a far less obvious, smaller ship, then gave him some of my own crew to finish the job on my behalf."

His explanation was plausible, but it didn't make her feel any better. "And I should trust you?"

"No, but you can trust that I hate Idril enough to destroy what he holds so dear."

"What did he do to you?"

Gunn laughed. "My dear old father? Why, everything, dearest."

Father.

Wren stared at the pirate in shock. Gunn was Idril's son?

Now that he mentioned it, she could see the resemblance.

You have a brother.

Did Gunn know they were half siblings? It was all too much.

"He's your father?" she croaked.

Her brother smiled, but it was anything but nice. "By blood only. I don't claim him, even though he keeps trying to rein me in."

Wren swayed and clutched at the railing behind her.

Gunn's smiled dimmed, a flicker of concern on his face. "Why? Are you that unhappy to see me?"

Wren shook her head, trying to get ahold of herself. Even if they were kin, Gunn wasn't her friend. She'd learned that lesson with Vienne.

He once again held out the handkerchief. "A peace offering."

But for all intents and purposes she could sense nothing from Gunn's behavior to suggest he was acting out of the ordinary, and hadn't he been keeping up his end of the bargain of feeding the rebellion thus far?

She took the cloth from his hands, unceremoniously dragged it over her face, then gasped in surprise when she pulled it away and recognized the name embroidered upon it.

"This is Arrik's," she ground out. Wren pinned Gunn with her eyes. "When did he give you this? *Why* did he give you this? Where is the prince?"

Gunn merely laughed once more. A little earring made from silver and quartz jingled from his ear as he did so. "So many questions."

"It's been a long day," she managed. "Give it to me straight. No more riddles."

"If you come with me, Princess, your questions will be answered." He gestured with his right arm toward a nearby ship. Wren stared at it, feeling stupid for having not noticed it the moment she ran into port.

It's okay to be weak. It's been a rough day.

She wiped at her face once more and pocketed the handkerchief, nodding at Gunn. He grinned and then turned on his heel, swaggering down the jetty like he owned the place. Wren exhaled heavily and looked down at Trove over her shoulder.

"I'll be back soon."

Quickly, Wren caught up with the pirate—a man who could very well be her brother—it was difficult to wrap her brain around that one. In silence, they made it to his ship, the waves lapping gently against the hull.

As they climbed aboard, she watched the carefree pirate with growing curiosity. "How do you know the prince? Have you been working with him since before Leif and I approached you?"

Gunn didn't answer.

She rolled her eyes as he led her to the prow of the ship. The pirate gave her a jaunty little bow and backed away.

"Where in the blazes are you going?"

He laughed. "To my study. Now be patient and behave."

"You behave, you cheeky devil," she muttered beneath her breath.

Wren leaned her cheek against the rail, grateful for the rough wood beneath her red, swollen skin, and let out a heavy sigh. Today had not gone as she'd planned. Blast it all, the last few months hadn't gone as she planned.

Her chest tightened as she thought of Rowen. She sank down, sitting on the deck. Since her capture, she'd held on to what they had to survive. But the fact that he'd been lying and using her from the beginning? It broke another piece of her heart.

"You're always worried about something when I find you," her husband said, his deep voice washing over her.

Wren didn't look at Arrik as he dropped down to sit on the deck beside her. She caught movement from the corner of her eye as he stuck his booted feet between the rails to dangle his legs over the side of the ship.

"A penny for your thoughts, wife?"

"Why do you call me that?" she muttered. They weren't truly married. They didn't even like each other that much.

"Because that is what you are. What would you have me call you?"

"Wren."

"Wren."

The way he said her name was like a caress.

Wren could barely stand to look at him. Her chest constricted at his mere presence beside her. The smell of his sweat on the air mixed with spice. She needed a safer topic.

He nudged her with his shoulder. "What is wrong? Your face is blotchy."

Lovely.

"How close do you think someone can get to breaking before they finally shatter into a thousand pieces?" she murmured, more to herself than to Arrik. She closed her eyes, still leaning on the railing as if it might ground her.

A strong breeze might be all it took to shatter her today.

"Tell me what happened, Wren. I find that talking things out helps me get my thoughts straight and levels my heart."

She let out a dark chuckle. "I wasn't aware you had one."

"Just as well, because that comment would break it."

She smirked and looked his way.

It was a mistake.

The late autumn sunshine softened all his haughty edges, making him even more achingly handsome than usual. But it wasn't just the way he looked that attracted Wren. He, out of everyone, had been honest with her from the beginning. Even when he was fighting her on the Dragon Isles or hauling her away to Verlanti, he'd spoken not a single lie.

True, he was a monster. A barbarian. But he'd never pretended to be something he wasn't. That was something she could respect.

"Can I trust you?" she asked, hating how her voice broke on the question. Wren felt so small. So vulnerable. But she was tired of trying to shoulder everything on her own. She had Leif, yes, but he had his own problems to worry about. Once Wren returned to the Dragon Isles—if she ever survived that long—she doubted her friend would come with her.

Arrik sidled closer and placed his hand over hers own. The warmth of his skin on hers rooted Wren in the moment.

She drew strength from the simple touch and blinked back the heat that pressed behind her eyes.

How had she come to this? Drawing comfort from her enemy.

"Yes, you can trust me. Just the way I know I can trust you. We will always do what's best for our people and each other."

That was enough for the floodgates to open.

"Why? I'm your enemy."

"No." He shook his head. "You are my partner, which is why I will entrust you with one of my secrets."

Wren held her breath, staring into his ice blue eyes. He brushed a strand of hair from her face. "You have a younger sister. The true heir to the Dragon Isles."

She blinked slowly, all her muscles locking up. He couldn't know.

Arrik slid his hand behind her head to cup her nape so she couldn't run away. "Breathe, Wren. Breathe."

But she couldn't. Everything she'd been fighting to protect was in danger.

He dropped his forehead against hers. "Don't fear."

"How?" she croaked.

"I had a notion," he admitted, his breath whispering across her lips. "Back in the palace, I spent many a sleepless night trying to work out why you would not break. If you had truly lost all that was important, you would have folded. But there was steel to your spine that I know from experience only exists when you have someone specific to protect. Someone you love."

Her stubbornness had given her away? "You will never find her."

"I have no plans to."

His admission floored her.

She pulled back slightly to look in his eyes. He meant it. The prince wasn't lying. She could read his sincerity in his gaze. "Why?" What could he possibly gain from this?

"Because any kin of yours is kin of mine."

A lump formed in her throat. "How long have you known?"

"Since I let you escape me the first time."

Her breath caught. The prince had known for months. "She gives you power."

"I will get it without her. I won't put someone you love in jeopardy."

He believed what he was saying but could she?

"What do you know of love? By all accounts it seems as if you love nobody."

If Wren had hurt him, he didn't show it. Arrik brushed the tip of his nose against hers, causing her belly to flutter.

"I don't know much of love. Regardless, my mother loved *me,* and until Soren drove her to her death, she did everything in her power to protect me from him. What I know is what I learned from her."

Oh.

She felt terrible for teasing him.

He pulled back and slowly released her, trailing his fingers along her neck. "Now it's your turn to tell me a secret."

"Yours wasn't much of a secret," she retorted, trying to deflect. She felt too exposed. "It was just one of mine you'd sussed out."

"Fine. I'm envious of you."

That wasn't what she expected. Wren cocked her head. "What do you mean? I'm homeless in a foreign land where everyone seeks to use me."

"You are so confident in your path," he replied gruffly, looking out at the sea. "You don't deviate in your path of what is right."

Wren didn't know what to say so she stayed silent.

Arrik smiled. "I see you brought your friend with you."

She followed his gaze and spotted Trove below them. The dragon was going to get himself killed. Wren whistled sharply and the dragon sank deeper until she couldn't see him any longer.

"Are we going to talk about your beast?"

"No, we are not."

The prince nodded. "Now, it's your turn. I demand a secret."

"Why do you keep pressing me?" she snapped.

"Because there's much you're not telling me, and you need someone to talk to."

That was the bloody truth.

Where did she begin? With Vienne? Lord Idril? Gunn being her brother? Or the rebellion's alliance with Vadon?

About Rowen.

It hurt too much to keep in.

"He's alive," she whispered, licking her salty lips.

"Who?"

"Rowen."

Arrik's entire frame tensed. "The man you were to marry?"

"Yes." Heat filled her eyes and she blinked repeatedly. "He survived and stayed away."

"Then he is a fool." A pause. "Perhaps not. If I'd seen him, I would have sent him to his grave."

Brutal but honest.

She swallowed hard. "What is more is that he's an agent for Vadon." Her voice broke and Arrik wrapped an arm around her shoulders, pulling her against his side. Wren leaned her cheek against his arm and let the grief come. "He'd been tasked to secure the crown. I never knew. He never wanted me."

Wren gasped when the prince lifted her onto his lap and held her close, his lips in her hair. He tipped her chin back. "Then he's a fool that's lost the greatest treasure this world has ever seen."

His words stirred heat in her chest and she found herself reaching up and skimming the tips of her fingers over his face to make sure he was real.

"I'm broken."

Arrik pulled her hand away and kissed her palm. "Fractured tiles on their own are ordinary, but mosaics are stunning pieces of art. We'll pick up the pieces together."

"Don't say such things." She trembled. "We're enemies."

"No, love. We're inevitable."

Her pulse leapt as he slid his hand through her hair, desire heating his gaze along with an emotion she didn't want to name. It was much too soon for such things.

He leaned close and Wren met him halfway, their lips colliding in a kiss that made her body tingle and her soul sigh.

Arrik's stubble scratched at her chin in an alarmingly good way as his lips eagerly molded to Wren's. It was a bit like dancing with a new partner. A few stumbles until one found the perfect rhythm. She bit at his lower lip just hard enough that he growled into her mouth, sending a thrill down her spine. His tongue flicked across her lip and she opened to him.

Wren sank her fingers into his braids, the silver beads tickling as she tilted her head and pushed closer, desperate for more. Heat spread through her body that had nothing to do with anger and everything to do with longing.

Kissing the dark elf prince brought her to life. Hot and startling life.

Wren wanted Arrik.

Needed him, in every sense of the word.

He groaned when she caressed the tips of his pointed ears, but broke their kiss and pulled away.

"No," Wren protested, panting heavily against Arrik's chest. "I want—"

"I want it too, trust me," Arrik murmured, voice so low it was barely audible.

She lifted her head, shaken to the core. There was no mistaking the desire painted across his flushed cheeks and dilated pupils.

"So then—?"

"When this happens for real, I want it to be about *us,* not because of the ghost from your past."

Wren flinched as if someone had doused her with ice water. Was that what she'd been doing?

She sucked in a breath through her teeth and untangled her fingers from his hair. "I'm sorry," she mumbled, mortified, "I don't know what came over me." Fraternizing with the enemy. Her mum would be ashamed.

Is he really the enemy?

"What came over you is the feeling I've had to keep restrained every time I've seen *you* from the very first moment I saw you flying through the sky on your dragon." She stared up at Arrik, hardly knowing who he was. The prince chuckled humorlessly. "I am not ashamed to admit it, but I'll be cursed if I take you to bed for the first time while you think of another."

This wasn't something Wren was sure she knew how to process. "First time?"

His gaze darkened and he gave her a wolfish smile. "There will be *many* times, my darling. Many times." He kissed her cheek. "Thoughts for another time, though. We have much to speak of."

She shivered. So many things had happened so fast, and now she had a moment to breathe, she realized Arrik was entirely correct. This very second was not the time for her to throw herself at him.

There would come another time. Another day, when Wren's mind and heart were far more settled and she could make a decision based not simply on pure impulse. The prince had saved her from regret and possibly shame.

"So what happens next?" she asked, keeping her eyes trained on the horizon. It looked as if a storm was brewing. Wren wiggled and Arrik hissed, causing heat to rush into her cheeks. She clambered out of his lap, avoiding looking at the prince.

"Considering the uproar after Cathal's murder—"

"So it wasn't a hoax?" Wren interrupted him.

"No."

Wren finally looked at Arrik. "Are you okay?"

His jaw flexed. "It is what it is. I didn't want him to die but he is one less piece I have to worry about."

Cold but true. "Do you know who was behind it?"

"No, but I have no doubt we'll find out in time," Arrik said. "My point was that I expected our plans to be thrown into the air because of it, but his death has actually worked in our favor. Everyone is acting recklessly. The rebellion plans to attack the port in the capital, for example. It will serve as an excellent distraction for...other things."

"What?" she barked. Vienne had never mentioned anything like that.

The prince laughed. "It will be a good distraction for my father." He reached out and laid his huge hand over the top of Wren's. "If you're willing, I need you to return to your aunt..." His jaw clenched. "...and that...good for nothing Vadonese spy. They cannot know we're working together." His thumb brushed her skin. "Can you do that?"

She had no desire to see Rowen, but that wasn't an option.

"I don't imagine anyone will doubt that I fled today out of shock." It was true, after all. "Will anyone get hurt during their attack? The people at the port, I mean. I don't want any innocent people to suffer simply so you can use the attack as a cover to deal with your father."

He studied her and squeezed her hand before letting go. "Even now, you can't help but worry about others before yourself. You don't *need* to worry," he reassured her. "I'll evacuate those in the port in the blast radius before the rebellion can hurt anyone."

The prince stood and held a hand out.

Wren stared at it. Their relationship had shifted today. She wasn't sure if it was for the better. If she sided with him and everything went south, there would be no redemption.

"I'm trusting you," she stated, placing her hand in his.

He helped Wren stand and stared down at her. "As I'm trusting you, wife."

Wren believed him.

Despite the fact everyone else was lying to her, or trying to manipulate her, or trying to use her, she trusted Arrik.

Her husband was a beast.

But he was turning out to be perhaps not nearly as monstrous as she'd once thought.

CHAPTER THIRTY-TWO

WREN

It took Wren longer than it should have to get back to the temple.

Each step felt like stepping closer to the edge.

The edge of madness.

She was a warrior, not a spy.

Heavy of heart, Wren returned to the tower. She hesitated as she reached the landing and inhaled deeply to steady herself.

The door to the small chamber opened up and her aunt stepped out onto the landing, her hazel eyes sympathetic, expression painted with relief. Wren didn't want her sympathy. She wanted the truth. She was so bloody tired of secrets.

"I'm glad you came back," Vienne said.

"I almost didn't."

Her aunt pursed her lips and nodded. "That's understandable. What changed your mind?"

"I have no other place to go." It was partly truthful.

"Come," Vienne insisted, wrapping an arm around Wren's

shoulders and bringing her inside the room. "There's much to speak of."

"Are you going to be honest with me?" she asked, pulling away from her aunt. Wren ignored the tall male near the window. She couldn't deal with Rowen quite yet. Bram nodded to her but she dismissed him. He could wait too. She gave Ever a small nod, which the woman returned and then went back to picking at her nails.

Several other men and women were packed into the room. They watched her like she was dangerous. Her skin crawled at all the attention. It was like she was part of a menagerie. A small part of Wren wanted to bare her teeth at them and growl.

"I am." Vienne squeezed Wren's hand and smiled. "We have some details to finalize. Together."

A few weeks ago, Wren would have done anything for the rebellion's approval. For Vienne's trust. Now it all felt hollow.

She moved to the fireplace and took a seat in one of the simple wooden chairs. Bram sat opposite her, scowling, though there was something about the way he glanced at her that suggested he no longer despised her.

Her lips thinned as she pinpointed what it was.

Pity.

Wren clenched her teeth and looked at the low burning fire. She didn't want his pity. She didn't want anything from them.

"She can't be here," Rowen commented, his voice a balm and a nightmare, murmurs of agreement following by the others Wren didn't know. "The princess is too emotional right now. It would be better if—"

"Don't you dare speak like I'm not here in this room." Her tone was dark, broken, and threaded with steel. "I'll be privy to all that you plan or I won't help you." She finally looked at her long-lost love and glared at him. She refused to be cowed by anyone. Not anymore. "I know you need me—more than I need you. So speak or I walk."

Out of the corner of her eye she saw a glimmer of approval light Bram's expression.

What was his problem? He hated how outspoken she was. Plus, he'd been treating her like a pariah since Wren had revealed her chance meeting with the prince. What had changed? It was odd.

Part of her brain guessed it might be due to the fact she and Leif freed Lord Idril's slaves. Leif had told Wren that Bram hadn't wanted to work with him.

Perhaps he knew there was no way Leif could free the slaves on his own. And if the original goal of the rebellion—releasing people from their Verlantian bondage—is more important to Bram than following Vienne, then maybe...

Maybe Wren could convince him to side with her.

Arrik had spoken truly when he said Wren needed friends. Now she had Leif, Josenu, Trove, Gunn, and Arrik himself. With such an accomplished spy as Bram working with her, they could rattle the kingdom of Verlanti.

Don't get ahead of yourself. Focus on the here and now. The attack on the port.

"I'm happy with her staying," Ever piped up from the

small bed. She smiled and glanced around the room. "She has proven herself over and over again. I trust the princess. She deserves to be here as much as any of us."

Wren shared a look of gratitude with the older woman. Perhaps she'd made a friend of Ever too.

"She stays or I leave with her." Ever's voice was resolute and it shook Wren to the core. She *had* made a friend.

"All in favor?" Vienne said.

A series of ayes were spoken around the room, including Bram. *What the devil?*

"Nay," Rowen interjected.

Wren flinched but stared up at her aunt, determined not to let him bother her.

Vienne clasped her hands behind her back. "The majority rules. The princess stays." She gave Wren a severe look. "Are you with us?"

"I am. I want peace for everyone." A lie with a truth.

Her aunt nodded and then looked to Ever. "Share the plan."

The rebellion's plan was simple but clever.

The attack on the capital port was to happen on the day of Cathal's public funeral which would be held in two weeks. She had to admit that a funeral would be the perfect distraction that would allow the attack to happen.

And that will in turn be the distraction the prince needs to deal with the king.

The plan was to return to Lord Idril's castle for a week and then head to the capital in four groups on different days. With Vadon's alliance, they had an escape route on a nearby vessel. It made Wren sick to think about the southern kingdom's involvement.

It hurt even more to know Rowen was part of it all.

The meeting wrapped up quickly as it was not safe for any one person to have all the details. Wren made note of the people she hadn't met before, and stowed their faces and names in the back of her mind.

They filed out of the room, their footsteps echoing down the stone stairs. Ever stood from the bed and walked across the room. She shocked Wren by stooping down and hugging her.

"I know today was hard. It will get better." The older woman pulled back and left with Bram hot on her heels.

Still Wren didn't stand. She had unfinished business with the silent man near the window.

Vienne glanced between Rowen and Wren. She finally sighed and headed for the door.

"Don't kill him," she muttered. "We need him." She disappeared from sight.

Wren would make no promises.

She stood from her chair and peered over her shoulder at Rowen. He watched her, his expression schooled. Her chest tightened to the point where she almost couldn't breathe. It *hurt* to look at him.

I can't do this.

Wren took two steps toward the door before Rowen caught her arm. She glared down at his hand but he didn't let go.

"Wren," he said, his voice ragged. "I'm sorry for earlier. I—

"

"You can be sorry all you want," she said, tone as icy as winter, "but that doesn't change things."

"I know, but I want to be able to explain myself."

"I think you've done enough of that."

"I haven't done nearly enough," he bit back.

She really couldn't have this conversation right now. "If we are going to talk, then it should be about the rebellion's plans and how you tried to cut me out."

"No. We need to talk about us."

She flinched and scowled up into his familiar face. "There is no us."

He didn't like that one bit. His grip tightened on Wren's arm and he spun her around until she faced him. "Just let me explain things!" he exclaimed, desperate and frustrated.

Feeling trapped, she whipped out her dagger on reflex—the one Kalles had bestowed upon Wren to kill her husband. Rowen stiffened but didn't release her arm, though his touch gentled.

"I've had enough of your excuses," she growled, straightening to stand tall and strong against him. Maybe one day she'd want to hear him out, but it wasn't today. She pointed the tip of the blade at Rowen's jugular. "Let me go and get out of my way."

"You've changed," he replied.

Wren snorted. "The loss of everything important will do that to a person."

His gaze dipped to the blade in her hand and he smiled. "Did you like my gift, then?"

What?

"What are you talking about?"

His smile widened. "Kalles passed on my gift."

She pulled back. "This is from you?"

Rowen leaned close. "Yes. I didn't want that monster getting his hands on you."

"You're working with Prince Kalles?"

He moved around her without an answer but paused at the door. "Too bad we aren't talking about anything personal, otherwise I might have told you."

He left without another word.

Wren stood there for too long, trying to sort herself.

Two weeks passed in a blur. Wren sent word to Arrik by way of Josenu about Rowen and the Vadonese dagger, and about how he was likely in cahoots with his brother. Arrik was yet to respond.

But now Wren and the rest of the rebellion were in the capital, so if Arrik had anything to say to her she reasoned he had been waiting to say it in person. Nerves flipped her stomach and threatened to make her vomit, though Wren hadn't been able to eat anything that morning and so had nothing to throw up.

Today everything would change.

They were swimming into the harbor from the derelict side of the city. That had been Rowen's idea, of course. The man seemed more fish than human at times, hence why he rose through the ranks of the Dragon Isle navy so quickly. But now even that memory was soured in Wren's mind: had

Rowen only done so to gain a position of power as fast as he was able? To make himself a viable marriage candidate for her?

She shook the thought from her head. There wasn't time to dwell on such things.

When they reached the ships they had to prepare the black powder beneath them to go off simultaneously. Arrik had assured her nobody would be around to get hurt. But as she was attaching the second-from-last charge, the one she had only just attached to a ship went off with a delayed, watery explosion.

She had no time to swim away from the blast, or even to cling to the ship to avoid being blown away. Before Wren knew it, she was being buffeted and tossed this way and that beneath the surface, the air she was holding in her lungs thoroughly knocked out of her with the force of ten punches to the gut. She was seeing stars, breathless and dizzy and in pain.

Then, through the haze, something very solid appeared beneath her. Wren grabbed at it with all her might, knowing it was Trove. He pulled her away from the explosion and the turbulent water, up to the surface, where he tumbled her out onto the dock. Wren barely had a chance to splutter in a breath and shake her eardrums free of water when she heard the *shing* of metal pointed at her.

Soldiers from the palace, their spears and swords aimed directly at Wren.

"Take her," the captain of the guard commanded. At once, Wren felt two pairs of burly hands unceremoniously grab her, dragging her to her feet and away from the docks. She didn't even have the opportunity to see if Trove had been seen or attacked. She could only hope his rescue of her had been invisible to the soldiers beneath the murky, uneven water.

Wren didn't bother to put up a fight as she was pulled up to the palace, then brought into the throne room to be dropped onto the marble floor in front of High King Soren. Just because one of the charges had gone off early did not mean Arrik couldn't use the attack to get rid of his father. There was still a good chance Wren would come out of this with ringing in her ears but otherwise unscathed.

So then why was Arrik standing to the left of Soren, stony-faced and immovable as the day Wren was first brought before the king?

"Ah, the barbarian princess," Soren drawled, though his tone belied the wicked delight on his face. He took a long draught of wine when a servant refilled his goblet. "Had you been upon land too long? Were you that desperate to swim with the oversized fish you call your friends?" The usual ghouls of the high court snickered. Wren went red with fury and shame. "Or did you mean to swim back home? My, how audacious of you. How precious."

Wren said nothing. Of course she said nothing. But she expected *Arrik* to say something. To defend her, or drive a sword through his father's chest. Anything but expressionless silence.

And then it occurred to Wren. *Had Arrik been playing with her?* Had all of this been some long game to amuse both himself and his father? Standing beside the elf, they looked so similar. Were they both rotten right down to their very core?

Wren shook with disbelief and white-hot rage. *He made me care for him. He made me feel* sorry *for him. He made me—*

"Has the dragon forgotten how to speak in human tongues?" Soren continued, laughing at Wren dripping seawater all over the floor, chest heaving with the effort it was taking her not to scream. "I think you have spent too long in the wild, my dear. There is no helping you. But now your people shall pay for your disobedience. Mark my words, if you thought things were bad for the isles already, then they are about to get a whole lot worse. I—"

The king paused, a hand going to his throat as a frown darkened his brow. "I—" He tried again, only to cough and splutter. The white of his eyes began to go red, and when he coughed again his spittle was crimson, too. He clawed at his throat, wildly swinging his gaze around for help.

Nobody came to his aid.

"Arrik," he spat out, through a mouth rapidly filling up with froth. "Help m—"

Arrik remained, as he had been the entire time, stony and expressionless. He didn't move. Didn't look at his father.

He did nothing at all.

With one final gurgle, High King Soren fell to his knees, then the floor, and then he was dead.

CHAPTER THIRTY-THREE

Wren

At first there was silence. Nobody dared move. And then:

Pandemonium. Chaos. People began screaming as they finally comprehended what had just transpired. With a clatter of spears, Soren's guards, who had been stationed outside the throne room door, barged in to attack their counterparts who stood by the throne. Arrik's men, going by the fact they did nothing as the king died, now drew their weapons to face the guards.

Wren knew she had mere seconds to decide what to do. She could risk being hauled to the palace to be humiliated by Soren had been all part of Arrik's convoluted plan… or she could run.

It wasn't even a decision.

Though Wren had no weapon—the Vadonese dagger had been taken from her the moment the captain of the guard pulled her from the water—Wren was a savvy enough fighter to elbow the guard who still held her squarely in the face, then in the groin. His hold on Wren loosened, and she wrenched away to struggle toward the door.

Forget Arrik. Forget all of this. All Verlantians are vipers.

But soldiers began blocking the door in order to keep the hysteria of the room at bay, so Wren careened to her left to escape through a window. The throne room was on the ground floor; there would be no drop for her to brace herself for.

Jump out and run, run, run.

A burly pair of arms curled around Wren and wrenched her away from the window when she was within touching distance of the frame. "Let me go!" she growled, kicking and clawing and screaming at Shane, Arrik's second-in-command. The dark elf tightened his grip before hauling her over his shoulder. She pounded her fist on his back and yanked at his black hair.

"Let me—" she drew up short as they passed the throne and its fallen king.

Wren caught Arrik's eye and all noise ceased to exist.

He, alone, remained motionless and blank against the chaos swirling around him. His face was hard, haughty, alien, even as he stared Wren down.

This was the Beast of the Barbarians.

This was the Dark Elf Conquer.

That was her *husband*.

Just when had Wren grown used to seeing him gaze at her with tenderness and laughter on his lips?

Everything was lies.

"Don't do this," she yelled.

He didn't react.

Arrik looked every inch the stranger to her now, though

by all accounts he was unchanged from the day Wren first had the displeasure of meeting him.

Heat pressed at the back of her eyes, but she didn't let the tears fall. He didn't deserve them.

It was as if everything that had happened between them never existed. That Wren had made it all up in her head.

"I won't forgive you a second time," she mouthed.

There is was. The smallest twitch of his lips downward.

Then Arrik dismissed her and turned to the queen.

So this was how it was to go.

The palace blurred by until Shane kicked open the doors to a familiar chamber.

Arrik's rooms.

Shane stormed across the room and dropped Wren unceremoniously onto her husband's bed and backed away.

He wasn't getting away that quickly.

She was quick to scramble after him to try to tackle him to the ground, her feet slipping on the marble floor.

"I don't want to hurt you," he said gruffly, sharp eyes scrutinizing Wren as she sank into a defensive position.

"Then run."

Her eyes narrowed as he spun on his heel and sprinted to the door. Wren screamed and bolted after him. He slipped though the doors and slammed them shut in her face. She pulled on them and slapped a hand against the wood. The blackguard had already locked her in.

"Let me out!"

"I can't, my lady," Shane's muffled voice came from the other side of the door. "You will be safe here. The prince will come for you."

She kicked the door in frustration and sank her fingers into her hair as she turned around and gazed at the room blankly. This wasn't happening.

Get yourself together.

Wren shook off the panic, casting her gaze wildly around Arrik's chambers in search of an escape. But she knew there was none. This was a prison of comforts that she was achingly familiar with.

One lone tear trekked down her cheek as she silently moved through the room to open wall that lead to the courtyard and bathing pool. Wren ran her fingers along the sheer white curtains and tipped her head back to stare at the sky.

"They all will regret this."

Heart aching, Wren wiped the tear from her face.

Wren was done with being a pawn.

She'd tried to play nice. To keep her honor intact, but enough was enough.

Her only choice left was to become something that *everyone* feared.

A dull chuckle escaped Wren.

She'd become something unexpected.

A transformation.

The Dragon Princess would become a serpent.

And swallow Verlanti whole.

CHAPTER THIRTY-FOUR

Wren

Two days passed before Wren was brought before her husband, the new king of Verlanti.

She was not at all surprised that he'd been crowned. Given the fact Soren's death had not been a shock to him, Wren had no doubt that poisoning his father's wine had been Arrik's plan all along. He had not returned to his chambers even once in the last two days, leaving Wren to stew in her own rage and betrayal until they threatened to bubble out of her like the poison had frothed from Soren.

But Wren hadn't been ignored, either. A servant had been assigned to bring her meals and clean her up.

Her hands flexed at her sides as she approached the throne room dressed in an emerald dress cut in a marginally demurer style than the typical fashions of Verlanti—not a see-through layer of gauze in sight. Wren had a sneaking suspicion this was Arrik's way of appealing to her better nature.

An olive branch.

It wouldn't save him from her wrath.

She had never been impressed by clothes though, so if he wanted her to be grateful that her dress was more comfortable than anything else she'd ever worn within the palace walls, he was sadly mistaken.

She heard her name announced to the throne room, and then she was allowed to make her entrance. Wren kept her black mask in place as she entered the grand airy room.

Arrik sat upon the throne, looking by all accounts a regal warrior king, resplendent in striking silver armor and a onyx cape that seemed to soak up the light around it.

It was the color of his rotten soul.

At his side sat Queen Astrid, looking altogether smug as she watched Wren approach. The queen winked and smiled encouragingly, but Wren didn't react.

Leif was correct. She couldn't trust anyone.

Least of all, her own judgement.

Astrid had shown her two sides. Now, she was prone to believe the kindness that the queen had shown Wren was just a façade. She suspected Astrid's behavior in Idril's castle was in fact her true nature. The queen was just a corrupt as everyone else.

"Thank you for joining us," Arrik said, pulling her attention to her backstabbing husband.

A beat of silence filled the room, booming off the walls as loud as the bang of cymbals. Wren's ears rang and her mask slipped as they stared each other down.

She'd say her piece, he'd expect that much from her and then she'd lock away her distain.

"I must have been a fool to believe you," she spat, straight at Arrik. Now she was seeing his expressionless face up close, she couldn't contain how livid she was. "If you thought I hated you before, it pales in comparison to how I feel now."

"Leave us."

She turned on her heel to storm from the door when his icy voice stopped Wren in her tracks. "Not you, *wife*. Everyone else."

Wren slowly turned around and breathed slowly to contain her anger that threatened to overwhelm her and ruin everything. Astrid plopped a grape into her mouth as Arrik glance in her direction and quirked an eyebrow at the queen.

"That includes you, Astrid."

Wren expected her to complain, but with a nod she got to her feet and swept out of the throne room. On her way past Wren, she gave her a small, genuine smile, but Wren didn't have it in her to question the woman's motives anymore. Astrid was out for herself, that much was clear, and that was all that mattered.

Trust no one.

Once the cavernous doors clanged shut, it was only Wren and Arrik left, staring at each other. Effortlessly, he rose to his feet, then descended the dais until he was on level footing with her. She gritted her teeth and forced herself to stand tall as he approached. He was still so tall that he loomed over her, long silvery braid framing his sinfully handsome face.

"You're angry." Two simple words spoken without any feeling.

"And you're simple minded." Not her best retort. "What

do you want with me?"

He blinked slowly and cocked his head. "Why are you so angry?" he asked, his non-expression finally breaking to show how irked he truly was. "Everything went to plan."

"To plan? *To plan*?" Wren couldn't believe what she was hearing. "You didn't tell me what you were doing! You didn't keep in contact at all over these last two weeks, and then you sabotage the rebellion's attack just to—what, humiliate me? To what end did it serve you to drag me in front of your father?"

"I wanted you to witness his death."

She felt sick. "I don't understand."

Keep it together.

Arrik's eyes were icy but determined. "It was the only way I could distract him enough not to notice the poison I slipped into his wine. He has someone test every bottle after it's opened, you see. I had to poison it right there beside him."

Wren felt like screaming. "And what about justice?"

At this Arrik barked out a short, humorless laugh. "Justice? Do you think justice would have been served if he'd been thrown into a dungeon while the council decided what to do with him? No. He would have been set free within a fortnight with a slap to his wrist." He took a step closer, blue eyes snapping with anger. "And then what do you think he would have done? Punished everyone around him. Justice was served today for all the people he abused in the past. Why can't you see that? I didn't think you were that naive."

She was going to punch him.

"Why didn't you tell me what you were planning in

advance?" Wren demanded, bristling at his insult but otherwise ignoring it. She needed answers, not to get into a match of biting remarks. She needed to play this just right.

"Because you act your most convincing when you *aren't* acting." He smiled softly – *intimately* – like he had that right. "You put on a wonderful performance."

Wren couldn't take it. She closed the gap between them and slapped Arrik in the face. Her hand stung as she pulled back and Wren tipped her chin up.

He let out a low chuckle and rubbed at his jaw, though his eyes were fiery. "I deserved that. Hit me again, if it will make you feel better." He turned his face for the other side.

So she did.

It didn't make her feel better. It made her feel grubby.

She took a step back and eyed his flaming red cheeks, the ornate silver crown on his brow. She had one more unanswered question. "You only became king because Cathal was dead," she murmured slowly. "But you seemed shocked that he'd been killed. Were you behind that, too?"

"I cannot answer that."

That was an answer of its own.

She knew he had blood on his hands – they both did. But murder?

It wasn't right.

"I thought we were supposed to be *in this together*!" She tossed her hands in the air.

Arrik grabbed Wren's right hand and interlaced their fingers. "We are. But I can't tell you about everything yet. I swear I will when I can. You can trust me."

No, I really can't.

And it broke her heart.

Wren gulped down a retort. She had to tread very, very carefully. "Now, you're the king."

"I am."

"Then our bargain has been fulfilled. Let me return to the Dragon Isles and free my people from Verlanti. I have done all you asked so far. It is only right."

He wouldn't let her go.

She expected it but it still hurt when Arrik shook no.

"I would love nothing more than to do so," he said, sounding genuinely sad.

"So do it," she replied. "You promised."

"With the political scene the way it is, I can't. At least for now."

"And what does that mean?" Wren demanded. She wrenched her hand from Arrik's and took a step back. Of course, she should have known Arrik would go back on everything he promised her. Of course. So why did it sting?

Keep it together. You almost have what you want.

"Vadon," Arrik said simply. "The moment you told me that Vadon had been spying on the isles, and that they were now working with the rebellion, everything changed. I cannot free your kingdom, but I *can* offer you something that suits our current situation far better."

The tantalizing sentence stopped the retort Wren had been forming firmly in her throat. She chewed over how to respond without sounding too eager. This is what she'd been leading him to since the moment she'd stepped into the throne room.

"What could you possibly offer me, Arrik?"

Arrik walked back up to his throne and held a hand out to the queen's throne at his side.

A shiver ran down her spine.

"Rule our kingdom with me. Be my queen. With the two of us together, Verlanti and the isles—think of what we can do, Wren. Think of the difference we can make."

"...and the isles?" Her heart raced in her chest.

"You can do what you want with the Dragon Isles. I will not stand in your way. You ruling your home only helps us both."

"So you wish for me to be more than your wife, but to be your queen and consort?"

A devilish smile tilted his lips that had her blushing in a way she didn't want to. "You will be my everything."

She brushed aside the words, not able to focus on them too closely. If she did, Wren might be tempted to believe his lies – to give him everything.

Wren had never wanted to rule, not once. But her sister was young—too young to sit upon the throne without being manipulated by people who would use her position to their own benefit. If Wren took Arrik up on his offer, she could help rebuild the isles so that, by the time Britta came of age, their kingdom would be restored to its former glory.

More than that: Wren could destroy Verlanti from the inside.

Arrik stretched his hand out to her. "Come, my queen."

It was now or never. She would not get another

opportunity like this.

To turn back now was to lose.

She took several slow steps to the dais, her skirts whispering as she ascended the steps.

Wren held her husband's gaze as she set her hand in his.

"Then let's rule together."

Continue the series with:

Throne of Serpents

LOVE READING ROMANTIC FANTASY?

Try my Twisted Kingdoms series!

A valiant huntress determined to prove herself . A dark shifter lord of the criminal underworld.
An epic love that should never have happened.

About the Author

Thank you for reading Queen of Legends
I hope you enjoyed it!

If you'd like to know more about me, my books, or to connect with me online, you can visit my webpage https://www.frostkay.net/ or join my facebook group FROST FIENDS!

From bookworm to bookworm: reviews are important. Reviews can help readers find books, and I am grateful for all honest reviews. Thank you for taking the time to let others know what you've read, and what you thought. Just remember, they don't have to be long or epic, just honest. <3

Also by Frost Kay

THE AERMIAN FEUDS

(Dark Epic Fantasy)

Rebel's Blade

Crown's Shield

Siren's Lure

Enemy's Queen

King's Warrior

Warlord's Shadow

Spy's Mask

Court's Fool

Prince's Poison

THE TWISTED KINGDOMS

(Epic Fantasy/Fairytale Retelling)

The Hunt

The Rook

The Heir

The Beast

The Hood

The Wolf

DRAGON ISLE WARS

(Epic Fantasy)

Court of Dragons

Queen of Legends

ALIENS & ALCHEMISTS
(Sci-Fi Fantasy)
Pirates, Princes, and Payback
Alphas, Airships, and Assasins
Blackmail, Bootlegging, and Bounty Hunters

www.ingramcontent.com/pod-product-compliance
Lightning Source LLC
Chambersburg PA
CBHW020338310726
48979CB00015B/2412/J

* 9 7 8 1 7 3 6 7 0 9 0 8 5 *